Praise for *Small Island*:

'*Small Island* is an astonishing tour de force by Andrea Levy. Juggling four voices, she illuminates a little known aspect of recent British history with wit and wisdom. A compassionate account of the problems of post-war immigration, it cannot fail to have a strong modern resonance' Sandi Toksvig, Orange Prize judge

'What makes Levy's writing so appealing is her even-handedness. All her characters can be weak, hopeless, brave, good, bad – whatever their colour. The writing is rigorous and the bittersweet ending, with its unexpected twist, touching . . . People can retain great dignity, however small their island' *Independent on Sunday*

'Every scene is rich in implication, entrancing and disturbing at the same time; the literary equivalent of a switc̲h̲ . . . . *̲ ̲mes*

'Wonderful . . . seamless . . . a magnificen̲t̲ . . . . ̲n̲t̲

'A cracking good read . . . I think . . . . st was the passion and anger in the writ . . . . yet it was always leavened with a particu . . . . r – the sort that, tho' you find yourself sm . . . . he time realise you almost shouldn't be' Margaret Forster

'*Small Island* is never less than finely-. . . ., delicately and often comically observed, and impressively rich in detail and little nuggets of stories' *Evening Standard*

'*Small Island* is as full of warmth and jokes and humanity as you could wish . . . Such a rich saga, stuffed full of interlocking narratives' *Time Out*

'Andrea Levy gives us a new, urgent take on our past' *Vogue*

'Levy's story is a triumph in perspective . . . a triumph of poise, organisation and deep, deep character – the sort of work that can only be achieved by an experienced novelist' *Age*, Melbourne

'Here is the book I have been waiting for . . . a book in which the author, Andrea Levy, never once forgets she is telling a story, delighting us, improbably, in this nasty tale of race, with the effervescent style of Dickens' *Globe & Mail*, Toronto

NEVER FAR
FROM NOWHERE

Andrea Levy

headline
review

First published in Great Britain in 1996 by
REVIEW

This edition published in paperback in 2004 by REVIEW

An imprint of Headline Book Publishing

19

ISBN 978 0 7472 5213 9

Printed And Bound in The UK by
CPI Group (UK) Ltd, Croydon, CR0 4YY

Headline's policy is to use papers that are natural, renewable and
recyclable products and made from wood grown in sustainable forests.
The logging and manufacturing processes are expected to conform
to the environmental regulations of the country of origin.

HEADLINE BOOK PUBLISHING
A division of Hodder Headline
338 Euston Road
LONDON NW1 3BH

www.headline.co.uk
www.hodderheadline.com

For Maya and Hannah

Vivien

We had marks on the door-frame that led into the living room. Olive's and mine. Scratched on the paintwork in pencil, because one day when it didn't matter what height we were or when our height didn't change weekly, then our mum was going to rub them off. But they stayed. Olive's ended higher than mine. I had to stand on tiptoe to see them properly. But Olive was older than me, three years. Olive was older and taller and I had to stand on tiptoe to see her all my life.

Three years is a long time in sister years. Three years meant Olive in the juniors with me one of the baby new girls in the infants. Her at secondary school in a smart new uniform, me in the juniors with scuffed knees and marbles. Her with boyfriends and kissing on the doorstep, me with socks and Sindy.

She was my big sister. I was her bloody little baby sister – annoying little sod sister – get out of my room sister – you get on my nerves sister.

We were sisters and we looked alike. We had the family resemblance passed down from our father's side. A large nose and correspondingly large ears, but somehow not out of place. Somehow looking right on our oval-shaped faces; Olive's more refined than mine, more symmetrical. But I had a light skin – a high colour. In a dim light I could be taken for Italian or Spanish. Olive was darker. Black. The Caribbean legacy.

Our parents were from Jamaica. My mother, a country girl brought up on a farm near Savannah-la-Mar in Westmoreland.

1

Her parents owned a shop and kept chickens and every Saturday would attend the Seventh Day Adventist church on the high street. Her great-grandmother was a slave, but in her freedom she married a fairer-skinned man. My grandmother married a man who descended from Scottish farmers. My mother had fair skin with strong African features.

My father's mother was part Spanish, part Indian, part African. She married a man of north African descent who lived in a large house in St Andrew, where they had parties and lived a socialite life. The Caribbean legacy left me with fair skin and black wavy hair. And Olive with a black skin, a head of tight frizzy hair streaked with red, and green eyes.

Newton Charles, my dad, was christened with two surnames. Often people called him Charles Newton. He didn't mind, he didn't care what way round his names went, they were only names after all, he said. He worked for London Transport. He started when he first came to this country as a ticket collector on the buses. 'No standing on top, hold on tight and tickets please,' being some of the only things my dad learned to say without a broad Jamaican accent. After a few years he got what he called a 'chance', and trained to be a mechanic. He then spent the rest of his life repairing buses, making them roadworthy. 'It's a skilled job, Vivien, a training.' Without him, 'them buses stop halfway up hill, 'em wheels spinning and not going nowhere, puffing black smoke.'

Without him, the fleet of London buses would be in very poor condition. So he got up at four every morning and came home stinking of petrol with his navy overalls black with oil up to the chest.

'The human dipstick,' Olive called him. 'Bet they dip him in to see how much oil's in the bus.'

'How you manage to get your clothes so black?' Mum always said, when he brought the overalls home for washing.

'It's me job nah – 'course I get black up.' Then he sat in his chair and read the paper while she washed the overalls.

Rose Charles, Mum, worked all the time. She had two

jobs. She helped prepare and serve the meals at the local school. Then when school was over she went to the hospital where she pushed a trolley round Out-patients and Antenatal, serving tea to anyone who wanted it. 'Not charity, Vivien,' she explained, 'they pay good money for the tea; it's business. We're buying new wings for the hospital.'

She always came home exhausted and would fall into a chair, legs splayed, with her coat still on. Then after five minutes in this undignified position she'd get up and start her jobs at home.

Olive and me were born in London. Not within the sound of Bow bells, wherever they were, but in Islington, north London. Our parents came over on a ship in the fifties and found rooms in a house. The downstairs of what is now a very smart dwelling near Gibson Square. But what was then, and as we grew up, just a notch above a slum. Cooking, eating and living in one room, sleeping in two others. Until the council housed us in a flat on an estate. A new estate that held the promise of decent living but didn't fulfil it.

We liked the estate at first. It was new and clean and the air around it felt fresh like days at the seaside, even though it was firmly in Finsbury Park. When we moved in there was hardly anyone else living there. On the first day we wandered round it – the fairy-tale kingdom of white concrete, radiant in the sun. Quiet with the sounds of birds and our footsteps echoing off the walls and corridors. It was like coming into the light after years underground. After years spent in a damp basement, where we could see the bottoms of people's legs as they went about their business on our busy road. Knees, ankles and feet in shoes all seen through railings – bars. But from our third-floor flat we could look down on people's heads and sometimes, when they were in the not too far distance, we could see them all.

All the blocks of flats sat at odd angles to one another, like a row of bad teeth. In between them were areas where grass promised to grow and places with swings for the children and benches for grannies to sit. Everything had been thought of, every need catered for.

Inside the flat was small, but full of things we'd always wanted. A separate bathroom and toilet. A kitchen you could sit in with a table and four chairs – for a proper family, like in the adverts. My mum and dad enjoyed their new home. Olive and me sat and watched them as they walked round discussing what was to go where and who should have what. Before, everything was just everyone's – squashed together, it was hard to get territorial. But with our own bedrooms and special places to eat and wash – then there could be privacy, and yours and mine and his and hers. Our dad made notes as mum called out that we needed two more wardrobes or a nice shelving unit with a light to show off ornaments to their best. Me and Olive watched them play house like we used to in our bedroom when we were young. My dad licked the tip of the tiny pencil before he began to write, and repeated the words as he wrote them. I didn't butt in with requests; neither did Olive – we didn't have to. Our parents covered everything we wanted and more besides. It was more fun watching than joining in. And everybody knew, but nobody said, that we didn't have the money to buy anything.

One morning Dad woke up with a cough. A great cough that seemed to have a life of its own beyond his chest. Like a demon living way down in him that roared every so often.

Emphysema, the doctor said. Brake linings, my dad said, and shook his head and coughed some more. 'Them brake linings finally get me chest.' They pensioned him off on sick-leave and he sat in a chair and wheezed and coughed. Then one day he ventured out for a paper and got caught in the rain. The cough became a fever and he died. Pneumonia.

Olive and me had to hold Mum up at the funeral. One either side as she leant heavily on us, trying not to let the tears run down her face. Holding them in by sucking at her top lip until it became red and sore. And I was surprised at how she missed him. All through his life she complained to us, 'Yer dad won't do this, yer dad can't do that, yer dad's no good for anything.' But she missed him.

When I was young I used to look at my parents as they sat exhausted in chairs, watching *On the Buses*, straight-faced but saying how funny it was, and I used to think how lucky this country was to have them. How grateful people should be that they came here and did such responsible jobs. And how if they went back – if they went back to Jamaica – well, who knows what would happen to the buses, to the children or the new hospital wings. My parents helped this country, I thought. I thought it as I lay in bed at night. I thought it at school. I thought it walking down the street or playing in the flats. But even when I was young, when I was still having my cheek pulled by passers-by and people winked at me on the tube, even then I knew that English people hated us.

Olive

I had a dream and I woke up sweating. The sheets were soggy. I should have changed them, but they were the only ones left. I don't know why I was sweating – it wasn't that it was frightening.

For some reason I was standing painting a picture. A canvas was propped up on the table in front of the window. And I was really excited by what I was painting. I can't remember what it was – just something out of the window. Something yellow and bright. I was nearly finished and it looked good. Really, nearly finished. Then I took the paintbrush to add the final touches here and there. As the brush hit the canvas it lifted paint off. Every time I touched the canvas with the brush, more little bits would come off until it was beginning to look unfinished again. I couldn't believe it and kept dabbing, and it just made it worse and worse.

Not frightening – frustrating. It was frustration that made me sweat. I'd been having a lot of bad dreams. Frustrating dreams. Like trying to get somewhere but I can't get my clothes on – everything's too tight or falling to bits. Or the bus breaks down. Or I end up in the wrong country. Mad things. Stupid things.

Vivien's the lucky one – always has been. She never had it as hard as me, although she says different. 'The black sheep of the family.' My mum said that once as a joke. 'Olive is the black sheep of the family.' She thought laughing and putting her arm round my shoulder made it all right. But everyone laughed. And the silly thing is, I smiled. Stupid really. I just didn't want anyone to think I didn't get the joke – that I had no sense of humour.

My mother didn't believe in black people. Or should I say, she tried to believe that she was not black. Although she knew that she and my dad were not the only people who came over here from Jamaica in the fifties, she liked to think that because they were fair-skinned they were the only decent people who came. The only ones with 'a bit of class'. And she believed that the English would recognize this. That in a long line of 'coloured people from the Caribbean', an English gentleman in his bowler hat with rolled-up umbrella would run his pointed finger up the line and say, 'Yes, her, Rose Charles, and of course her late husband Newton Charles – they are what we in this country are looking for. They are the truly acceptable face of other people from the Commonwealth. Welcome to our country, which is now yours too. I hope you and your offspring enjoy your stay.' (Then he'd turn to everyone else: 'And the rest of you can stay if you don't make a noise and don't breed.')

She used to talk to me about what she thought of the black people here, looking me straight in the face, telling me how they were like this and like that – nothing good of course. But she sat looking in my black face telling me. And I thought if anyone looking at us sitting at the table talking had to describe the scene, they'd say, 'There are two black women talking.' But my mother thought we weren't black.

'I'm black,' I used to say, when I was old enough to butt in.

'Don't be silly, Olive, you're not coloured.'

'No, Mum, I'm black.'

'No Olive, you're not black, and that's enough of this stupidness.'

'Well I'm not white, I have to be something.'

'You're not white and you're not black – you're you,' she would say, leaning her face right into mine, and that was the end of it.

I tried to explain that now I was a grown-up I liked being

black. I wanted to be black. Being black was not a bad thing, being black was something to be proud of. That I am black, and so is my daughter.

'You mustn't say that, Olive – she'll grow up confused.'

And I said – I said at last: 'No, *I* grew up confused – she's growing up black.'

And I tell Amy that she is black. But she has a very pale skin. Her dad was a white man. English, and she's inherited his colouring. Lots of people don't believe she belongs to me – but she does, every last little crack and hair of her. When she came out she looked silver-blue and slimy like a huge slug. Then she went pink and I thought she'd darken up, but she didn't. But I tell her she's black. It's a political statement, not just a fact.

But my mother would never understand that. She doesn't want to. She got the world sorted out, aged nineteen, somewhere on a ship between the Caribbean and here. She sorted it out and that's the way it's going to be. Like an unwritten religion: just follow the laws and you'll never have to think about anything again.

But I like to think about everything. I like to work everything out. I'm sure Mum and Vivien think I go on about colour too much. They probably think I've got a chip on my shoulder. Chip – make mine a big one! I mean, bloody hell. But they don't know – they haven't lived my life, they haven't gone through what I've gone through.

Vivien

Before we moved to the flats, I was young. A little girl really, a little girl that liked dolls. I had loads of them, twenty-eight, and I knew them all by name. There was Sandy, Toddy, Penny, Teddy, Mandy, Fluffy and all the others. I kept them on my bed and when I went to school I put them all inside it and covered them up with the blankets so they didn't get cold. And I believed that all the old clothes I dressed them in – the jumpers that needed the sleeves rolled back so much that they couldn't put their arms down, the skirts I had to tie round their waists with string, the nappies that slipped off when I lifted them up – I believed that my dolls would grow into them, that one day they'd fit.

Olive used to laugh at me and call me a baby. She only had an old teddy with one eye and no fur. She persuaded me to let her cut off all my teddy's fur. 'Like a haircut – it'll grow back, honest,' she said, crossing her heart and hoping to die. And, of course, I knew it would, one day. Olive always got her way with me because if I didn't obey her she would hold up one of my dolls, hold it high in front of her with one hand and make a fist with the other.

'Will ya?'

'Put her down.'

'Go on and I'll put her down.'

'Put her down and I will.'

And if I didn't she would punch my doll right across the room, then laugh at me as I fetch my doll back, sobbing.

Olive and me shared a room. We had bunk-beds until one

night Olive threw herself from her top bunk in her sleep. She landed with a bump on the floor, too bewildered to cry. But she twisted her ankle, so our dad separated the bunks and squashed the two beds side by side in the room. In the night I could feel Olive's breath on me.

But in the flat we had our own room and I was different. I could laugh when she held up my doll to punch it, and I stopped putting them in my bed. They lay all over the room and would get regularly thrown about in the hunt for shoes and socks.

At fourteen I was an old maid. I'd never been out with a boy. I had never really spoken to a boy, not since primary school, which didn't count because I was too young. I went to an all-girls' school, Lady Stanhope, a grammar school, so I didn't meet boys there. My friend Carol knew boys. She said she always played with them down her street, in a gang. She said that she had never actually slept with a boy but she'd had some of that – at which she held up her middle finger. I was too embarrassed to ask her what 'some of that' was. I asked Olive who told me not to be so dirty, so I gathered it was something sexual.

Carol knew a lot more than me, at least I thought so. Before we were friends I used to watch her in the playground at break-times, because she frightened me. It was like being fixated on a spider you couldn't bear the sight of. She was more like a boy than a girl. She had long straight mousy-fair hair, a turned up nose and small slit eyes that made her look Chinese. But she was English, a working-class Londoner, her family going back generations, all brought up on the same street. She was the same height as me, although she seemed to take up more space. She played football like a boy, pushing girls out of the way and shouting, 'You stupid bitch, get out of my way, fucking cow. Fuck you. Fucking cow.' She smashed things against the wall when she was angry, saying, 'Fuck it! Fuck it – cunt!'

But then the next minute she'd be calm and friendly, with

her arm round the girl she'd just demolished. And she would be able to make it all right so people would play with her again and choose her for their team.

I became her friend for fear that if I didn't, she might become my enemy.

Carol was mad about boys. It was all she wanted to talk about.

'Let's go down the youth club – you know, the one in the boys' school.' She nudged my elbow and winked, 'Eh, what do you think – for a laugh.' I wasn't sure but she looked pleadingly into my face, willing me to say yes by nodding her head.

'All right,' I said, 'but I ain't staying if it's crap.'

It seemed odd actually walking into the boys' school. Carol and me walked past the school as often as we could. We hitched up our school skirts and took off our ties as we went by. We pretended not to notice the throngs of boys. Boys hanging around the playground. Huddled in groups with cigarette smoke rising from them. Or sweating fast on the football pitch, screaming out names and holding their arms in the air wanting a pass to them. Sitting on walls, talking but not looking at each other, and every few seconds hawking phlegm up into their throats with a neanderthal sound and 'gobbing' the spit as far as they could get it. In their black and white uniforms, 'They look like a load of skunks,' Carol said.

But we'd never walked down through the playground. If we did that during the day we'd be eaten alive with just our hats left as proof we'd been there. But in the evening it was quiet: there was nobody around.

The outside of the club looked grotty, just a glass door with mesh over it and over the windows. You couldn't see in because of the crusted dirt. As we approached the door it was pushed open.

'Hello girls – you come for the club?' A middle-aged man stood grinning at us. I wanted to turn and run and Carol could tell because she held my arm firmly and pushed me a little.

'Come in, don't be frightened,' he said, showing us a row of perfect yellow stained teeth. We walked in through a waft of Old Spice. There were boys everywhere. Rows and rows simply looking, waiting silently for us to walk in. It was too late to run, they'd seen us – those thousands, those millions of boys. I looked at Carol who had the grin of Billy Bunter in a tuck shop. But subtle: only I knew.

'You'll have to fill in a form,' the man started saying, as the room filled up with noise; shouting and banging and laughing.

'Come in the office – follow me, girls.'

We followed him through a door which had a skull-and-crossbones sticker on it and *poison* written underneath, and some big letters that obviously said 'Fuck off wankers' and which somebody had tried hard to scrub off.

'I'm Ted – and who have I got the pleasure of meeting?' Carol and me stared.

'What?'

'What are your names,' Ted tried.

'I'm Carol.'

I said, 'I'm Vivien,' although nothing came out of my mouth. My lips moved, but – nothing. Then Carol said, 'This is Vivien,' and nudged my arm. I coughed and repeated *Vivien* audibly.

'Fill this in then, girls.' He handed us each a piece of paper. 'I'll get you pens,' he said, pulling biros out of a tin and rubbing them on a scrap of paper on the desk. He found one that worked and handed it to me. The form said Name, Address, Date of birth, School and Education authority. I waited for Carol who was waiting for her pen. I wanted us to fill the form in together in case I didn't really understand – in case it was more difficult than it looked.

'It's for the council,' Ted went on, finally handing Carol a biro. 'They like to know who comes here. It's a membership. I'll give you a card that you bring every week and get the tutor at your lesson to sign to say you've been. Have you thought what lessons you'd like to do?'

Lessons! I tried to catch Carol's eye. I didn't want any more lessons, I got plenty at school. More history, more physics. No thank you. I spelt my last name wrong and crossed it out. I can't hand this in, I thought, he'll think I'm a right prat who can't even spell her own name.

'There's table tennis and drama or you might like badminton – what else, let's have a look.' Ted hunted through papers on his desk. Carol finished her form and I nudged her to show me. She'd left out education authority but she handed it in anyway.

'There's football,' he went on, 'but you won't want that – have you finished, love?' he said, holding out his hand for mine.

'Table tennis,' Carol said. 'We'll do that, eh Viv.' I nodded. And drama, I wanted to say, but couldn't. I couldn't because I knew that if I spoke, whatever I said would be stupid, dumb, meaningless and Ted would look at me and frown and all those boys would laugh and point and Carol would say, 'What d'you say that for, stupid.'

'Table tennis it is then. I'll do your card and take you up to the room.'

'Innit in here?' Carol asked.

'No, this is the coffee bar and TV room. Table tennis, in fact all the lessons, are upstairs in the classrooms. I'll show you.' Ted started writing on cards. 'You can get drinks in here and there's a television in the little room down the bottom and football machines, but you're meant to do lessons. I shouldn't tell you this, girls, but seeing how you're both so pretty,' Ted winked at us and smiled, baring his teeth, 'most of the boys out there don't go to their lessons much but there's not a lot I can do. But you'll go, won't you girls. You'll like table tennis. You played before?'

Carol nodded – I shook my head.

'Well.' Ted took out a rubber stamp and pushed it on to the backs of the cards. 'Bona fide members, girls – now off to table tennis. You sure you don't want to do anything else, drama perhaps?'

Carol shook her head; so did I.

'Well, you think about it: you can always change your mind.'

The table-tennis room was up a long staircase that smelt of disinfectant trying to hide piss. The room was big and bright, probably a geography room during the day, with posters of sheep-farming in Australia and an Indian woman picking tea. There were five or six large green tables. And at all the tables were boys. One boy at each side, dancing and jumping around after a small white ball. Round the edges of the room were girls, standing together in twos and threes laughing or watching a game silently or talking to other boys who sat on the school desks which were piled up at the end of the room. The sound was punctuated by the click, click, click of the ping-pong balls hitting the tables.

Ted interrupted a game. 'Billy,' he shouted, holding his hand in the air. Billy stopped playing. He was tall and blond and not much younger than Ted, but he was dressed like all the other boys in the room. Ben Sherman check shirt, Levis rolled up at the ankles, big boots and braces. Ted talked to Billy as Carol and me tried to look as if we always stood in this room, as if it was nothing unusual. Carol bit her fingernail and I whispered, 'They're all skinheads.'

'They're not,' Carol said, without moving her lips.

'Look at their boots and jeans.'

'They've got long hair,' Carol said, 'that's not skinhead, that's crombie.'

'He ain't got long hair,' I said, trying to show her a boy at the other end of the room without moving or pointing in any way. 'They're all skinheads.'

I hated skinheads. If Olive could have seen me. Olive hated skinheads even more.

'Racist bastards,' she'd say, 'they hate everybody, them and their Paki-bashing and queer-bashing – who do they think they are?'

She told me, and I read in the *Daily Mirror*, how skinheads behave. Going round in gangs and beating people up. Leaving them for dead. How they love reggae but hate 'wogs' and wear steel-toe-capped boots so they can give a good kicking – even the girls.

I saw skinheads round our flats – not many at first but more and more came. They all dressed the same and looked frightening – tough. And Olive said that one day she met two on the stairs and they stared right at her, in her eyes, and started laughing. Then as she walked by them they said 'Fucking wogs.'

'Are you sure they said that?' I asked.

'Yeah,' Olive said, 'I'm sure – I hate skinheads.'

Since Olive told me that I'd always walk the other way if I saw any of them coming – even girls – or I'd cross the street or not look up. But here I was now in a room full of them.

'This is Carol and Vivien – am I right, girls?' Ted was saying. 'They want to learn to be champions. This is Billy – he'll teach you. I'll see you later girls: I leave you in Billy's capable hands.'

Billy didn't look at us. 'D'you know how to play?' he said, looking at the ground and around. I moved in closer to Carol. I felt like a bright light that everyone had to turn and look at. Carol's face went red as she nodded to Billy, who handed us a bat each.

'You can play on this table,' Billy said, indicating an empty table with his head and looking for a brief moment at Carol. Then he went and resumed his game.

'You go up that end,' Carol whispered.

She looked embarrassed, the most embarrassed I had ever seen her. More embarrassed than when she caught her skirt in the top of her knickers and walked into assembly like it. But she did then what she did now. Suddenly she changed. 'Come on Viv – you go up that end,' she said, loud and confident, although she was still scarlet.

I walked to the other side of the table from her. She picked up the ball that was lying next to the net and hit it across to me. I went to hit it with my bat but missed, and it tinkled on to the floor. Carol laughed. It rolled over near the legs of two boys. I looked at it. I looked at Carol. 'Go and get it.'

I looked at the ball again and the boys. I looked round the room. My ears became full of noise, like rushing water, and I felt hot and so bright. I leant over to Carol, 'I've got to sit down.'

'Get the ball then.'

I took no notice of her and went and sat on a chair behind me. Just as I did a boy rushed in through the door. He ran past Carol, pushing her out of the way. I was startled. He ran up to another boy in the room who started to back away from him, tripping over chairs. A girl screamed, 'No, Johnny!' The boy punched the tripping boy which made him fall harder back into the desks. Another girl screamed. The tripping boy got his balance and tried to punch the boy back but he missed. Somebody picked up a chair and held it in the air and girls screamed. Then boys were holding other boys apart and the air was thick with screaming and swearing.

'Fucking cunt, fucking, fucking, cunt. I'm going to 'ave you, fucking cunt.'

Then Ted ran into the room.

'Out! Come on you, break it up – I've told you.'

He picked up the boy who'd run in and pointed his finger. 'I've told you – you're barred,' he shouted into his face as he held him by the shirt with one hand. 'I don't want to see you here again.'

'Fuck off,' the boy screamed, struggling out of his grip.

'Out,' Ted shouted, pointing at the door. The boy began to straighten his clothes, tucking his Ben Sherman back into his jeans. He spat on the floor.

'You're fucking dead, John,' he growled, ' you're a fucking dead man.' He stomped out of the room, tipping over a chair as he left.

'Johnny, you're bleeding, oh, God, he's bleeding!' a girl shouted. Johnny held his hand up to his nose.

'I don't want this trouble, John, I've told you before.'

'It's not my fault,' Johnny said, looking at the blood on

his hands. 'He fucking jumped me.'

'And I don't want that language,' Ted said. Johnny rolled his eyes as a girl handed him a tissue. He held it up to his nose.

'I don't want this, Johnny,' Ted went on. 'You lot can kill each other outside, not in here, not on my time – in here you play table tennis.'

Ted started to straighten up the chairs with help from Billy. 'You all right, girls?' Ted said as he approached us. 'It's not like this all the time. You can carry on now.' He felt in his pocket and handed Carol a ping-pong ball. 'Come down to the bar when you've finished, I'll buy you a cup of tea,' he said smiling, and left. Carol put the ball and her bat on the table; so did I. We followed Ted downstairs.

'Let's go,' I said.

'In a minute,' Carol said. 'Let's just see what it's like in the bar bit.'

'I wanna go.'

'In a minute – don't be such a spoiler.'

I was shaking, but only on the inside I hoped.

Coffee bar sounded good. Coffee bars were where hip kids in chunky-knit jumpers hung round listening to jazz and clicking their fingers to the rhythm. This coffee bar was a smoky, loud place. Loud with shouts and screams coming mainly from the two table-football machines which had great big boys hanging on to them. Picking them up and trying to get the ball to roll their way. Slapping at the handles till they spun and someone shouted, 'No spinning, you fucking cheat.' Then someone lifted it again, banging it down hard on the floor. 'Goal – yes!' A boy threw his arms into the air. 'I am the greatest,' he shouted. 'Wanker,' came a reply.

There was a record-player playing something but the record was so scratched that the sound was distorted beyond recognition. Just the thud, thud, thud of a bass. And chattering.

''E never.'

''E did, on my life 'e did, I wouldn't lie, honest 'e . . .'

17

'They gave that goal away – he's a tosser that . . .'

'Don't, Mickey, you're such a . . .'

'Oi, Sandra your boyfriend's got a filthy . . .'

'No I can't tonight – I've got to take 'er down the Sporran.'

Ted beckoned us to a small counter with a glass cabinet on it full of Mars Bars and Dairy Crunches.

'Cup of tea, girls?' Ted said, feeling in his pocket for change. 'Two teas, Sandra – I'm paying, just put it on my tab.'

'You ain't got a tab – give us the money, you tight git,' the girl behind the counter said. Ted laughed as he placed the money down.

'You've got a wicked tongue. You can't pull one over on our Sandra,' Ted said, grinning and winking at us. 'Well, I'm going to have to love you and leave you girls.' He walked off to his office.

Sandra pushed two teas, in plastic cups, at us across the counter. She wasn't dressed like everyone else. She had on a long flowery print dress and black lipstick. 'You just come today?' she said to me. I nodded.

'Do you like it?' she asked, like an adult would to a child, although she looked my age. I smiled.

She beckoned us to pick up the teas. 'Go on, Ted's paid,' she said before turning her back.

Carol picked up the tea and I followed her over to two chairs by a wall. The room was painted green, blue, orange and red with no apparent logic. Circles mostly, overlapping and going over doors and round windows. The floor was grey lino, pock-marked with cigarette burns.

Carol and me didn't talk, we didn't have time. Every few seconds our eyes would be drawn to another shout or crash or someone jumping in the air. Startled like puppies on firework night.

A door in the middle of a wall opened. Covered with a blue circle, I hadn't noticed it was there. Inside the darkened room I could see the glow of a television.

'Shut the door,' a loud voice boomed, and Pamela from

our class came through. She saw us.

'Aaahh,' she screamed quietly.

'Aaahh,' we replied. This was the traditional greeting at our school.

'What you doin' 'ere?' Pamela said, coming over to us.

'What you doin'?' Carol said.

'I've been coming here ages,' she said, flicking her hand at us. She sat down.

'God, I can't believe it – you never said nothing.' We both shrugged. We had deliberately not told anyone about our adventure in case we got cold feet or it was rubbish.

'You never said you come,' Carol said.

'How long you been coming?' I asked.

'Ages,' Pamela screamed.

'They all skinheads?' I whispered.

'It's not skinhead – got long hair – it's more crombie – some skinheads but nice ones, you know. I can't believe it – come in the telly room – oh hang about, I've gotta get a drink for Linda.'

'Linda?' Carol said.

'Yeah,' Pamela screeched, 'Linda's in there – aaahh.'

'Aaahh,' we replied. I sipped at my tea which tasted of coffee. Pamela went to the counter. 'Got any orange?' She looked around her and patted her grown-out cropped hair. 'Hello, Gary,' she said to a boy who walked up to the television-room door and went in.

'Al'right,' Gary said.

Pamela quickly sat down in front of us. 'Oh I don't believe it. He's gorgeous, ain't he, don't you think?'

Carol and me looked at the door.

'Don't tell anyone, but I really fancy him.'

Sandra pushed the orange drink on to the counter.

'Oh hang about,' Pamela said getting up. She took a sip. 'Eh, it's warm,' she said. She patted her hair again. 'Oh, God I'm embarrassed now – do I look all right?' She was wearing a pink check Ben Sherman and short two-tone mohair skirt and white tights with a pattern of holes up them. It was almost like our school uniform but not quite. Carol looked at me and rolled her eyes.

'Come on then,' Pamela said, leading the way.

'She gets on my nerves,' Carol said to me. 'D'you wanna go in?'

'Yeah, all right,' I said.

I was comforted that I knew other people there. Pamela and Linda were in our class and sometimes they hung round with Carol and me at break-times. Sitting round Carol's desk at eleven o'clock eating the sandwiches her dad made her for lunch. I always got a sandwich, best friends first, and Carol gave Linda one once, but Pamela usually only got a bite.

Linda looked up as we walked in. 'Aaahh,' she said.

'Shut up,' a boy said.

'What you doin' here?' Linda said in a whisper.

'Shut the bloody door,' the boy in the corner growled. I quickly shut it behind me. Linda rolled her eyes and grinned.

'Sit down,' she said, pulling at a chair beside her. Carol nudged me to sit down. 'I'll get another one,' she hushed. Most of the other chairs were overturned.

'This is Tony,' Linda said nodding her head to the boy who had his arm round her. Tony was definitely a skinhead. Short crop and all.

'How do you do?' he said, smiling at me and Carol. He held out his hand for us to shake it. I wasn't sure what to do until Linda pushed it away and laughed. 'Take no notice of 'im – he's not all there.'

'I am,' Tony said, 'wanna see?' He grabbed at his fly and started to undo it.

'Get off you dirty git,' Linda said laughing.

'Shut it!' the voice boomed again. 'Or go outside – fuck ya.'

Pamela sat down and handed the drink to Linda who took a sip and pulled a face. We all looked at one another, then sat in silence watching Z Cars on the telly. I couldn't make out what was happening. Then the music for the credits came and everyone in the room, except me and Carol, started singing along. Someone got up and switched on the light. The room was suddenly bright and filthy with crisp-packets and cigarette-ends. Tony stared at me, then said: 'Give us a sip of yer drink, Linda?' He got down on one knee in front of her as she moved the drink out of his reach. 'Who's yer friends?'

'Carol and Viv,' Linda said.

'Hello Carol and Viv, I run this club – I'm the boss,' he said. He was short and fat but with impish good looks.

'Skinny!' shouted Linda. She held her little finger in the air.

'He *thinks* he's the boss,' said Pamela.

'You coming, Gary?' Tony called over to the boy Pamela fancied. He turned round slowly like an owl and looked at us. He was as pretty as a girl. His hair was long with a fringe, like Davy Jones in the Monkees. He may have been a skinhead but he was gorgeous.

Suddenly the door flew open.

'Fucking Rolly jumped me.' Johnny stood in the doorway still holding the tissue up to his nose. 'He fucking came right up to me, cunt – I'm goin' to 'ave 'im.' Johnny looked at the dry blood on the tissue. His nose had obviously stopped bleeding, but he put the tissue back. Two boys walked in behind him. One looked Greek or Turkish or something and he had large, deep green eyes, like Olive. The other was tall, fat and spotty with a lower lip that was too big for his face. He was grinning as Johnny went on.

'You comin' to get 'im?' Johnny said to Tony and Gary.

'Where's he gone?' Gary said reluctantly.

'Probably down the Oak.'

'Well they'll all be there, the 'ole Quadrant.'

'So – I'll just go in the pub, do 'im and get out.'

'They'll jump yer – you'll be dead,' Gary said.

'Well, let's wait outside – pick 'im off before he gets home and give 'im a kicking.'

'He might not be on his own,' Tony joined in.

'So there's . . .' Johnny looked at his gang, '. . . there's five of us.'

'There's fucking hundreds of them, and most of 'em are mad bastards,' Gary said.

'You bottling out on me?' Johnny said, looking straight at Gary.

'No,' Gary said throwing back his shoulders. 'No, just get 'im when he's on 'is own.'

Johnny kicked a chair and sat down. He looked at the tissue again but it hadn't changed since last time.

We girls sat in dumb silence, watching. Then a girl with short blonde spiky hair and a crombie coat walked into the room, sat down beside Johnny and slid her arm in his. Johnny shrugged away from her. 'Not now Dor,' he said, 'this is serious – go and sit with the girls.'

Dor got up and came and sat by us.

'You all right Dor?' Pamela said.

'It was bloody awful,' she said. 'He just came in and jumped him.'

'Why?' Linda asked.

'I don't know, he ain't done nothing.' Dor looked at me and Carol. 'You saw it, didn't ya?' We nodded. She whispered, 'He's bleeding and everything.'

Ted put his head round the door. 'Ten minutes, you lot, then out – we're closing up early tonight.' He looked around the room but no one replied. 'Ten minutes – all right,' he said, and shut the door.

'Let's get down the flats,' Tony said.

Everyone moved except me and Carol.

'You comin'?' Pamela said.

'Where?' Carol asked.

'The flats, you know, the Fields.'

Carol looked at me and grinned. 'That's where you live, innit, Viv.'

I nodded and smiled.

'Oh, really,' Pamela said, 'what block?'

'Wheat.' I said quietly.

'Oh, we hang round Corn and Fallow – it's round the block at bit.'

'What d'you do there?' Carol asked.

Pamela shrugged. 'Dunno – just hang round really.'

Carol and me looked at each other then followed them out.

Olive

Me and Vivien went to the same school. But I always thought of it as Vivien's school, not mine, even though I went there long before she did. In fact if it wasn't for me she'd have found it harder to get in, or she may not have got in at all. I had to pass my eleven-plus, which I did. But she, but Vivien, and this is typical really, didn't have to. When it came to her doing the eleven-plus, the powers that be decided to suspend the exam that year as an experiment. They decided that Vivien's year should be judged on merit – the year's work and that. So she didn't have to do it and got into the grammar school anyway because they like to keep sisters together.

That exam was horrible. I remember doing it, clear as anything. The day – there was something odd about the day. It was quiet, really quiet on the streets. No dogs or birds singing or cars. The only people about were scared-shitless kids like me, waving goodbye to their families and walking off, like they were going to war.

I was scared, but I wasn't that scared. I didn't really care whether I got into the grammar school or not. It was my mum's idea, she said it was a 'respectable' school, with 'decent girls'. I thought it was a right stuffy place. Strict uniform. You'd see the girls in their hats, not a hair out of place. And no black girls. All white. So I knew if I got in that straight away I'd be odd. I told Mum that there were no black girls, but she just smiled and said that that was good. And when I said that I'd be the only one, she sucked her teeth and changed the subject.

I passed, even though I didn't want to go to the school. I just wanted to show them that I could, that I wasn't thick. My teacher at primary school said I'd never come to anything because I couldn't stick at things, see them through to the end. He said I gave up too easily – which was rubbish. They were wrong and I showed them. They all looked surprised when I passed and nodded and smiled when I got into Lady Stanhope. Then they started giving me lectures on how I would have to knuckle down and work hard to keep up with the other girls.

I stuck two fingers up at that school when I left, and I stuck two fingers up at Lady Stanhope the first day I walked in.

The uniform was like a strait-jacket. There was tons of it. Vests, knickers, hockey boots, and they all had to be worn and worn 'correctly'. I hitched up my skirt on the first day. I was not going to be seen in that long skirt. The fashion was short, up your arse, and here was this skirt stopping on my knees just before my fawn socks started. I rolled it over and over at the waistband and tucked it under my purse belt. The deputy head, this mad old grey woman, caught me and made me kneel down so she could measure from the floor to where the hem was. It had to be less than six inches or she said you could see my knickers when I went up the stairs. Well don't look then, I thought. Mine was well out anyway, so I had to take it down and show her.

And you had to wear a hat. You had to wear this hat home – all the way. You were not allowed to take it off. Once you'd closed your front door behind you, then you could take it off. That was good of them: I didn't have to sit watching *Crossroads* in my bloody hat. If they saw you, the prefects or teachers, in the street without your hat, you'd get a detention. And in the rain the bloody thing would run – blue dye would run down your face in great streaks, but you had to keep it on. That was the sort of school it was. It was rules like that – stupid, dumb rules – that really got me. I mean, you couldn't ask why, couldn't discuss it. You just had to do it, like little kids.

My best mate at school, Maggie, was like me. She didn't

make jokes about wogs or coons and then say 'Sorry Olive, I don't mean you, you're all right,' in some prissy little posh voice. She lived in a council house, not a very nice place. She got suspended for dangling a pair of knickers out of the window on a pole. The headmistress saw them from her office. The old bag blamed me at first, but Maggie said it was her. She only had to stay away from school a few days: her dad made such a fuss they had to let her come back.

We used to get reports and I'd sign my mum's name on them but never show her. I never looked at them either, really, I just opened the first couple of pages. 'Olive does not apply . . . Olive should try to . . . Olive's attitude needs . . .' I didn't have to read them – I knew.

But there was nowhere to do homework at home. I couldn't put my books out for long without someone wanting to sit down or use the table or switch the telly on. And I couldn't go into the bedroom because it was freezing and Mum didn't like us to put on the electric fire for too long. It didn't seem to matter to her that it was my education.

When I left I didn't get one exam, but I didn't care. I broke a stink bomb in assembly on my last day. The smell was disgusting. I was choking. I had to run out but then so did everyone else. It was so funny. The headmistress said she was glad to see the back of me. And I was glad to see the back of her, even though the back of her was worse than the front because she had such a fat, wobbly arse with big thick wedge legs like two triangles stuffed up her skirt.

I hated that school.

Vivien

We started hanging round. There was Tony, Gary, Arthur, Johnny, Salvo and Carol, Pam, Linda and me. There were loads of others that came and went. Other Garys, Barrys, other Johns, the odd Frankie and even a Ralph. And other girls who came round on a boy's arm and stayed for a couple of weeks, and who then got packed in and we didn't see any more. Or people's cousins who came to stay or friends from work or school. We went up the youth club when it was open which was three nights a week and on the other nights and during the school holidays we hung round the flats – in the porch and on the stairs of Corn block or on the grass in front of Fallow. Sometimes outside the chip shop on the main road or round by the swings or on the low wall near the bins. Two of us would go and sit, and gradually through the night everyone else would come and—

'Pooh, who's farted?' Johnny says.

'Not me,' Arthur says.

'Something's crawled up you and died.' Carol to Arthur.

'I can't smell nothing – it must be your top lip stinkin'.' Arthur to Carol.

'Your mouth open more like.' Johnny to Arthur.

'Blimey, I can smell it now – fuck, it stinks.' Salvo, waving his hand in front of his face.

Arthur grins.

'It is you, you dirty git,' Pam says. Everyone waves their hand in front of their face.

'Silent but violent,' Arthur says.

'Loud but proud.' Tony lets off a loud fart and turns his

bum towards everyone. Linda and me jump back and hold our noses. Everyone else laughs. Salvo sticks out his bum and does the same. The girls scream, the boys laugh.

'Got any money for chips, Linda?' Tony asks.

'I'm skint,' Linda says.

'Get off, everyone knows you're rollin' in it,' Johnny says. Skinny,' Linda says, putting her little finger in the air.

'Where's Gary tonight?' Pam to Johnny.

Johnny shrugs, 'He's out with that slag.'

'Who?' Pam asks.

'That muff from up the Sporran.'

'Which one?'

'Her with the hair,' Tony says.

'He don't fancy 'er, does 'e?' Linda says.

'He's after what he can get,' Johnny says.

'Well she's had more pricks than a dartboard,' Carol says.

'She's a right goer – she'll do it with anyone,' Tony says.

'Yeah, she gave that wog a blow-job last week, made me feel fucking sick when I 'eard,' Johnny says.

'Who?' Pam says.

'That one that hangs round with that cunt Rolly, thinks he's God's gift, think's he's hard,' Johnny says.

'He's got at least twelve inches,' Carol says, laughing, indicating inaccurately.

'Oh yeah, how do you know?' Tony says.

'All wogs got big dicks,' Carol says.

'Get off – they ain't that big,' Linda says.

'It's a well-known fact,' Carol says.

'You measured the ones you had?' Johnny cups his hand and shakes it, the wanker sign.

'Get off, I can't stand 'em,' Carol says, holding her nose, laughing and nudging me. I smile.

'Twelve inches would come out her mouth,' Salvo says, making a choking sound.

'Oh yes, you queer bastard.' Arthur walks along with one limp wrist.

'He's wearing a pink shirt,' Pam says, laughing.

28

'Hampstead away colours,' Tony and Johnny chant together, then put their little fingers in the air and say, 'Skinny.'

'Bollocks,' Salvo says.

Tony grabs his crotch. 'You ain't havin' mine.'

'Fuck off, tossers,' Salvo says.

'Dunno what she's going out with Gary for – pencil-dick,' Tony says. 'She needs a man like me.' He goes to undo his fly.

'Oh, get off,' Pam and Linda shout. Tony laughs.

'Any time you wanna, girls, I'm always ready.'

'We're fed up, not hard up,' Carol says.

'You're a dirty git,' Linda says. Tony blows her a kiss.

I stood round with them. I laughed and jumped about. I patted my hair and bit my fingernail. I smiled, looked horrified or puzzled, whatever was required. I nudged Carol and bought chips and passed them round. I did everything like everyone else did. Except that I didn't speak. When the boys were around I couldn't speak. It was too great a leap, like jumping into a spotlight and taking a bow. I wanted to stay unseen. Because they all hated wogs. And I had nothing to say.

Olive

I liked going to clubs. I used to go up the West End to Birdland or to Whisky-a-Gogo. I loved the music, loud, thumping music that you could just let yourself go to. Just run round inside it every night, forget about everything. Forget about the fact that I worked in a crummy shop all day. Chelsea Girl on Holloway Road. Sounded good, assistant in a boutique. Sounded swinging. But it was so boring.

I got bossed about by a stupid white bitch whose only ambition in life was to work in Chelsea Girl, to work her way up to being manager. Big deal. I wanted better things for me. I only did it for the money, so I could go down the clubs and forget who I was during the day.

And I was popular down there. I got asked out all the time. People used to say I could have been a model. Some people thought I was, and they'd come up to me and say 'Aren't you that model?' or, 'Didn't I see you on the telly?' And sometimes I'd say yes and they'd look at me with respect, a shy respect. But if I said I worked in a shop, their eyes would roll and glaze over.

Most of the blokes at the clubs were French, although some were Italian. But the main thing was that there were hardly any English blokes and the ones that there were were nice. Not like the blokes that hung round our flats. No little creeps who came up to your chest and would ask if you'd give them a blow-job. French blokes have a sort of charm. They mostly didn't speak English or they were here to learn. I only knew one word of French, *merde*, so we didn't have many great conversations. But I understood; we used sign language and you couldn't hear much anyway because of the music. French blokes were more sensitive, more intelligent.

I stayed at the clubs all night or sometimes Maggie and me would wander through Hyde Park or Regent's Park in the early morning and wait for the tubes and buses to start. Sometimes we went back to people's flats and had a laugh until it got light.

I went with a bloke once. He was Italian, said he was an actor. Everyone fancied him but he just bought me drinks all night. I really liked him. He even paid for a taxi back to his place which was miles away. He had a nice flat, big and posh with carpets on the walls. He said it belonged to his family who were counts or something in Italy.

We sat on the settee and started kissing. He started to get really heavy, breathing deep and grabbing up my jumper and trying to get his hands up my skirt. He was all over me. I was a bit pissed, but not that pissed. At first I just laughed and pushed his hands off but he wouldn't stop. And it got harder and harder to keep his hands down – he began to use force. I started shouting 'No' and 'Get off'. And he stopped, looked at me surprised and said, 'What did you expect?' He grabbed me again, saying I owed him. I tried to push him off. Then he slapped me hard round the face. I was so stunned, I looked at him and it got me off guard and he pushed me down on the floor and knelt on my arms. I was screaming, but he didn't seem to care. He was leaning on my arms and looming over me when he started undoing his fly. He got his prick out. It was huge – I'd never seen one look like that before, fat and red. He tried to stick it in my mouth. I kept turning my head and wriggling around as much as I could. And this thing kept hitting my face but I kept my lips tight shut. He yanked up my jumper and pulled at my bra until my tits fell out the top. Then he stuck the thing between them and started rubbing it on them. It was like he was pushing an iron bar on me.

I stopped struggling. I just lay there looking at the carpet on the wall, picking out little creature faces in the pattern. He rubbed himself and grunted and dribbled on my neck. Then he came over me, a great whoosh of sticky, warm slime, and he went limp all over like a great sack of shit. I pushed him off – it took a couple of goes. And I called him every name I could think of. But he just lay there with his eyes shut. He didn't even look at me.

I wiped the spunk off with his jacket and threw it on the floor. And as I went out of the room he said, 'Thank you.'

I just ran out of there. I forgot my coat. It was dark and I hadn't got a clue where I was. I just started walking in the hope I'd find a bus-stop or a tube. Eventually I found a tube and sat by the gates and waited for it to open. I was freezing and I couldn't stop crying. I could smell him on me. I felt so stupid.

When I got home my mum was up. She looked at me – I must have looked such a state. I was shivering. She sat me down in the kitchen and made a cup of tea. I was so pleased to be home that I told her what had happened. She listened, then she looked at me and said, 'If you ever do that again, I'll kill you.'

Vivien

Olive laughed her sarcastic laugh when she heard that school-days are meant to be the best days of your life.

'I'll kill myself now then,' she said. 'I'd kill myself now if I really thought that was the best bit of my life. Don't you believe it, Vivien – school-days are shit and whoever says different is mad.'

I thought school was great, although I snarled and rolled my eyes with Olive and everyone else when they talked about it. The uniform – what crap. The school dinners – disgusting. The rules – bloody stupid.

We had assembly in the mornings, the whole school together. Rows and rows of maroon and black, fidgeting and rippling like a gentle sea. We sang hymns and then listened to a sermon given by Mrs Baker the Baker's Bum, our headmistress.

'Girls must not run in the corridors. Girls must not boo at the swimming gala. Girls must not fraternize with boys at the school gates. Girls must not chew gum.' There seemed to be no end of things we girls must not do. It only took one person to do something before it became a school rule to stop doing it.

Lessons sometimes got in the way, except when I sat next to Carol and she'd say, 'Sir,' to Mr Olman our religious knowledge teacher, 'why have you got hair in your ears?' The whole class would laugh and we'd watch his face creep from white to pink and his bald head glow with the embarrassment.

'Don't worry about that, young lady,' he said.

33

'But, sir,' Carol went on, 'you said we could ask you about anything we didn't understand.'

'About religious matters, Carol and you know it – you can be a sensible girl when you want to.'

'Well, sir, I really have got a question about something I heard from the Bible in assembly. I have, sir, it's a real question, innit Viv?'

I nodded because she was my friend. Mr Olman sighed. 'What is it then?'

'What does intercourse mean sir?' Carol asked, as most of the class suppressed a laugh behind their hands. Mr Olman smiled and said, 'It means to meet with other people.'

'Is that all?' Carol shouted. Mr Olman nodded and remained quite pale until Carol said, 'What about sexual intercourse, sir?' We all laughed out loud as he glowed as red as a squeezed spot.

At break-times the whole school had to go into the playgrounds. The only exception was when wind, rain or snow made it impossible for Miss Forsyth, our deputy headmistress, to stand upright when testing the air outside with her finger. Miss Forsyth thought that we north London girls did not get enough fresh air. So break-times, including dinner, were spent trying to avoid sampling the weather. Trying to stay attached to a warm radiator discussing our favourite topic, boys.

'Tony's nice,' Linda said, 'when he's on his own.'

'He's lairy,' Carol said.

'Only when he's with his mates – honest, Carol – he's really nice when you get him on his own, really shy.'

'Johnny's the lairy one,' I said.

'Yeah,' Carol agreed, rolling her eyes.

'He's like Tony, though – I walked down the flats with him the other night and he's quite shy,' Pam said.

'You said he tried to get you to hold his dick,' Carol said, laughing. We all laughed.

'Yeah, but he was shy about it,' Pam said. 'He didn't just plonk it out.'

'Oh, fuck-me-gently Pam!' Carol shouted, 'You don't 'alf talk some crap.' We all laughed again as Pam said, 'What, no what – tell us what – what'd I say, what?'

Prefects and teachers patrolled the corridors looking in classrooms for signs of life. We hid under tables, in cupboards, toilets. If they saw us, made eye contact, they wouldn't speak, just stand in the doorway and wait for us all to file out past them. Then we'd walk outside through one door and back inside through another and go back to our last hiding-place, safe in the knowledge that they wouldn't look there again for a while.

We all had ambitions. Carol wanted to be a solicitor.

'My mum wants me to do law,' she said. 'It's a good profession and you'll always have a job.'

Linda wanted to be a nurse, because 'I like helping people. I always look after my baby brother when he's ill and I really like it. It's all I want.'

Pam wanted to be as happy as her mum. Get married young and have a flat with a washing-machine. She said, 'I don't wanna be one of those old parents, I can't stand that. I wanna be young so I can still understand my kids. I just wanna be like my mum.'

Pam's mum always looked haggard to me. She had three kids. Pam was the eldest and the other two were boys. I'd see her down the shops screaming at her sons, 'You get 'ere.' And if they didn't come,' You get 'ere now or I'll fucking brain yer.' My mum said she was common and that I shouldn't hang round with Pam too much in case some of that 'rough' rubbed off on me.

I wanted to be a film director. And when I told Miss O'Keefe, my English teacher, my favourite teacher, about my ambition, she didn't laugh. She looked at me seriously and asked me what exams I was taking. Then she talked to me about film school and said she could see no reason why I shouldn't try.

I was taking O-levels at school, GCEs, hundreds of them. English Literature and Language, Geography, Art, History and Food and Nutrition and CSE French and Maths. We had exams first to see how good you were at the subject. If you passed you were allowed to take the O-level, and if you failed you were made to take the inferior CSE.

'Do you know it?' Pam always asked me outside the exam-room door.

'No,' I'd say.

'Have you studied?' I'd ask Carol.

'No,' she'd say.

'Have you, Linda?'

'No, I went out. We went out last night, didn't we, Pam.'

'I bet you've swotted, Viv,' Carol would say.

'I haven't – don't know any of it,' I'd lie.

I always looked at my books for weeks before. I slept with them under my pillow in the hope that the knowledge would seep out of them and into my head in the night. I sang history dates to myself because my mum said it was easier to remember things as a song. And I asked Olive to test me on my French verbs. She'd sit with the book next to her cup of tea saying, 'To jump, to give, to sleep' in an uninterested monotone. Eventually she'd throw the book at me and say 'That's enough, swot.'

When the exam results came out, I came top of my class in everything. Carol looked at me and winked, proud to be my best friend. 'You're really clever, Viv,' she said. 'You should be a solicitor too.' She told everyone about my brains saying, 'You should listen to Vivien, she's brainier than you,' if anyone disagreed with anything I said.

But I couldn't understand how I came top. I looked at Carol, Linda and Pam and the rest of my class and wondered what was going on in their heads. It didn't make sense. I mean I even came top in Food and Nutrition. The task I got was to take Jewish old-age pensioners on a picnic where I had to supply all the food. I had to say what I'd make them. And I forgot a golden rule and put down egg and cheese flan with salad. It was only as I handed the paper in that I could hear my teacher's voice in my head saying, 'Old people have difficulty chewing, so never give them something that requires a lot of mastication, like, for example, a salad, because bits may get stuck under their dentures and cause them problems later.'

But I still came top. What did they all give them, roast pork with crackling?

Olive

My dad died at an awkward time for me. I was planning to leave home, get a place of my own, maybe with Maggie or some other people. He got ill, and I just couldn't stand to see him sitting in a chair all day coughing. It's no life. It was the best thing really. Sad of course, but . . .

I didn't really get on with him anyway, not since I was little. When I was small, really small, he used to hit me with his slipper. Sometimes for no reason. He'd just get mad and fly at me and push his big face into mine. When I got up to run he'd chase me, hopping to get his slipper off, then he'd hit me with it, sometimes four or five times. Hopping mad, that's what I thought it meant, my dad running after me trying to grab his shoe. When he'd finished, I'd sit in a corner or behind the settee and try and think what I'd done. Sometimes I knew – I'd spilt something or lost something. But sometimes I just didn't know.

Well, if you're going to get hit, get hit for something. Stupid git. After a while I used to laugh. He never hit Vivien. Not once. If anyone had to be hit, anyone had to be shouted at . . . oh, he saved it up for me.

When he died my mum was really upset, wailing at the funeral. She wanted to throw herself down on the floor and sob. If it was just me I'd have let her. It was embarrassing, really.

I couldn't leave then, not straight away. I felt sorry for Vivien, leaving her with Mum. She was only young – still played with her bloody dolls. I thought it might be quieter now anyway, without my dad. But my mum just starting hopping for two instead.

Mum was always chasing me round the flat – it was driving me mad. I'd stay out later and later in the hope that she'd be in bed or at least too tired to fight. I dreaded coming home, I just knew I would get such grief. When I thought of my mum all I saw was this big contorted angry face with slit eyes, fat cheeks and a mouth open with a pink tongue flapping furiously. That's all I could see. I couldn't remember what she looked like when she smiled, and as for laughing – no – just a childhood memory along with Noddy and Big Ears.

She wanted me just to stay in every night, sit in the chair Dad used to sit in and watch the telly. And then when I matured, when I was just like her, then I would miraculously find a husband. She worried about me she said, it wasn't safe outside. Well it wasn't safe inside, either.

I met Peter down a club. Pete everyone called him, but I insisted on calling him Peter. I think that's why he noticed me. I didn't fancy him at first: I didn't like English blokes. But he was different. He had a beard for one thing. It made him look mature, like someone you could tell your problems to, someone who'd look after you. He had long, straight dark hair which was parted in the middle, like the bloke in the Kinks, only nice. And blue eyes that were so pale they were almost nothing.

He could talk too. Not just about himself like most of them. He talked about workers' rights, exploited labour and the right to strike. He was passionate about politics. I'd never really thought much about it. But on the first night we talked and I listened to him. We wandered through Hyde Park up to the fountains as the sun was coming up. It was magical – so romantic.

And when he asked me where I came from, I didn't do what I usually did – stick my hands on my hips and shout London, England – I told him my parents were from Jamaica. And he said he thought so. Then he talked about how black people were exploited and how we should get together with the workers to overthrow all oppression.

He didn't even kiss me that night – he had too much respect for me. Women, he said, were special because we were the bearers of children, the givers of life.

'Workers of the world unite – you have nothing to lose but your chains,' he shouted, standing on the side of the fountain with his arms up, silhouetted against the water like the statue of somebody who was going to change the world.

Vivien

Friday night was disco night at the youth club, so me and Carol bunked off school after lunch to get ready. I sat for a long hour in a hot bath listening to the unfamiliar DJ on afternoon Radio One. Then I went to Carol's where Linda, Pam and me squeezed into her bedroom to get ready together, listening to Percy Sledge singing, 'When a Man Loves a Woman' over and over again.

No one was in at Carol's house until late in the evening. Her brother was much older than her, grown-up and living in a flat with a wife and child. She lived in a big house, but her family only seemed to occupy a little bit of it: the kitchen which was also the bathroom, the living room and two bedrooms. The rest of the rooms had doors that were kept firmly shut and when you asked about them Carol would shout, 'Don't go in there – it's haunted.' When I stayed with her she would wake in the night and lift her head from our shared bed and say,' Can you hear that?' Then she'd go back to sleep and leave me listening to the strange dragging and thumping noises coming from the mysterious rooms. Several cats sat alert at holes in the floorboards, and an old smelly Alsatian dog lived behind a dilapidated twin-tub washing-machine in the kitchen. It never seemed to be walked, and only moved a few feet from its spot to go into the backyard and crap.

Carol's parents were 'Bloody ancient – my dad was mates with Noah,' she said. And they did look old, but they stayed out of our way except that Carol had to be home earlier than anyone else. Her dad would wait outside the youth club in an old Ford Anglia. She'd see him and groan: 'Bloody stupid old fart.' She'd get in the car and shout, 'Go, then, if you're going,' before he had a chance to finish his smile and sentence about whether she had enjoyed herself. He never seemed to complain. But if she got in late or he saw her with a boy then he would roar at her and she'd be cowed.

Different to my mum. My mum was . . . not uninterested, just tired. 'Vivien, you're late nah,' she'd say from her chair in front of the telly. 'Try and get in sooner, you hear me – I have the worry.' I spent most of my evenings watching her chasing Olive round the flat, shouting and flailing her arms. Our flat was designed so you could run round it: through the kitchen into the hall, round past the bathroom, through the lounge and back into the kitchen until you got dizzy. 'You get back here now, child!' she screamed, running past with a shoe held high. Olive coming past pulling off her coat in a well-practised manner and shouting, 'Shut up, you silly cow.'

'Don't talk to me like that,' my mum now with a tea towel that she whipped out in front of her in the hope of reaching Olive. Then Olive grinning at me as she ran past for the third time. And my mum eventually collapsing puffed on to the settee muttering, 'That child will be the death of me – I don't know where she came from, she's the devil's child, the devil's.' And Olive calling, 'Goodnight,' from her room before she locked the door behind her. My mum was spent.

'Look at all these split ends,' Pam said, holding up a clump of hair for Linda and me to look at. Carol came into the room with a bottle.

'Here it is,' she said, triumphant, 'Protein 21.' Protein 21 mended split ends.

'Quick, give it here,' Pam said, grabbing for the bottle.

'Get off,' Carol said, giving Pam a withering stare. 'It's bloody expensive.'

'Can I borrow some?' Pam asked.

'Just a bit,' Carol said.

'It don't work,' Linda said, 'I used it, and I've still got 'em.'

Linda handed me a bunch of her long dark hair. I looked at the tips and could see the rogue ends with their two strands that so plagued our lives.

'Oh yeah,' I said, 'you've still got some.'

'I mean, it's better,' Linda went on, 'but it's not like what they say – they're not all gone.'

Linda lifted up my hair. 'Ohh, Viv, you've got terrible ends – look at these ends,' she said, holding my hair up and yanking my scalp a little. 'You need to cut those off, Viv.'

'I know – I don't care though,' I said.

'Don't care,' my friends said in unison.

'You can try the shampoo, Viv – go on, take it – you can wash your hair in the kitchen.'

'No,' I said, 'I only washed it last night – it gets ever so dry if I wash it too much.'

'Dry!' they all shouted.

'You're lucky, Viv, I'd give anything to have dry hair. Mine's so greasy,' Pam said.

Carol ran her hand across Pam's hair and said, 'Frying tonight, Pam?' We all laughed.

My hair was a lie. It wasn't really straight. It shouldn't have hung down my face like it did. It should have been frizzing up around my chin. Olive and me straightened our hair. But I didn't like people to know. My mum said people would think it was naturally like that. When me and Olive were young it was a big secret, going to the hairdresser's. We didn't brag about it like girls with perms or crop cuts did. We just had it done, and when it lay lank round my face I'd say I'd had it thinned. And after washing it I would have to roll it up carefully in hair rollers and sit for hours under a hair dryer hood until it was dry. At night I wore a cut-off stocking with a knot in the end, pulled down tight on my head to keep my hair in place. Rain made it frizz up, damp made it frizz up, and as for going swimming . . . well. Olive and me wore a lot of hats: woolly ones, plastic ones, rubber ones, anything to keep our hair straight.

'It sort of sticks the ends together, I think, it feels sort of sticky,' Carol said, coming back into the room after washing her hair. She rubbed a towel over it and showered us all with water, then she combed it through and pushed it into the desired shape.

We were all too busy to reply. Nail polish takes concentration so you don't get little bits round the outsides of your nails. We swapped make-up, looking in each others' bags at Miners mascara in black and midnight blue, Miners white cream eye-shadow in little tubes, Revlon blue powder eyeshadow and blushers in vivid pinks. We all put on our make-up in the same way – the proper way – the only way, as taught by *Fab 208* and *Jackie* magazines. Blue or green eyeshadow on the lids, then white shiny stuff under where your eyebrows were, but which were now either plucked off, in the case of Pam, and replaced by a drawn line, or shaped into neat half moons. Then the white shadow continued under the eyes to help give you a wide-awake look. Finished by at least three layers of mascara. 'You're so lucky, Viv, you've got such lovely long eyelashes,' Linda said, and she was right. When I'd finished with the mascara wand my eyelashes could get caught in my eyebrows. I was proud of my lashes. 'They're great,' Carol said, 'they look false.'

We all got dressed. Pam in her new two-tone green and red mohair suit with short skirt and long jacket. Linda in a blue Ben Sherman and navy sta-prest trousers. Carol didn't like the shirts. 'Not for a dance – it's too hard-looking,' she said. She wore a multicoloured striped jumper with short sleeves over a long-sleeved mauve satin blouse. I wore a tight pink angora top and borrowed Pam's black and white Prince of Wales check skirt.

'Vivien!' Olive had shouted when she saw the skirt on my bed. 'What's this?' She held it out in front of her like it had a bad smell. 'Since when have you been a skinhead?'

'I'm not,' I protested, 'I only borrowed it.'

'I've seen everything now,' she went on, oblivious to me, 'I've seen everything. But I never thought I'd see the day when my own sister would turn into one of them.'

I wasn't sure if she was joking.

'I'm *not* a skinhead – I just borrowed it.'

She took no notice. 'I never thought I'd see a Prince of Wales check skirt in this house. You getting a mohair suit next, or, or . . . Oh my God, you getting Doc Martens, eh Vivien, with steel toecaps . . .'

'No,' I screamed.

'. . . Going beating up Pakis, Vivien, eh, kicked any heads in?'

'I'm not – it's not like that, I only borrowed it.'

She flung the skirt at me and walked out. She wasn't really angry, but she wasn't really laughing. I gave the skirt back to Pam after that, saying it didn't fit. But tonight I was staying at Carol's, and it did.

We looked in the full-length mirror in Carol's parent's room. Adjusting skirts and pulling on our white tights to get the holes in a straight line down the sides of our legs. Taking it in turns.

'So just say hello,' Carol instructed me.

'I mean, we all get shy – I'm shy,' Pam said.

Carol gave Pam an disbelieving stare then turned back to me.

'I mean, you're not shy with us,' she said. 'Just lift up your head and say hello – it's easy – then you won't feel so shy.'

'Yeah, 'cause people think you're a snob,' Pam said. Carol gave her another look.

'Do they?' I asked.

'It's just 'cause you don't say anything,' Linda said. 'They don't know you like we do – I tell 'em – I say you're just shy . . .'

'I don't know why I am,' I said.

'Just lift up your head and say hello – go on, practise – pretend I'm Gary.'

We all laughed. 'Not him, I hate him,' I lied.

'Why?' Pam asked.

'Thinks he's God's gift,' I said.

'Don't you think he's good-looking though?' Pam said.

45

'Not as much as he does,' I said. Pam looked hurt but Linda laughed.

'Well, not Gary then,' Carol went on. 'Oh, just say hello, that's what I'm saying – just say hello then you won't feel so bad.' My friends all looked at me and nodded like three maiden aunts. Then we all sprayed on Carol's Kiku perfume in turn with her shouting 'That's enough!' and left.

Olive

Peter and me started spending a lot of time together. All our time when we weren't working. He was a postman so he worked from very early in the morning until the afternoon. I used to take days off work, calling in sick with headaches and stomach-aches and dentist's appointments and so many period pains that I would have been haemorrhaging, not menstruating. But I just wanted to be with him.

He lived a long way from me in south London, Lewisham. I'd never really heard of Lewisham before I met him. In fact all of south London was just a great 'down there' region to me – I knew it was there, I just didn't want to look. He lived with his mum and loads of brothers and sisters. So many that I lost track. Some older than him, some much younger. His dad was a long-distance lorry driver. 'Very long distances,' Peter used to say, 'so long we hardly see him.' They lived in a council house, a big house. But there were so many of them. Every room I looked in seemed to have four beds in it. And the noise – thumping, shouting, screaming non-stop. It made my house feel like a nunnery.

We spent more time at my house. At first we used to get in and sit in this embarrassed silence with my mum and Vivien and watch the television. My mum didn't take much notice of Peter. She wasn't rude, in fact she smiled at him and offered him cups of tea. But that was it. And he was just happy being somewhere where you could sit down without a flying toddler landing in your lap. But then one day Peter made a comment when we were watching the news. He said, 'The Labour party are selling the workers down the river.'

Me and Vivien took no notice but my mum said, 'That's right – they want to get rid of all those Communists. I'm a Conservative. They know what they're doing. They're decent people. Not like that riff-raff in the Labour Party who can't even dress properly.'

And that was it. From then on most evenings were spent listening to Peter trying to persuade my mother out of being a fascist. Impossible. She'd rant on about people looking after themselves and how people didn't want to work because 'they're bone idle, Peter, bone idle.' And Peter would talk about the workers working together to overthrow bosses in factories and idleness would end because workers would control the means of production.

At first I got worried when they started arguing; all night they'd go on. But then I realized they both liked it. My mum was all for ending idleness, and Peter liked my mum because she was working-class. Although when he said that to her, she looked at him like he just spat in her face.

I started getting on better with Mum. Nothing major, but she stopped chasing me round and didn't seem to mind what time I got in as long as I was with Peter. She pretended he annoyed her 'with all his ideas'. But whenever he was around she wanted to talk to him. Then it started to get on my nerves. She wouldn't let us be alone. If we went into the bedroom she'd soon come knocking on the door. Not asking us in a suspicious manner what we were doing in there, but offering Peter fried chicken or 'did he want to try her bread pudding.'

I began to take afternoons off work too so we could go home and be by ourselves, well, at least until Vivien got home from school. Peter would meet me and we'd walk home arm in arm. He hated being a postman but said that at least he had some control over his job – when he was out delivering letters no one could see what he was doing, he was his own boss. But he always looked forward to the day when he'd be truly free. After the revolution.

One day he picked me up in a car. He'd just bought it and

wanted to surprise me. It was an old Oxford Cowley but I was really impressed. It was all grey and round outside and had leather upholstery inside that was cracked and worn with age. He said he bought it for me – so he could show me a new life. When he said that I knew I loved him.

I never felt like that for anyone before. When he wasn't there I missed him so much. I thought about him all day, and kept looking at the clock until he'd pick me up. I'd see him, and I know this sounds mad, but he was like a knight come to take me away. I'd float out of the shop and give everyone dirty looks as I got into my car.

I didn't need anyone else, just him. I stopped seeing Maggie. All she wanted to do was go down the clubs. But I went off clubs. Too many people, too much noise. It seemed so childish. I just wanted to be alone with Peter. Somewhere where I could listen to him and hear him say, 'Oh you silly wombat,' when I didn't understand something or asked him questions. I was mad about him, I was crazy about him. I wanted to get as close to him as possible – right down inside him and curl up and let him take care of everything.

He didn't make me have sex with him – I wanted to. I wanted to make love to him. It started gradually and he kept asking me if I was sure. Was I sure I liked him feeling my breast? Was I sure I liked him fingering me? Was I sure I wanted to be naked with him in bed?

It hurt me the first time we actually did it. There just didn't seem to be enough room inside me to take him all in. I thought there was something wrong with me. It stopped hurting after a while but I couldn't understand how it could be nice. I writhed about and panted; I knew that's what you had to do and I wanted it to be good for him. But I kept thinking about stuffing chickens whenever we did it. I couldn't get the image out of my mind. A great fat hand stuffing wodges of goo up a chicken's arse.

Once we started having sex, that's all he wanted to do. He stopped asking me if I liked it. Stopped kissing and cuddling with me on the settee before anyone came in. It was always straight down to it. And sometimes in the afternoons I didn't want to, not really. I wanted to listen to him talk about what the world would be like when inequality was banished for ever. But it got to be a quick fuck then put the telly on. I didn't mind though – I loved him.

Then I missed my period.

Vivien

The disco was at the top of the school in an unfamiliar room. We followed handwritten signs that said 'Youth club dance' and a wobbly arrow that always pointed upwards. The signs were unnecessary as the music was so loud and alien to the grey-walled corridors that you couldn't possibly wander into another room by mistake. The deep thudding bass of 'Remember Me' by Diana Ross kept us on track.

'You know what this song means?' Pam said, as we turned up another flight of stairs. Nobody answered, we didn't have to.

'It means,' Pam went on, 'that she's dying of cancer, you know.'

'Who said?' Carol said.

'It's true – everyone knows it.'

Linda nodded. 'It's true Carol – I've 'eard it too.'

'Yeah, but what's that gotta do with it?' I asked, as Carol rolled her eyes so only I could see.

'It's to her fans – you know – remember me after she dies, that sort of thing,' Pam said with authority.

'Really,' I said.

'Yeah – it's sad innit,' Linda said.

'Yeah,' I said. I was always happy to believe anything tragic about the world of pop.

'When's she going to die then?' Carol said, but there was no answer because we'd reached the disco door.

'Hello girls,' Ted said. He was sitting on a table that blocked half the doorway. 'You all coming?' he grinned.

Carol looked down at her crotch and said, 'No, it's just the way me skirt hangs,' and we all giggled.

'How much is it?' Linda asked.

'Well to you, my special girls, who all look so lovely, it's two bob each.'

'Yeah, and a shilling for everyone else,' Carol laughed.

'You gonna let us in for free then, Ted, 'cause you love us?' Pam asked.

'I wish I could, my beauties, but it's only two bob and you're in.'

'As the actress said to the bishop,' Carol said, and went 'Boo-boom.'

We gave Ted our money in turn and he took it and pressed a date-stamp on the backs of our hands which printed a blue smudge on our skin.

'You can go in and out now girls,' Ted said. We all looked at one another and began to giggle again.

'Dirty git,' Pam said, and we giggled some more.

Ted looked hurt. 'I know I've just said something funny, girls, I'm just trying to figure out what,' he said.

The room was empty apart from the DJ who stood over in one corner behind his console of traffic-lights wired up to flash the beat. We put our bags and coats in a pile in another corner.

'Right,' Linda said, 'When good music comes on we'll show you how to dance.'

You couldn't just get up and boogaloo any more, that went out with the Monkees. And you certainly couldn't just do your own thing, waving your arms in the air. 'Because,' Pam explained, 'people will think you're hippies and you'll probably get beaten up.' Carol and me cautiously showed them how we intended to dance. They looked at us gravely and shook their heads.

'No, you can't do that – you'll look like spasses – everyone'll stare,' Linda said. They showed us what we could do.

'Well, first there's the moonstomp,' Linda explained, as 'Montego Bay' started playing. 'That's easy.' They stood side by side then suddenly jumped into the air and landed hard on both feet, then jumped again but landing with one foot on a heel, then jumping and landing on the other heel. They did it a few times. 'It's peasy,' Pam said, 'come on, 'ave a go.' Carol and me got in line and jumped.

'Land harder,' Pam shouted. 'Really hard – right on the beat,' she said as we began to get the idea.

'You can do this to reggae,' Linda said, wrapping her hands round her braces.

'You put your hands on your braces,' Pam said, copying Linda.

'But you ain't got braces,' I said, 'neither have we.'

'Well girls sometimes don't – you just pretend.' Carol and me followed the instructions and hooked our thumbs through our bra straps for support.

'There's loads of others,' Linda said when the record had finished. The opening chords of 'Wild World' by Jimmy Cliff started playing and Pam screamed.

'Ooohh, I love this – look, look, I'll show ya what to do on slow ones.' They stood in their line again but this time they swung their hips and arms slowly one way, then turned on their toes and swung them the other.

'You can do this if no one asks you for a slow dance,' Pam explained.

'Do this one a lot then, Pam?' Carol said, as we took our places on the line. Pam gave Carol a dirty look.

'That's it,' Linda encouraged. It was easy. But then two boys we didn't know came into the room, and we stopped and went into a huddle of nail-biting and looking around.

The room began to fill up. Diana Ross, the Four Tops, the Temptations, Stevie Wonder, the Jackson Five and—

'Hello . . .'

'What you doin' 'ere . . .'

'Get off . . .'

'Oh, is he looking at me . . . ?'

'Don't embarrass me . . .'

'You gonna dance . . .'

'Skinny!'

Then we heard, 'Oi slags,' called out from across the room, and we all looked round.

'You answer to your name then,' Arthur said. Tony, Johnny, Gary and Salvo laughed.

'Takes one to know one,' Carol said.

I smiled at them all but it seemed a bit odd to say hello after that entrance. Nobody else did. And they were always together in a deep-voiced male lump; it made it worse.

Tony pulled Arthur's braces so they pinged back on his chest. 'Me nipple,' Arthur screamed, trying to catch Tony's braces. But Tony moved, leaving Arthur stretching the braces so much they fell off his shoulder. Then Salvo tried to get Johnny's braces and Gary just stood with his hands firmly pressed against his chest. This kept them entertained for quite some time until rows of mohair suits, jeans and boots started forming on the dance-floor. We got in line. The smallest line you could make was of two people – one was free expression – not allowed. Boys mostly lined up with boys although some straggled in girlfriend's lines looking a bit uncomfortable. We moonstomped, the whole room jumping with the beat and landing down hard until the room shook with the collective pulse. Soon you could hardly hear the music but just the violent tribal thud, thud, thud. Precise and sharp – no one jumped off the beat, no one heeled when they shouldn't.

Then the music changed and people started doing unfamiliar dances that me and Carol didn't know. Steps back and skips forward, turns to the side and patting knees and clapping. All in time, all together. But we soon picked them up and before long there was no twist or jump that we couldn't master after a few bars.

'You're good, Viv,' Carol shouted at me.

'So are you,' I replied.

Sometimes I'd show her when I got it quicker and sometimes she'd show me and we'd smile. We danced for ages and began to sweat. Then suddenly a slow record came on and within seconds the dance-floor was empty. 'Each day through my window I watch her as she passes by,' The Temptations sang. The room came alive with heads turning and eyes darting and elbows nudging. Gradually boys started going up to girls, whispering and walking slowly with them out on to the floor again. The boys put their arms round the girls' waists and the girls put their hands on the boys' shoulders and they moved round in a small circle. Most boys followed the beat for momentum but some liked to follow the rhythm and they moved their girls faster. We watched and waited.

'D'you think he'll ask me?' Pam whispered to Linda.

'He's looking over here,' Linda replied. I bit my nail and Carol pretended to tie up her shoelace.

'He's comin' over,' Linda said, through the corner of her mouth.

'Oh, don't, I'm gonna die,' Pam said. 'Am I red? Oh don't, oh don't, oh don't, I'm so embarrassed – do I look red, Linda? Don't look, do I look red?'

Linda didn't have a chance to reply before Gary was in hearing distance.

'D'you wanna dance?' he said in a monotone. He was asking Carol, who was just getting up from tying her shoe. She looked flabbergasted and flushed red that shone out even in the dark of the disco. She nodded her head and then went confidently on to the dance-floor and waited for Gary to come and move her around. We watched as he put one arm round her waist and let his other arm drop by his side as he held her close. It was too late for the rest of us to be asked to dance now, so we three wallflowers started our swaying dance in a line, trying not to look upset.

'Cow,' Pam muttered, and looked away when I looked at her.

Gary and Carol didn't dance for long before the record came to an end.

They parted company without a look and Carol came back

to me. 'Let's go to a toilet,' she said with urgency. 'I'm touching cloth 'ere.'

There are no girls' toilets in boys' schools. I looked at the urinals halfway up the wall. 'What are they?' I asked Carol.

'It's their piss-hole – it's where they piss.'

Suddenly water flushed through one of the urinals and splashed me.

I screamed, 'Did you do that?' at Carol. She was laughing, clutching her stomach and hopping on the spot.

'How did you do that?' I asked.

'I didn't, it does it itself,' she laughed.

'What?' I said staring at the bowl. 'How?'

'I gotta go,' Carol said, running into a cubicle.

I looked in the mirror and adjusted some of my eyelashes that were sticking together. Three girls walked in as Carol came out of the toilet.

'Oi you,' one of the girls said, pointing a finger at Carol. She was small and looked younger than us with spiky blonde hair and spiky features. Carol smiled.

'Yeah?' she said innocently.

'You goin' out with Gary?' the girl asked.

Her two friends stood behind her, one biting her nail, the other with her hand on her hips.

'What?' Carol said, still smiling.

'You 'eard me,' the girl said. The tone of her voice made Carol look at me, worried.

'No,' she said defensively.

'You better fucking not be,' the girl spat, pointing a finger close into Carol's face.

'I'm not,' Carol shouted.

'You were dancing with him.'

'He asked me, that's all.'

'D'you fancy him then?'

Carol was red again. 'No, I don't,' she said slowly, shaking her head.

'You better fucking not – he's going out with my friend, so you fucking stay away from him, d'you 'ear.'

'I don't wanna go out with him, I don't even like him,' Carol said, backing away from the girl's finger.

'You better fucking not,' the girl said. She pulled out a steel comb from the back pocket of her jeans and held up the handle which was sharpened to a point. 'You fucking stay away from him else I'll cut ya,' she said. Then the girls left the toilet.

Carol was shaking. She began to cry. I'd never seen her cry before. I stared at her waiting for her to change but she kept crying, so I hugged her tight. 'I don't even like him,' she said, into my shoulder.

'Take no notice, fucking bitches,' I said. I was shaking too. Carol straightened up. 'I don't even like him – he's a creep.'

'Oh come here, all your mascara's running,' I said to her. I went to get some toilet paper for her eyes but they only had the hard stuff with GLC stamped on every piece. 'Come here,' I said, as I started to wipe at her face with my fingers. She wasn't crying but sniffing and breathing hard. 'Take no notice.'

'I don't even like him,' she repeated.

'D'you wanna go?'

'Yeah, hang on.' She looked in the mirror and started wiping at her face.

Linda bounced in. 'Pam's gone home, she says she's not talking to you, Carol.'

Linda looked at Carol and her tone changed. 'What's happened?' Linda said in a high sympathetic voice. She put her arms round Carol as Carol began to cry again.

'These girls just threatened her.'

'Why?' Linda asked, wide-eyed.

'For dancing with Gary.'

'You're joking,' Linda said.

'On my life – they threatened her with a comb.'

'Bloody hell! What'd they say?'

'They said he was goin' out with her friend.'

'Oh, not that spiky-haired girl,' Linda said.

'Yeah, the blonde one.'

'Oh my God she's hard, that one. Yeah, course, she's the friend of that girl with the hair,' Linda revealed.

'Should we tell Ted?' I asked.

'Oh, he can't do nothing. I think we better go,' Linda said, solemnly. 'Your dad's outside anyway, Carol.'

Carol went and got some of the hard loo paper and blew her nose in it. Linda looked at me and bit her bottom lip.

'I got a tissue 'ere,' Linda said, looking through her bag.

Carol looked in the mirror and laughed through her tears. 'I look like a bloody ghost,' she said and we all laughed.

We ran out of the toilets and I went and got our bags and coats from the disco. I didn't look at anyone and went straight past Tony, Arthur, Gary and Salvo without a word, which was nothing unusual.

The night air was cold and raw and my teeth began to chatter as we stood in a huddle, stamping hard on the ground.

'He was here a minute ago, I came out with Pam – he was over there,' Linda said, pointing to the spot.

'Where's she gone, anyway?' Carol asked.

'Pam? She went home – she's fed up 'cause Gary didn't take no notice of her, and Dor said he was definitely gonna ask her to dance tonight. I think she was a bit pissed off he asked you.'

'I can't help that,' Carol shouted. 'Bleedin' 'ell, he's the one that asks me to dance, but I'm the one in bovver.'

'It's not your fault, Carol,' I chipped in. I put my arm round her as her teeth began to chatter too.

'God where is he, stupid old fart,' Carol said. We all started jumping up and down together in our huddle.

'I'll fucking cut ya,' Carol said, imitating the girl's voice. 'Ugly cow – I thought she was gonna comb me bloody hair at first.'

We heard laughing behind us and saw Tony and Arthur playing a sort of leap-frog, where one jumps over the other but tries to get the other one on the ground. We all rolled our eyes.

'Hello slags,' Arthur laughed.

'Yeah, yeah, you've done that – yawn, yawn,' Carol said, putting her hand up to her face and patting her open mouth.

'What y'doin'?' Tony asked.

'Waitin' for Christmas,' Linda said.

'That's funny, 'cause I'm Santa Claus,' Tony grinned.

'Oh shut up, will ya,' Linda snapped.

'Need to!' Tony and Arthur chanted sarcastically.

'Carol got threatened in the bogs thanks to Gary,' Linda said.

I looked around for signs of Carol's dad's car.

'What's Gary gotta do with it?' Arthur asked.

'Her with the hair's friend didn't like her dancing with him'

'What's it gotta do with her? Slag. He dances with who he likes,' Tony said.

'He's goin' out with her, i'n he?'

'He ain't goin' out with no one,' Tony went on. 'She don't fucking own him, he's only getting his end away, stupid slag – what'd she say?'

'She held up a steel comb to my face,' Carol said.

'Stupid whore – you wanna do 'er.'

We three girls sniggered. 'Skinny,' we muttered.

'I fucking hate them girls,' Tony said. 'They're not like girls, more like blokes – they'll beat anyone up. I'd rather stick my dick in a hole in the wall.' Tony and Arthur started laughing.

'Excuse me,' a voice said. We all looked round to see a middle-aged man in an overcoat looking at us. 'Excuse me, you are blocking the road.' We all moved a bit so he could get by, but he didn't walk on.

'You are still blocking people's right of way,' he said with authority.

'What?' Tony said, throwing back his shoulders.

The man spoke with slow precise words. 'Other people cannot get by.'

Tony looked up and down the empty street. 'What other people, mate?'

'Don't you mate me, sonny,' the man said quickly.

'You got a problem?' Tony frowned.

'Yes I have,' he said. 'I am a police officer, so watch your mouth, all right son? Now just stop blocking the pavement, people can't get by. Come on . . .' The man started to pull at Tony and pushed him against the fence by the school, then he pulled Arthur and flicked his hand at us girls showing us where he wanted us to stand. When he'd finished we were all in a line along the fence.

'We can't talk like this,' Tony said, stepping out of his position.

The man pointed an angry finger. 'I've told you sonny – you're blocking the Queen's highway: it's an offence. You stay like that or I'll take the lot of you in – you got it?' Tony got back in place.

'What are you lot doing out here anyway?' the man asked.

'Waiting for her dad,' Linda said, nodding towards Carol.

'Well you just wait like this,' he said, indicating all of us along the line. We stood silently and watched the man walk on down the street.

'Fucking wanker,' Tony said, when the man was well out of earshot.

'What a cheek,' Linda said blinking. She opened her mouth and put her hands on her hips.

'All coppers are cunt-stables,' Arthur shouted down the street, then ducked down low when the man looked round.

'There's your dad's car, Carol,' I said with relief. The little maroon Ford Anglia was driving past the man. We quickly ran away from Tony and Arthur and hailed the car down, waving our arms. Carol put her fingers in her mouth and let out a loud piercing whistle. I wanted to get away before the man came back and decided that it was an offence for us to move at all.

Carol opened the car door and lifted up the seat for me and Linda to get in the back. She sat down in the front and looked forward as her dad started to say, 'Did you have a nice—' but was stopped by Carol shouting, 'Well go if you're goin'.'

Olive

I got the sack. I was going to tell them I was leaving anyway and that they could stuff their job, but the stupid white bitch got in before me. She sort of puffed out her huge tits and said how she couldn't put up with all my 'absenteeism'. That was probably the longest word she'd ever said in her life. I smiled as she went on about head office needing a note for all the days I was sick or else I had to go. When she'd finished I told her to piss off, and that I was leaving anyway because I had another job, a better job, with more pay and prospects. I didn't want her to think she could upset me.

I didn't tell anyone I got the sack, not at first, not even Peter. I made him meet me somewhere else, because I said they were getting a bit funny about him hanging round the shop. He didn't think it was odd, and I was going to get another job and surprise him anyway.

I hadn't had a period for a long time. It was quite nice – a relief. I thought it was because there was something wrong with me inside. I felt sure of it – there was something out of place or missing that meant I couldn't enjoy sex, and certainly couldn't get pregnant.

Peter always said he'd be careful when we did it and that I shouldn't worry. He used to pull out just before he came and squirt that slime over me and the sheet. But if it was my period or something he wouldn't bother. He said I couldn't get pregnant then because it was the wrong time of the month.

I didn't really understand about all that stuff. I'd never been told. Not at school, where I never got told anything important. And certainly not by my mum who thought 'relations', as she called it, was 'a cross we women have to bear'. I knew the basics, we all did at school. I knew that you could only get pregnant if spunk got in your womb. Once spunk was in your womb then your womb closed up and formed into a baby. I knew that. But when Peter said about the time of the month, I sort of nodded and said yes, like I knew what he was talking about, but I wasn't sure and it would have been too embarrassing to ask him. Just another thing I didn't know. So I didn't. After sex I just used to drip all the time, like I was wetting myself without knowing. I was always wet. So I thought no spunk ever stayed inside me, so nothing would happen.

I began to get sick, but not in the mornings – at night usually, or when Mum was frying chicken or fish or something. I went to the doctor who asked if I ate a lot of fried food. I said yes and he said I should stop eating so much of it, then I'd stop being sick. I was relieved. I thought at least I can't be pregnant if the doctor doesn't think so.

But my stomach started to get fat. Not the sort of fat you could just breath in to hide. This was a hard lump that was really part of me.

When I told him Peter said he thought I was on the pill. But he knew I wasn't. He knew. He made me an appointment at a clinic to get a pregnancy test. He was going to go with me but at the last minute he had to do another shift at work because it was near Christmas. So I went on my own.

I said my name was Mrs Flynn, which is Peter's last name. I felt so adult – Mrs Flynn. I even wore a ring. They asked me everything, where I lived, how old I was, how long I'd been married, how often I had sex. I couldn't believe it, but I just sat politely and answered with a pack of lies. But I think they asked everyone the same things. Then I peed into a bottle and they said I should telephone them in a couple of days.

'Congratulations,' the woman said when I phoned. And I had to sound pleased.

* * *

I would go into the bathroom and look at my belly in the mirror. It was so big. I was always able to stick my stomach out so I looked pregnant. I used to do it for Vivien to make her laugh when she was small. She used to poke it with her finger and I'd tell her I was having a baby and she'd look shocked, but a naughty shocked that was funny.

But this was real. It was getting hard to hide it with the corset I bought. I had to strain it over the lump and I got scared that the thing inside me would be crushed. I kept thinking of people's faces when they squash them against glass – how their cheeks and nose get all flattened and distorted. I could feel it moving about. Wriggling. It was horrible. Like an alien living in me. Something I'd swallowed that just grew and grew. A giant fart with arms and legs.

I wanted it to go away at first – that's what I really wanted. That I'd just wake up and everything would be back to normal. But Peter thought that abortions were a sin. He was a Catholic. I didn't realize he was religious, I didn't know revolutionaries could be. But he said he believed that all life was sacred. He said that we could get married. That we could get married and have the baby and everything would be great. So that's what we agreed. He didn't propose or anything. Didn't go down on one knee or bring me flowers. It was just that we were going to get married. Mrs Olive Flynn.

We had to tell my mum, of course. I was all for leaving her a note and going to stay at Peter's for a week. *Light the blue touch-paper and retire.* I could see her running after me with her shoe, screaming that she knew I'd come to no good. Calling me a whore. Telling me I'd be the death of her. I had a dream that she was walking on the ceiling in a shop, pointing at me everywhere I went, so everyone stared. I couldn't get rid of her.

But Peter thought we should sit down and talk to her like adults. I said, 'You don't know her like I do.' And he said, 'She's all right.'

It was good the way Peter did it. It sort of took me by surprise so I didn't get nervous. We were watching the telly, just my mum, Peter and me, when he suddenly said, 'There's something we need to talk to you about, Mrs C.' I wasn't really ready: we were in the middle of *Coronation Street*. My heart went boom like it was coming out of my chest. I had to breathe in hard and sit up. I'm sure my mum thought it was going to be one of Peter's lectures about the proletariat. She smiled and looked at him.

'Olive and me are getting married,' he said, calm as anything. I sat in closer to him and looked at the hair on the back of his head, which was beginning to thin. My mum's smile twisted into a puzzled look. A why-do-you-want-to-marry-Olive look. But Peter went on. 'And Olive's going to have a baby.' Her head then tipped back slowly and her mouth opened in an *I see* sort of way.

'I thought she was getting fat,' she said, like I wasn't there. I wanted to punch her. There was a long silence. All I could hear was Annie Caldwell talking to Ken Barlow in the Rover's Return. And I held my breath. The banger was lit – it just hadn't exploded yet.

'I'll make a cup of tea,' she said after a few minutes, and got up and went into the kitchen.

Peter squeezed my hand and said, 'See, that wasn't too bad.' And he was right, it wasn't, except that she didn't care. After all those times of being shouted at, the names she called me, the 'You'll come to no good.' All the 'devil's child, devil's child.' All the keeping me in to keep me safe. After all that, I got pregnant at seventeen without being married, every parent's worst nightmare, and all she could say was, 'I thought she was getting fat'. I mean, bloody hell.

She came out with the tea things. 'So when the baby due?' she said to us both.

'Four months,' I said.

'So soon,' she said.

I kept staring at her, expecting to see a tell-tale sign of real fury, a throbbing vein or a twitching eye. Anything. But she poured the tea like we'd just told her we were going down the pub.

'What do you think then, mum?' I finally asked.

'It's your life,' she said, and handed me a mug of tea. Peter got up to go to the toilet and my mum sat down beside me and looked at me.

'I can't say I'm surprised, Olive,' she said.

'Is that all you've got to say?' I said.

'What d'you expect me to say child – what's done's done.' I sat back and folded my arms as best I could and looked at the television. My mum sucked her teeth and took a sip of her tea, then she leaned in closer to me and whispered: 'But you have a good man there Olive – there's not many that would marry you.' Then she pointed her finger: 'You see you keep him, you hear me nuh.'

Vivien

'Right, that's Mayfair with two hotels on it,' Peter said as he looked down at the little Monopoly cards. 'That's four thousand pounds, Mrs C.'

'What!' mum shouted. She looked dejectedly at the ten-pound note in her hand. 'I haven't got that sort of money, Peter!'

Peter puffed on the fat cigar Mum had got him for his Christmas present.

'Well, sell something. What you got to sell?'

'I only have this,' she said, holding out the Water Works and Electric Company.

'That'll do,' Peter said, grabbing them.

'It's all I have,' Mum whined.

'Oh dear,' Peter said, as he picked up the dice for his throw.

Olive had long given up on this game, when all her money was gone and she had to sell her 'get out of jail free' card to me. Winning second prize in the beauty contest just made her shout 'Second – cheek!' and slump back on the settee and doze off.

Mum was banker: we decided at the beginning that she was probably the most trustworthy out of the four of us. Although whenever you thought she was really done for she managed to buy her way out of it. But after playing the game for three hours most of the bank's funds had transferred into Peter's hands. I clung on with my Regent Street set and careful savings.

'Well, I'm out then,' Mum said, as she looked under the lid

of the box to see if any spare cash was lurking.

'Let's finish then,' I said.

'Oh, it's just getting good,' Peter said, taking another puff of his cigar.

'It's all right for you, you own everything,' I said.

'Not quite, Titch,' Peter said to me, 'not quite.' He grinned. 'This capitalism lark's quite easy,' then took a big puff on his cigar and laughed to himself.

It was the first Christmas we'd spent without my dad. It was unusual not to have the television on all day and sit in a bloated stupor in front of it, passing a tin of Quality Street back and forth. But this year my sister's boyfriend came and cooked a turkey and roast potatoes and insisted we play Monopoly instead of watching Morecambe and Wise.

It seemed right that everything should change if my dad wasn't there, but I missed him. I missed him sitting with his glass of beer that went down painfully slowly through the day. I missed watching him eating Christmas cake sent by his sister from Jamaica. How he pushed the black gooey cake with his finger, then put it in his mouth and ate it with his mouth open so you had to turn away from the sight. I missed him grinning when he gave you your present. Always money in a little envelope with your name in careful childish handwriting on the front. I kept looking up to his chair where he always sat, expecting to see him snoring with his head back.

And sometimes I'd think I'd see him in the street. And sometimes I'd expect him to turn up again. Suddenly to walk through the door so I could say, 'Hello Dad, you've been a long time,' and watch him screw up his face and say, 'I know, it's terrible, Vivien, terrible, they working me to death.'

But now there was Peter instead. Olive had lots of boyfriends before she met Peter. She'd tell me about them as she was getting ready to go out. She told me about their height, their hair, their eyes, but always ended by saying: 'But big ears – looks like the FA cup,' or 'Bad breath – could strip paint with it,' or just 'creep'. But she never brought any of them home with her. She always sneaked round our house, wary of corners and doors in case my mum was there waiting to scream, 'You'll be the death of me too, just like you kill yer dad.'

Olive woke me up at seven in the morning the night she met Peter. She knelt by my bed puffed with excitement.

'His name's Peter and he's gorgeous,' she said hugging herself. She pulled off one of her false eyelashes: that made one eye look much smaller than the other. She leant close to my face, and the happiness and her little eye made me wonder if I was still dreaming.

'He's quite tall and really intelligent, Vivien, really intelligent. He makes me feel a bit thick.' I waited for the bad point but it never came, she just knelt there smiling and pulling glue off her eyelid.

It was about four weeks later that she brought Peter home. The way she talked about him I thought he'd be a cross between John Lennon and Jesus Christ. But he was quite short and ordinary-looking. A bit of a hippie in fact, with dead straight hair and eyes like a couple of marbles you wouldn't have minded losing down a drain-hole.

'Never trust a man whose eyebrows meet in the middle,' Carol always told me. And I wished I had told Olive, because Peter only really had one eyebrow that formed a shelf on his face. Nice teeth though, perfect white, and he smiled a lot.

My mum liked having Peter around, he filled the space my dad left. He spent most of his time with us, sleeping on the settee.

'Is Peter coming tonight?' my mum always asked Olive in the mornings. 'Only I'll wash the sheets so they're nice,' she'd say. Or 'I'll get him a nice bit of chicken,' or 'Because I have a question for him.' Olive usually just rolled her eyes but my mum never noticed. When she heard Olive's key in the door she would jump up and run into the kitchen to put the kettle on.

'Peter – I'm making a cup of tea,' she'd shout.

'Thanks Mrs C.,' he'd call back, and Olive would roll her eyes again.

Peter and my mum started having conversations. Rows really, but not the sort of yelling rows she had with Olive. She and Peter would talk for hours about things: I never quite knew what they were going on about. I'd just hear my mum scream, 'Give the working classes guns – are you mad, Peter?' She'd shout, but then she'd laugh and Peter would go on and on about something else and she'd laugh some more. Olive and me usually sat trying to listen to the television, saying, 'Oh shut up,' every so often.

Peter cooked, and my mum would smile and say how she liked a man who could cook. He made us things we'd never had before like spaghetti bolognese, which my mum picked at and said, 'It's very nice, Peter, very nice, but I don't like foreign food.'

He helped me with my English homework. He'd look over my shoulder when I was working, asking me what I was reading or what the question was. It got on my nerves at first, but then he told me to put in the words 'conventionally mundane' when I was trying to describe Billy Liar's girlfriend. I didn't know what it meant, but when I got the essay back the teacher had written 'excellent vocabulary' in the margin next to Peter's words. So I started asking him what Shakespeare was going on about and he'd tell me and I understood. And I began to think that Olive was right – Peter was very intelligent.

Olive stayed home most of the time and sat on the settee. She began to get fat. She could hardly sit down without opening up her legs wide first.

'You're getting fat, Olive,' I said. 'Shut yer gob,' she shrugged. 'None of your business.'

Then the whispering started between Peter, my mum and Olive. Hushed conversations in bedrooms. And everyone stopping talking when I came in. It went on for days. Sometimes Olive would look like she'd been crying and sometimes she'd look so happy that she almost hugged me.

'What's happening?' I asked my mum.

'Ssshh child – it's none of your business.'

'What's going on?' I asked Peter.

'Nothing's going on, Titch.'

'Why are you always whispering?' I asked Olive.

'Mind your own business.'

There was definitely something going on but I didn't know what. Then my mum called me one day. She was in the bedroom sitting on the bed. 'Sit down Vivien,' she said. I got worried. She looked so serious and concerned. I was scared Peter had told her about Carol and me and the tights we pinched. I told Peter one day that Carol and me nicked things from Woolworths. 'Everyone did it,' I said. Some days you'd just see people picking handfuls of stuff off the counter and stuffing it in their pockets. I told Peter about the tights thinking he'd find it funny and pat my head. But he didn't, he gave me a lecture.

'You're stupid to shoplift. If you get caught, they'll call the police and you'll end up down the nick. You'll have a criminal record. And that will last for the whole of your life. It's not worth it for a pair of tights or bloody eye-shadow.'

I was surprised and embarrassed when he said it. He was so serious and I was still smiling. But by the time he'd finished the smile felt odd on my face – out of place.

'It's not that bad,' I said, 'everyone does it. We don't do it a lot.'

'Don't do it at all,' he said.

Mum patted the spot beside her and I wanted to cry.

'Your sister's going to have a baby,' she said.

'What!'

'Ssshh, child, don't make so much noise.'

'Olive's going to have a baby?'

Mum looked agitated. 'That's what I said, child, don't make such a fuss.'

'But she's not married.'

'She's getting married.'

I laughed, 'You're joking – who to?' I felt stupid as soon as I'd said it.

'Peter, of course,' Mum shouted, then put her hand up to her mouth. 'Ssshh.'

'When?' I asked.

'Soon, Vivien,' my mum said, getting up. 'That's enough now – no more questions. You can go. But Vivien,' she said, 'don't go telling any of your rough friends now – you hear me nuh.'

Olive

We started making plans, Peter and me. Started getting the *Evening Standard* every night to look at the 'Flats to rent'. There were loads of them. I thought we'd get a place easily. Peter rang a few of them up but when he said how old he was they weren't interested. So he started saying he was twenty-five but then they said they didn't take children. No children and no pets. There was always a problem; I couldn't believe it. I mean, I can understand about pets because they smell and leave hair everywhere, but children don't. Everybody has children, eventually.

We went to see two flats. They were both in south London. I didn't really want to move down there. I didn't know my way around – it all looked the same, a wasteland of council estates and derelict shops and people with string shopping bags. But luckily the flats were awful.

One of them was just a room, not that big, but dark, with this horrible flowery wallpaper and a big cupboard. Only when you opened the cupboard it was really the kitchen – well, a sink and cooker. And you had to share the bathroom which was miles down a hallway that stank of piss. The other flat wasn't much better.

Peter went to see some without me, but he said they were awful too. We were so excited when we saw an advert for a place we could afford. They always sounded so good over the phone. At first we used to celebrate before we'd seen it. But Peter just didn't earn enough money for us to get a nice place. Well, not if we wanted to have enough money left to buy food and look after our baby.

73

I went down to the council, the housing office. Peter said I should go on my own. Because I was pregnant and everything, he said they'd probably take pity on me and give me a place there and then. I had to take a number and sit and wait. I waited nearly three hours. There were loads of people there and kids running about. And no magazines to read, just leaflets on head lice and contraception. When I finally got to see someone all he did was take my name and age and make me fill in a form where I had to repeat everything I'd just told him. He asked me if I had anywhere to live. I said not really, because we were staying with my mum and it was overcrowded. I tried to make it sound worse than it was – I said that I had to share a single bed with my fiancé. Then he wanted to know when the baby was due. So I told him and said that I'd like a place before it was born to give us a chance to settle in. The man looked at me like I was mad, but I think he looked at everyone like that. He said I'd have to go on a list.

I got a card saying that they'd received my application and that I'd be hearing from them. I got quite excited about that, but Peter said they do that to everyone. He said that we'd probably have to stay with my mum until we could save up enough for a nice place. I cried. But he said it wouldn't be for long because he could do overtime for some extra money.

He asked Mum if we could stay with her. She seemed pleased. Pleased at gaining a son even though she'd rather have lost a daughter. It won't be for long, I told her, and I showed her the card the council sent.

I began to get on with her. We had something in common now. We were both mothers, at least I nearly was. She was looking forward to the baby, I could tell. She kept buying it things – things she 'just picked up' in the market. She even found an old shawl that was mine, that she'd 'put away safe for her first grandchild', she said when she gave it to me. And I began to like my lump too – I could feel its head. The nurse at the hospital told me what to feel for and sometimes

I'd pat it. In the mornings it liked a good stretch. I could feel it pushing out its tiny arms and legs, like it had just woken up. Yawning. The nurse said they do yawn and suck their thumbs. She showed me diagrams.

I was looking forward to having it. Dressing it up in its little clothes. Little jackets, little booties, wrapping it in the shawl. I didn't believe in all that pink for a girl and blue for a boy stuff. Although my mum, kept saying, 'What colour shall I get?' I didn't care – we mostly got yellow anyway. I wanted to take it for walks in the park. I never went to the park just for a walk, didn't seem any point, but when you've got a baby you have to.

I started going to bed early: I was tired, but also I wanted to start taking care of myself. I stopped drinking and smoking although I'd never really smoked much. Peter tried to stop smoking too but it wasn't as easy for him, so he started again. I tried to eat vegetables and drink plenty of milk. It was all important, not just for me, I had to think about my baby now.

Peter stayed at our house nearly all the time. After a while he started staying all night in my bed because we were getting married. So we did end up sharing a single bed. We were really squashed because I was getting big. He still wanted to have sex. I didn't like him to get on top of me, so he'd do it from behind – at least I didn't have to look as if I was enjoying myself. Sometimes I got worried because sex can be quite rough, and I kept thinking of my baby. I kept wondering if it could see what we were doing. If it was horrified and tried to turn away or cover its little eyes. Or if it could feel Peter's prick poking and banging it, again and again. I made him stop if he was doing it too hard. I said it hurt, but really I was scared for the baby.

Vivien got jealous, I could tell. She kept looking at me, staring, because I was getting all the attention for a change. 'You're only seventeen,' she said to me. I let her feel when the baby was kicking so she wouldn't be too left out.

Peter's mum just said 'Oh dear,' when we told her. Peter made it sound like we weren't pleased. 'Olive's pregnant,

Mum,' he just said, like he was admitting to breaking one of her best cups. But when she found out we were getting married and that we were happy, she was different. She took some Scotch out of the cupboard to celebrate. She insisted that we have the wedding reception at her house. I thought that was really nice of her, but Peter said it was because his younger brothers demolish everywhere else they go. We agreed anyway, and Peter went to book up the civic centre for the wedding.

Vivien

Nothing stopped Carol and me going up Chapel Street market on Sunday mornings. Nothing. Not rain, not snow, and definitely not Olive standing sideways in the mirror, puffing out her huge pregnant belly and saying 'Vivien, come and feel, quick, quick, it's kicking.'

Now everyone knew she was pregnant she would spend hours looking at her bulge – fiddling with her protruding belly button, fascinated with every new line and wrinkle. All she wanted to talk about was her wedding, her husband-to-be, her baby. She started every sentence with, 'When I'm married,' as if she was going to be born again in a better form. 'I can't believe I'll be a married woman and a mother,' she'd say with a vacant stare. My mum stopped shouting at her altogether and started smiling instead. Occasionally I would hear them in the kitchen discussing things.

'The baby will need a little cot and a pram, Olive, I can get you one from the catalogue – a sort of wedding present.'

'Thanks, Mum – and Peter said his mum's still got a baby bath.'

'Ah yes. You know, we should make a list.'

'Yeah, I've got one – look . . .'

I made Carol swear not to tell anyone about Olive. Made her cross her heart on Upper Street. 'On your life – no, on your mother's life – no wait a minute, on . . . on . . .' I tried to think who Carol really wouldn't like to see dead, but I couldn't.

'On my nephew's life,' Carol said helpfully.

'Yeah, on Jason's life.'

'What?' she shouted.

'My sister's going to have a baby.'

Carol didn't look as shocked as I'd hoped.

'I thought she was getting a bit fat,' she said, without even opening her eyes wide and shouting, 'But she's not married.' Or screaming that I was going to be an aunt. Or laughing and asking me when Olive had done it. I looked at her, ready to answer any further questions, but none came.

When we got to Chapel Street we went straight to Otis. Otis was a clothes shop, a boutique it said above the door, but there was also a record shop at the back. Paul, the man who ran it, was famous. Or at least we thought he must have been because he was in a group in the sixties called Yellow Sun. There was an LP tucked away in the Y section of rock and pop that had a picture of him and his band. Four smiling men standing around in suits with neat haircuts and guitars.

'I look different now,' Paul said, when he showed us the picture. And he was right. Now he had grey hair, 'prematurely grey,' he said, and wrinkles round his eyes when he smiled. Carol said he was mature, 'Not like the tossers down the club.' When she was around him she didn't swear. She laughed at his jokes, even sat on his knee, giggling. Or she'd look at record sleeves and ask him what sort of music it was and if he thought she'd like it.

'I like Ray Charles,' she said, although I knew for a fact that she'd only just heard of him. Olive had his Greatest Hits record and Carol said 'Eh, what's this rubbish,' when I put it on. But Paul liked Ray Charles, so Carol listened on headphones to him singing 'The Long and Winding Road' and declared it better than the Beatles version. Sometimes Carol got on my nerves.

We stayed with Paul in the shop for a few hours, until it got really busy and he didn't have time to talk to us and 'educate our ears'. We walked up the market, in the middle of the road looking at the stalls on either side. Then on the pavement past Manzies café and Carol breathed in heavily and sighed, 'Oh, smell that pie and mash – I love it.' And I breathed in the sweet fumes and felt sick.

'It's dirty food,' my mum had said. 'Don't you go eating that dirty food, you hear me, you don't know what they put in those pies, and what is that green stuff? Disgusting.'

We watched people eating bacon sandwiches in De Marco's café.

'You see him?' Carol said, pointing at a young man who was pushing egg on toast into his mouth. 'He's the one that killed a bloke with a pole.'

I remembered the story going round the club about the boy who hit another boy in a fight with a pole you use to open high windows. It knocked him out and he never regained consciousness. So he was being done for murder. He got the nickname Polar, and the boys bragged about how they knew him. 'He's hard. He's a wanker. He's mad in a bundle.' And girls stared at him and his girlfriend often cried in a corner.

'He looks normal, dun he?' Carol said. And he did, sipping tea and looking around.

We got a lemon ice-cream from the window at the side of the café. No matter how cold the weather we always bought a lemon ice-cream when we were 'up Chap'. My fingers went numb holding the little tub and scoop. And when we passed the apple fritter stall I wished I'd got two of the hot, sugary fried fritters instead.

'Rock 'ard yer tomatoes – come on ladies, rock 'ard tomatoes,' Tony sang out from a vegetable stall.

'This one's soft,' Carol said, pretending to squeeze a tomato as we approached.

'Al'right,' Tony said. He looked pleased to see us. I smiled.

'Get us a cup of tea, Carol?' Tony asked.

'Get off,' she said. He looked at me but didn't say anything.

'Well give us some of your ice-cream then,' he said, trying to grab at Carol's tub. Carol twisted out of the way, stuck the scoop in her mouth and bumped into Dor.

'Where'd you come from?' Carol said, surprised.

'I was behind you all the time,' Dor laughed. She opened

her mouth wide so she could eat a hot apple fritter using only her front teeth.

'Get us a cup of tea, Dor?' Tony said, as politely as he could.

'Get your own,' she said.

'Oh, come on Dor, I can't leave 'ere and it's fucking brass monkeys.' He put his hands up to his face and blew his breath into them.

'Come on then,' Carol said, holding out her hand, 'I'll get you a tea.'

Tony smiled and felt in the blue pouch round his waist that had a little sprig of leftover mistletoe pinned to it.

'I'll let you kiss me under me mistletoe when you get back,' Tony said, sticking his crotch forward and laughing.

'I'll bring me tweezers – help you find your dick,' Carol grinned. She grabbed the change from Tony's hand and before I had time to say, 'I'll come with you,' I could see her back disappearing through the crowds. I turned back to Dor who was wiping sugar off her chin. I looked at Tony and prepared to smile, but he started serving a customer.

'Where's Pam and Linda?' Dor said.

'Dunno,' I said, 'I don't think they could come out.'

'They working?'

'No.'

'Have you got a job?' Dor asked, as she screwed up the fritter bag and threw it on the ground.

'No, I'm still at school.'

'I've got a job,' she said. I looked around for Carol and nodded.

'Oh,' I said, 'you left school then?' Tony pushed Dor gently out of the way so his customer could get by.

'Yeah, I couldn't stand it. I got a job now though.'

'What you doing, then?' I asked.

'When?' Dor said, looking puzzled.

'In your job – what job you doing?'

'Well,' Dor took a breath and started. 'I get this box and get this label and what I have to do is put the label on the box and then close the box up with this tape stuff and put it back on the belt and then get another box – you know.'

I stared at Dor not knowing what to say next. Then Tony came close to Dor and whispered out the side of his mouth. 'Here Dor, look at that.' He nodded his head out into the crowd.

'What?' Dor said, straining to look.

'Over there – that wog with that white bloke – I hate that, I fucking hate that.'

He turned away from her and started stacking tomatoes and serving a woman with a pushchair. Dor was still looking into the crowd when I saw Olive and Peter walking towards us. I turned my back and pretended to look at the cauliflowers. Dor started nudging me and giggling. 'Oh yeah, look Viv, over there.'

I didn't turn back. I could feel myself warming up. I closed my eyes. Then I felt a tap on my shoulder. I jumped.

'What's a matter with you?' Carol said, when I turned round. I looked into the crowd but couldn't see my sister. She hadn't seen me.

'Nothing,' I said.

Tony took the tea.

''Ere Viv,' Carol said, giving Tony some change. 'I think I just saw your sister.' She looked into the crowd and pointed. 'In't that your sister over there?'

'No,' I said, without looking.

Olive

Wednesday! What was the matter with Wednesday? Everybody made such a fuss. Maggie said she didn't think she could get the time off work. My mum kept moaning about losing a day's pay. And even Vivien loved school so much, all of a sudden, that she didn't want to miss art. All the Saturdays were booked up at the civic centre until well after the baby was due, so Peter booked a Wednesday. He asked for the day off all right. I told him to make sure to have the revolution at the weekend because nobody would come if it was in the week. It didn't seem to matter to anybody that it was my wedding. I felt like calling the whole thing off and giving birth to a bastard.

Peter stayed at his mum's house the night before the ceremony, because I'm a bit superstitious about things like that. I hadn't even shown Peter what I was going to wear. He'd shown me his made-to-measure suit. In fact he'd done nothing but show it me all week. He kept putting it on and holding bits of it and saying, 'This doesn't fit – do you think this fits?' He said the only place he could feel it touching him was under his left arm.

I bought a lovely off-white all-in-one catsuit with a polo halter-neck. It was designed to be a bit baggy, so once I'd got it on I didn't look pregnant, just fat.

I took ages getting ready, I wanted to look really beautiful. I rolled my hair up and left it in curls all over my head. Bubbles it was called, I saw it in a magazine. I put on my make-up properly, with foundation and powder. I even used body make-up on the bits of my arms and back you could see.

Mum wore a hat and stupid white gloves. Vivien wanted to wear her black velvet midi-coat, but Mum said 'it's not done,' to wear black to a wedding. So Vivien got all huffy and sat on the settee with her arms folded and her bottom lip sticking out.

We ordered a taxi to take us there. When the driver found out I was getting married he tied a white ribbon to the aerial of his car. It looked a bit odd on a red Cortina.

The ceremony was at two-thirty and we got to the building at about a quarter to two. It didn't look like somewhere to get married in, it looked like a swimming-pool building. We waited in this big reception area that had nowhere to sit. There was another family waiting to go in. The bride was all in white, with a veil, bouquet – the lot. She looked really out of place.

We all stood around with everyone talking in whispers, when this man came in and in a strong Jamaican accent started complaining about his toilet overflow pipe. The receptionist kept pointing him somewhere else, but he kept shouting that the water was 'drownin' him'. Mum started rolling her eyes and muttering about him being embarrassing. Acting like she knew him. And the other family, who were all white, kept sniggering.

'What if Peter don't come?' Vivien kept saying and laughing. It started getting on my nerves and I said, 'For Christ's sake, shut up.' And my mum said to me, in a loud voice so everyone could hear, 'Don't take the Lord's name in vain, Olive.' I felt so stupid. Everyone looked at me. I felt like a little kid, not a woman who was about to get married. I gave her such a look.

People kept turning up for the other wedding. Every time the door opened it was another fat, white couple with red faces and flowers.

Eventually Peter came rushing through the doors with Maggie following. He came up to me panting and going on about places to park, but I was more concerned about Maggie, my witness, who was still wearing her Marks and Spencer's overall. She saw me staring at it and started unbuttoning it – luckily she had a dress on underneath. But she said she didn't have long because it was her lunch-hour.

Peter gave me a kiss and said I looked beautiful. The other couple went in for their turn and their huge family followed them, making jokes all the way. Peter went over to the doors to look for his mum and brother and have a cigarette. While Maggie started telling me all the gossip from the clubs. I started getting nervous, my hands were sweating and Maggie kept jabbering in my ear about Claude and the new DJ and looking at her watch and saying, 'Bloody hell, I thought you were going in at half two – it's a quarter to three.' I wished she hadn't come.

I could see Peter's hands shaking and my mum still tutting at the Jamaican man, who was refusing to move.

The other couple came out of the ceremony room really quickly. I thought they'd changed their minds, until everyone started throwing confetti on them. A woman started shouting at them and pointing to the sign which said 'Please do not throw confetti in the building.' But it was too late, it was all over me.

Someone called out 'Flynn and Charles.' Peter tried to explain that his witness wasn't there, but the woman just pushed us through the door, saying they were running late as it was. We sat at the back of the room. It was all pink – pink chairs, pink curtains, pink lights like a little girlie doll's house. And it smelt sweet, like a toilet after pink air freshener had been sprayed. I began to feel sick. There was a table at the front, with pink flowers on it, and a woman sitting behind it.

'Who's getting married?' she called out. Peter and me put up our hands. 'Well, come down the front,' she said, like the teachers at my school. We walked slowly towards her and I half expected her to say, 'Come on, hurry up, we haven't got all day.'

Peter explained again that his witness hadn't arrived, and the woman said we could hang on for a few more minutes. Then there was silence and the only movement in the room was people's eyeballs in their sockets – it was so embarrassing!

The woman was just about to say something when the double doors were flung open and Peter's two little brothers came running in making a noise like aeroplanes, with their arms outstretched.

'Sit down over there,' Peter's mum shouted as she walked through the door. She had on her old beige mac which only had one button that she strained to do up across her chest. She was puffing and saying, 'Sorry, sorry.' Then she pulled the kids into a row near the back. Peter's older brother marched up to the front and said, 'Not too late, I hope.' He had on a saggy grey cardigan which had a white stain down the front. He stood there grinning. My mum said, 'Oh God,' when she saw him, and he looked at her hat and white gloves and straightened his cardigan.

The woman said, 'Shall we start?'

Everything went all right except when Peter had to say his bit and his little brother called out, 'Don't talk, Peter, you shouldn't talk, Peter. Mum, Peter's talking.' His mum hit him across the head with a loud thwack, and my mum sucked her teeth.

Maggie ran out as soon as we were pronounced man and wife and had signed the register. I only had time to wave goodbye. The woman whispered something to Peter and he put his hand in his pocket and gave her some money. She opened a little drawer under the table and gave him some change and a receipt. 'I had to pay her for the wedding,' he said. I mean, bloody hell!

Peter's mum said, 'Oh, you don't look like Olive,' to my mum when Peter introduced them. My mum held out her gloved hand for her to shake, like she was the queen or something. And nobody had brought any confetti.

There was a black fingerprint right in the middle of the white icing on the wedding cake. And there was no food or sandwiches out when we got to Peter's mum's.

I sat with Mum and Vivien in the front room, listening to

the din Peter's two little brothers were making in the room above our heads. It was so loud that Mum kept ducking, thinking they were about to come through the ceiling and land on her.

Eventually Peter and his mum came in with plates of food and bowls of crisps, and Peter's brother brought some beer and two bottles of champagne. The cork from the champagne ricocheted round the room and we all ducked and laughed and for a moment – when everyone held up their glasses and toasted me and Peter – it felt like a wedding should.

Vivien

Pam got off with Johnny. Linda started going out with Tony. Dor tried to get off with Gary, to get on Pam's nerves, but he was going out with Mandy, although everyone knew he fancied Carol. But Carol started fancying Lenny who was Tony's cousin. Salvo started going out with a girl that nobody knew and Arthur walked Dor home, but she only let him to make Johnny jealous. And nobody fancied me.

At the end of the evening down the club everyone would pair up. Girls linking arms with the boys going two by two down the road home. I was left walking up to the bus-stop on my own or with Maureen. Nobody fancied Maureen either. She had a huge red birthmark down the side of her face and her mouth and jaw were crooked.

'It's horrible to say,' Pam said, 'but she's really ugly. But I don't understand why nobody wants to go out with you, Vivien, you're not ugly.'

'They're all thick anyway,' Carol said. 'You don't wanna go out with any of them – you're too clever for them.'

'Someone'll ask you out one day,' Linda said, nodding at me sympathetically. They all felt sorry for me.

'It's because you're shy,' Carol explained.

'Where d'you come from?' Pam asked.

'She's from here,' Carol said for me.

'Yeah, but your mum and dad and that,' Pam went on. They all looked at me.

'They came from Jamaica,' I said.

'Yeah, but you're not coloured like them others,' Linda said.

I didn't answer.

'You're different to them, Viv, you're not really a darkie.'
Carol giggled. 'You're one of us.' She put her arm round my
shoulder. 'You look Spanish or Italian anyway.'

'Do I?' I smiled.

'Oh, yeah – nobody would know,' Carol said, and my
friends nodded. Then Pam added, 'But your nose is big,
though.' And Carol gave her a dirty look.

I'd never even kissed a boy, although Carol said I wasn't
missing anything. I used to practise on my knee in the bath so
I'd be ready if it ever happened. Or I'd try French kissing,
poking my tongue through the gap left by my thumb and
index finger when I put them together. It was the waggling of
the head that seemed odd to me. But Linda said you have to
move your head around when you snog.

Everyone thought the club was getting boring.

'That Ted gets on my bollocks,' Johnny said. 'Him and his
fucking table tennis.'

Tony imitated Ted saying, 'If Hitler had played table tennis
we'd never have had a war.' They started hanging round
down a pub called the Swinging Sporran instead.

I'd only ever been in a pub once before, when Carol
suddenly said, 'My mouth's like the bottom of a birdcage. I
need a drink.' It was at night and the sweetshop was shut. So
she marched into the pub and hoisted herself on to a bar
stool. I followed her when she turned round and beckoned
me in, but I was ready to run at a moment's notice. The
barman came out, looked at Carol and said, 'What can I get
you, young lady?' She ordered half a pint of shandy and
drank it down, only stopping to give me a sip when she was
near the bottom. She said she went into pubs all the time with
her mum and dad. My mum had never been in an English
pub. She said they were dirty, loud places, full of gin-soaked
working-class people who were free with their bodies. She
got her ideas about them from reading Charles Dickens at
school in Jamaica.

The Swinging Sporran had a dive bar. That meant it was in

the basement and had no windows. You couldn't tell how big the room was because it was packed out with people and you couldn't see the floor. We had to push through the crowd to get to the bar. I followed Carol as we squeezed up tight against people and slid our bodies past them. It was like being on a tube train in rush hour. You couldn't look into anybody's face because they might realize that you were pressed so close together you could be having sex.

The bar stank of cigarette smoke, alcohol and Brut aftershave. There were no flashing lights but the room was lit with a dim red and blue glow. The music was loud – so loud I had to put my ear close to Carol's mouth as she shouted into it and I still couldn't hear properly what she was saying.

'What do you want to drink?' I finally made out.

I looked at her. I didn't know why she'd asked me. We'd been rehearsing this all week. Carol said it would be good if I knew what drink I liked before I went in the Sporran because then, if anyone asked me, I wouldn't look a spas trying to decide. I said I'd ask for a Coca-Cola but Carol laughed and so did Pam and Linda. They said no one would go up to a bar in a pub and ask for such a wanky drink as Coke. They said it had to be alcoholic.

'I drink rum and pep,' Carol said, and told me that it was rum with peppermint cordial.

Linda and Pam both drank barley wine. 'Because,' Pam explained, 'it's cheap, it lasts for ages and it makes you really pissed.'

'I drink port and lemon,' I said confidently.

'Oh, that's a nice drink,' Carol smiled. I didn't know about that, I'd just heard someone order it on *Coronation Street*.

'Port and lemon,' I shouted down Carol's ear about four times before she understood me. She pushed her way up to the bar and held a five-pound note high in the air to attract the barman's attention. She looked like she'd been doing it all her life. She passed the drink back to me, holding it high above people's heads. I took a sip. It was sweet and warm and pungent as piss.

'D'you wanna try mine?' Carol said, holding up her glass. It tasted like Polo mints, until the rum hit the back of my throat with a smack. I coughed and snot came down my nose so fast that I had to hold it back with my hand. I hoped nobody had seen, although a girl gave me a dirty look.

Carol stood on her toes and held on to my shoulders while she looked around the room. 'They're over there,' she said pointing. I could see Linda, Pam, Tony and Johnny standing over in a corner. 'Witch Queen of New Orleans' started playing as we pushed through the crowd in time with its thudding bass.

'I love this song,' Carol said to me. She started singing along. I couldn't hear her but I could see her lips moving and her neck muscles straining. It was quieter in the corner and I could see a bit of floor.

'Al'right?' Carol said, and I said, and everyone said to one another. Pam handed her drink to me and I handed mine to her and Linda and Carol did the same. We all took sips, pulled faces of disgust, and handed them back. There were notices all around the walls saying 'Patrons are requested not to dance as we do not have a licence for dancing on these premises.' Tony tapped Carol and pointed to the notice and laughed when she swung her hips, as 'Maggie May' started playing. We all stood there, sipping our drinks and looking around. Occasionally someone would lean and listen to someone shouting in their ear. Table tennis seemed much more exciting to me.

Then Carol shouted, 'Lenny's just come in.' She waved her hand at him and he waved back from the other side of the room. Lenny went to the bar and his friend Bobby walked over behind him. Bobby had been to the club before with Lenny, and Carol wanted me to fancy him. She said it would be good because we could go out in a foursome. But I didn't. He had curly hair and was too tall and too quiet. But tonight, after a few sips of port and lemon, he didn't look too bad.

'Bobby's quite nice actually,' I shouted in Carol's ear. Carol looked at me and slowly smiled.

'D'you fancy him?'

'No,' I said.

'You like him, though?' she said with a cheeky grin.

'He's quite nice,' I smiled.

'Shall I tell him?'

'Don't you dare Carol,' I said, and we giggled.

I saw Lenny straining his neck above everyone trying to get Carol's attention. I nudged her and pointed at Lenny, who made a drinking gesture with his hand. Carol mouthed 'Rum and pep,' but he didn't understand. So she started moving through the crowd to the bar.

I watched her with Lenny and Bobby. Touching them, putting her arm round Lenny's waist, laughing and talking. I wanted to do that. They all suddenly looked over to where I was standing. Then Bobby turned to Carol and held his nose and Carol hit him on the arm and started laughing again.

Pam nudged Linda and Linda nudged Tony and Tony nudged Johnny. They all looked to the stairs that led into the bar. Rolly, the boy who jumped Johnny at the club, was coming down them. A black boy dressed in a mohair suit and Ben Sherman followed in behind him. They were smiling at people and saying 'Al'right.' And the black boy grinned a wide toothy grin and slapped Lenny on the back and shook his hand. Everyone laughed, including Carol.

Tony and Johnny put down their drinks and started straightening their clothes. Johnny spoke into Tony's ear and they moved away from us, looking serious and hard. Something had changed. The room felt smaller and hotter. I looked around me: the only way out was up the stairs we'd come in by. And the music was loud and thumping and other people just stood around, tapping their feet and singing and talking as if nothing had happened. I looked at Tony and Johnny again, who were now talking to some other boys and pointing their fingers over to the bar, but low down so no one could see. Pam and Linda looked at me and Linda bit her lip.

I saw Carol coming back through the crowds and behind her were Lenny, Bobby, Rolly and his black friend. Pam turned her back to them but Linda said 'Al'right' and smiled. Rolly looked around him all the time and kept pushing the knuckles of his hands, but his friend looked very relaxed. He smiled at me and I smiled back. Then he leant over to me and shouted in my ear.

'I haven't seen you in here before.'

I was surprised and before I had time to think I said, 'First time I've been,' as naturally as anything. It didn't seem odd, I just said it. It must be the port and lemon, I was thinking, when he said: 'You know this lot?' and tossed his head towards my gang.

'Yeah,' I said.

'You go up that club?' he asked.

'Yeah,' I replied.

Then he said, 'Oh, I might start going then,' and laughed. I laughed, and realized I was being chatted up. Carol caught my eye and momentarily held her nose and stuck out her tongue.

'D'you like this music?' the black boy said, looking into my eyes. I turned away from him a little and didn't answer.

'Don't be shy,' he said, and grinned a smile at me, charming, like a beautiful naughty boy.

A glass flew through the air just missing our faces and smashed on to the floor. I jumped back and fell on Pam who pushed me back. Then another glass came from nowhere and splashed me with beer. I began to trip over Pam's feet, but she was falling too. She held her arm on the wall to steady herself and I was pushed again hard into her and she screamed out and I began to fall until Carol caught me. I looked up and saw Tony pushing his hand into the black boy's face and cracking his head against the wall. The boy started kicking Tony and punching out at him as Tony smashed his fist into his stomach. Everybody was being pushed around and tripping over and trying to get to the stairs. Lenny and Bobby and more boys joined in. There didn't seem to be any sides, just a muddle of punches and kicks and glasses smashing and everyone pushing. And the music played loud but the shouts and screams and the cracks and the fucks and the cunts became louder.

Carol and me were trapped in the corner watching Johnny pull a bent-double Rolly round by his shirt; punching up at his face until blood began to drip on the floor. Carol held herself over me like a hero as she yelled, 'Lenny don't! Lenny, Lenny, don't!'

'I wanna go! I wanna go!' I shouted. Carol pulled me by my jumper round the side of the fight but a boy landed hard on her and pushed her against the wall. She screamed and pushed him back hard and he turned round to hit her, but stopped himself when he saw she was a girl. Then someone shouted, 'He's got a knife, he's got a knife!'

Suddenly the music went off and bright white lights came on and a thud of black uniforms started bobbing down the stairs. A policeman caught a boy and twisted his arm up his back until his face contorted with pain. Another policeman pushed through the crowds, knocking people over and pulling at boys' shirts and swinging them round towards the door. The fighting stopped. And Lenny and Bobby who were, a moment before, smashing, kicking, thumping, were now standing still, tucking their shirts back into their jeans, looking for their drinks. Johnny put his hand up to his nose and cursed when he saw the blood but turned his back when a policeman approached him. Other boys turned away from the police as the officers started moving through the crowd looking fierce and angry. Everyone was standing still now, like a game of statues, watching the police move round the room and look nose to nose into people's faces.

'You. Out,' they said every so often, flicking a gesture at the stairs.

'How old are you?' they said, and then went, 'Out!' before the reply came.

They didn't take any answers. They pointed violent fingers and said 'Shut your fucking mouth.' I'd never heard a policeman swear before.

Then a young policeman, not much older than Peter, came

up to me. I smiled. He looked straight into my eyes without a hint of kindness. With pure hate.

'Out,' he spat, and moved on.

I ran to the stairs and joined the procession of people waiting to get up and out. Pam and Linda were nearly at the top. I looked round for Carol and realized that the policeman had let her stay. They thought she was old enough. I could see her grinning a little to herself. But then she came up to me and said 'I'll come with you anyway – let's go home.' We shuffled to the top and out on to the street.

'That was your fault,' Pam said to me when we got outside. She stood with her hands on her hips.

'What d'you mean,' I said, realizing I was still holding my drink tight.

'Johnny couldn't stand that coon talking to one of his women.'

I wanted to hit her. I wanted to run my nails down her face. I was shaking.

'What are you going on about?' I shouted.

'What's it gotta do with 'er?' Carol yelled, and pushed Pam's shoulder.

Pam looked scared but shouted, 'She shouldn't have talked to him, that's what I'm saying. My Johnny's nose is bleeding again and he'll probably get taken in this time.'

'He started it,' I said.

'Only 'cause he couldn't stand to see you with that wog.'

'You shouldn't have talked to him,' Linda butted in in her reasonable tone.

'Oh, shut yer face, the both of you,' I screamed and turned away from them, before the tears came down my face.

'It's nothing to do with her, you silly cows – piss off,' Carol said. And we walked away from them, off down the road, in silence.

Olive

I thought I'd wet myself. I woke up and everything – the sheets, the mattress, my nightdress – were soaking wet. Peter was still asleep. I sat up to get out of bed when the pain started. It took my breath away, made me gasp. It wasn't like normal pain, a headache or a toothache. It came from right inside me, twisting its way up. Like every period pain I'd ever had, all in one go. I wanted to scream. I thumped Peter in the back and said, 'I think the baby's coming – Peter, the baby's coming!' And he said . . . and he said, 'Can't it wait till morning?' The pain seized me again and my lump pushed up and moved to one side and I screamed 'No!' He looked really panicked then.

There was no position I could get in to make the pain go away. Then it stopped. Peter said he'd phone the ambulance, but I felt all right. I could feel it starting again though and I screamed and Peter ran out of the room.

My mum came in with her hair in rollers and started telling me to breathe deeply. I didn't want her there. I'd got my own family now. I didn't want her going on. 'I know how to breathe,' I told her. But when a cramp came I clung on to her and she held on to me, tight.

Everything happened so quickly at the hospital. It was just a blur of uniforms and lights and rushing along corridors. And a gas-mask thing that they kept pushing into my face. I wanted to breathe air, fresh air, but they kept holding this thing over my nose and it made me feel sick and dizzy. Every time I went to push it away they thought I wanted more and held it on me. And everybody kept saying, 'There's a good girl – there's a good girl – there's a good girl.'

When we were in the delivery room Peter kept patting my hand. That's all he did, pat my hand. And I kept thinking, it's your fault I'm here, you bastard.

Then this great big football started to try and squeeze out from inside me, from between my legs. 'I'm going to split in two – it's going to kill me,' I yelled, but nobody took any notice. Peter just kissed my cheek. I heard someone screaming, 'I'm too young to have a baby, I'm too young!' It was me. The nurse laughed and told me I was nearly there. But it was just getting bigger and bigger and bigger. I wanted to faint. I wanted to die. I wanted my mum.

Then the pain stopped – just like that – and a baby cried. And Peter said, 'It's a girl.'

The nurse held her up to show me her shiny blue head. I thought there was something wrong with her. But the nurse said 'She has a caul, see – she's lucky.' I held out my arms to take her but the nurse took her away. I shouted, 'Give me my baby,' in a deep voice that even frightened me. But the nurse took no notice and started roughly wiping my baby's head.

She wrapped her in a towel and handed her to me, and Peter sat on the bed and we looked at our baby. A happy family. Peter was crying. We looked at her fingers with little nails – real but tiny. And at her face that was screwed up like a little old man's. She was looking around, trying to look at our eyes, and a minute before she was looking around deep inside me.

Peter stood up and his trousers were covered in blood. I was lying in blood, my blood. Other nurses came in and the baby was taken away and Peter was asked to leave. Suddenly everyone was moving fast around me. I began to feel really sleepy. All I could see were nurses coming to my open legs, peering inside me, touching, prodding, poking. Like they owned that bit of me. I could feel myself being yanked from the inside. Someone was trying to pull my stomach out. I felt so weak, I couldn't even move my mouth. It was horrible.

I woke up in a bed with my mum looking down at me. If

I'd died I'd gone to hell. Then I saw my baby in a little cot beside me, sleeping.

Peter managed to squeeze a double mattress on to the floor of my tiny bedroom. It was a surprise for when I got out of hospital. He even managed to get the little wooden cot in too. There wasn't much room for anything else. It looked all cosy, with a pink lampshade lighting it.

I got straight into the bed and Peter and the baby got in with me. We all cuddled up and Peter told me how things would be when we got our own place to live. He was so gentle with the baby. Always being careful to hold her head when he picked her up.

Amy, we called her. I heard someone shouting it out in the hospital. It was like an omen. It means beloved.

I was really sore everywhere. They had to keep me in longer than normal at hospital because I lost so much blood. The doctors said that if I was giving birth a hundred years ago I'd be dead now. That's how serious it was. I was still very weak. I had four stitches in my fanny, it was disgusting. And my tits were huge and kept dribbling sticky milk. I couldn't get out of bed, I was too exhausted.

But Peter had to work during the day. And the baby cried. She cried and cried. Mum was in, but she wouldn't come. I called her, she must have been able to hear. In the end I had to get up. I tried breast-feeding her but she didn't want that. I looked in her nappy, I did everything, but she wouldn't stop crying. I didn't know what to do. The nurses always took her away when she was like that because I was so ill. I only told her to shut up once but my mum came in the door.

'What's all this noise?' she said.

'What do you think it is?' I said. I handed her the baby and told her I didn't feel well. She started rocking it and saying stupid goo goo words and singing.

Then she looked at me and said, 'You must learn to take care of the baby properly.' I told her I was tired, that I'd just got out of hospital. And she said, 'You wanted the baby,

Olive – it's your responsibility now.'

It was all right when Peter was around. He'd change her nappy or get her dressed. But he hated being woken up at night. He had to get up early, and once he was asleep he didn't like anything disturbing him. He got up to see to her a few times, but then he just started nudging me and I'd have to get up and take her out of the room. But she was always waking up in the night. I'd have to walk round with her and I was so tired I couldn't even see properly. And one night as she screamed, Peter just kicked my leg really hard and said 'Shut that fucking baby up!'

Vivien

'Have you thought about doing A-levels, Vivien?' my English teacher asked me.

'I'm not clever enough to do them,' I said.

'Oh I think you are, Vivien – I think you should think about it. Talk to your mother,' she said.

My mum said, 'If your teacher say you can do it, you should do it. You have a good head on your shoulders, Vivien. Not like that sister of yours. You want to get a good job – a teacher or a nurse. They're good jobs. You'll always have work. You should work and earn your own money. You want to be a teacher or a nurse?' she asked.

'No, a film director,' I said.

She looked at me, rolled her eyes and sucked her teeth long and slow. Then she went back to stirring her pot on the stove, mumbling about big ideas. 'How you going to be a film director?' she asked me, squinting her eyes and looking into my face.

My plan was to get a job in a film company and work my way up. I thought I'd get the name of one from the telephone book and write to them to see if they had any jobs. My mum listened and said, 'Don't go getting too many big ideas, or you'll end up like your sister. But if your teacher say you can do these level things, then you must do it.'

I didn't want to end up like Olive. I didn't want to be at home all day surrounded by steaming nappies, watching a baby playing on the floor. I didn't want to be too tired to get dressed, shuffling around in my dressing-gown and slippers. I didn't want to have a baby sucking at my tits every minute. I wanted better things for me.

But A-levels meant going into the sixth form at school, and the sixth form was full of A-stream girls. Posh girls who came from nice homes and lived in houses like me and Olive grew up in, only after they'd been done up, after they'd moved all the riff-raff out. It was full of girls who spoke Latin. Or were intimate with the insides of white mice which they pegged out for open days, showing proud parents all the different parts.

B-stream girls didn't usually do A-levels – they went straight into the commercial class. A room full of typewriters, where they learnt office skills, typing and shorthand. They got certificates from Pitman's and went on 'to be some of the top secretaries and personal assistants in the country', the teacher always proclaimed. 'One girl,' she said with pride, 'is even working for the BBC.'

I was in the B-stream. B-stream girls handed out the programmes or did the cloakroom at the open-day concerts, where the A-stream girls played their string instruments. We weren't as bad as the C-stream girls, who had to perform gym and show what uses can be made of a Victoria sandwich. A-stream girls went to university and studied English or History. B-stream girls made good wives and C-stream girls . . . well, Olive was a C-stream girl.

Pam was going into the commercial class – she couldn't wait. 'At last I'll be learning something useful,' she said.

Linda was leaving to train as a nurse. 'SEN,' she said.

'SEN? Ain't that when you're a bit funny in the head?' Pam asked.

'That's ESN, stupid,' Carol told her.

Carol said she needed three A-levels to become a solicitor.

'So you going in the sixth form?' I asked her.

'I have to,' she said with a resigned sigh. 'You should do A-levels, Viv, you're much brainier than me. We could do them together.'

Olive

Someone asked me whose baby Amy was. It was a woman in a shop. She looked into the pram and said. 'What a lovely baby.' Then she looked at me: 'Are you looking after her for someone?'

'She's mine,' I said, and the woman looked away, embarrassed. Amy's hair was curly, but her eyes were brown. I kept looking at her eyes every day hoping they'd turn green like mine. I just wanted her to have something that was like me. She didn't cry a lot. Well, not like some babies. She was quite good. But when she screamed, oh God, the noise used to go straight into me and rattle my ribs.

Nobody knew how hard it was looking after a baby all day. In the mornings, Peter, my mum and Vivien would just get up and rush about, having a wash and getting something to eat. I used to watch them. I'd sit on the settee feeding Amy and see them running in front of me, speeded up, like they were in one of those silent films. Peter said he wished he could stay home all day. He thought it was fun. But once everyone was gone, the flat felt so quiet. There was no one to talk to, no one to ask anything. Amy was nice, and I'd talk to her and she'd smile and the little dimple would show in her cheek. But.

I used to put the telly on as soon as everyone had gone. I'd prop Amy up on a chair and stuff cushions all round her, then put her in front of it so she could see. We watched all the schools programmes, some of them were quite good, and Amy loved *Playschool*.

I was really tired all the time. But I had to feed her, change her nappies, get her dressed, stop her crying, play with her, change her nappy again, feed her again, try and get her to sleep, walk round with her, give her a bath, wash her hair. I couldn't just leave her alone while I went back to bed; she'd cry.

And there'd be a mound of washing. All her little clothes that she'd been sick on or spat her food over. And nappies, nappies, nappies!

I wanted to get a washing machine. But Peter said we didn't have the money and my mum said we didn't have the room. So they decided. *They* decided, that I should go down the launderette. I tried it once. It took nearly all day. I had to get dressed and get the baby dressed. Get her in her pram, then get the pram down the stairs, with all the washing balancing on it, in this big bag. The bag kept tipping over and I had to run up and down the stairs to get the things back that dropped out. Then Amy kept screaming in the launderette and people looked at me and tutted like I should stop it. I tried giving her a bottle but she wouldn't take it. She liked my milk better, but I couldn't breast-feed, not in front of everyone, I was too embarrassed. I had to take her outside and push her round the park until she fell asleep. Then go back and do all the washing and stuff.

I was nearly crying when I got home. And there was no one in to help me. I had to feed Amy and try and get her to sleep so I could put all the washing away.

'I want a washing-machine!' I shouted at Peter after that, but he said I had all day to do the washing. So I had to wash the nappies by hand. All of them; if I just dried one without washing it, it went hard and gave Amy a rash. Then everyone kept moaning about the nappies drying all over the place, but what could I do! My mum didn't want the airer in the front room because it got under her feet. Peter said the bedroom wasn't big enough for drying nappies as well. And Vivien just threw them out of the bathroom.

No one thought about me. Everyone loved the baby and bounced her on their knee making stupid noises. But when she needed changing, or feeding, or shutting up, my mum would just say, 'She's hungry . . . she's wet . . . she looks dirty,' and hand her to me. She wouldn't do anything for her.

Peter kept saying that he could do things better than me. And when Amy went to him she did get quieter. He could get her to sleep or get her to take a bottle which she wouldn't with me. It wasn't fair. When she started to cry, he'd watch me with her, then start tutting. Eventually he'd say, 'Give her here.' And he'd look at me like it was my fault. He thought he knew bloody everything.

He still wanted to have sex. 'I'm knackered,' I'd say, and he'd say, 'Why, what have you been doing?' We didn't even kiss any more, he'd just get on top of me. I didn't have to do anything. I just lay there and let him get on with it.

Since the baby I could hardly feel him inside me, like he wasn't touching the sides. He said, 'You've gone all slack.' But it didn't stop him wanting to do it nearly every night. I just wished he'd leave me alone, especially when Amy was still awake.

Vivien

Pam and Linda now officially got on my nerves. After the night down the Sporran Carol and me didn't hang round with them so much. We saw them at school and they'd still sit with us and go on about Tony and Johnny and how gorgeous and funny and hard they were. But Carol and me didn't really listen, we didn't really care. We didn't see our old gang any more. We stopped going to the porch and stairs of Corn flats, stopped hanging round the chip shop and the low wall near the bins. They all went to the Sporran still, to the dive bar, but Carol and me went somewhere else.

We started going to a pub called the Oak, where Lenny and Bobby went. We'd buy a barley wine each when we got there at seven in the evening and still be sipping it when the bell was rung at eleven. It was an art. The Oak was an old pub with brown wood everywhere and coloured glass like you get in churches. It had a room at the back, away from the bar, where you could listen to a DJ who sat by a double deck choosing tracks from LPs. There was different music on different nights. Monday was reggae and ska. Tuesday, Thursday and Friday were Tamla Motown, and Saturday and Sunday were soul. Wednesday, well, we went on a Wednesday once by mistake. Carol bought the drinks and we walked straight into the middle of the room without really looking: we were too busy talking. Then, when we looked round, the whole room was full of people in cowboy hats and cowboy shirts, leather trousers and patterned boots – all the gear. Wednesday was country-and-western night. 'Fuck me, we're in the OK corral!' Carol said really loudly, and everyone looked at us. We nearly wet ourselves laughing. We never went on Wednesdays again.

Lenny and Bobby used to be part of the Quadrant. The Quadrant was a gang, a big gang that even had a girl's section. In its heyday everyone was scared of them and all their members. They used to go up the Arsenal together – up the North bank. One big group of bovver-booted blokes with the girls following on behind. The crowds used to part when they came through. Or at least that's how Lenny and Bobby said it was. But then most of the blokes got jobs and some even had families. So now they went about in twos and threes and only remembered their glory days.

Carol started going out with Lenny. Although she never seemed to go anywhere with him. She'd just meet him, go down the Oak, and then he'd walk her home. She was mad about him before she got off with him. She kept going on about his long blonde hair, his big baby brown eyes and the great clothes he wore. But after going out with him for one week and three days, she started saying his hair was like rats' tails, his eyes were two piss-holes in the snow and 'Fuck me, what does he look like?'

Lenny was always with Bobby and I was always with Carol. So when Lenny and Carol walked arm in arm to the pub, I had to walk with Bobby. Bobby didn't fancy me. Carol said he liked me, said I had a nice personality. Although most of the time we just walked along in silence or . . .

'Where do you live?' he'd ask me.

'Finsbury Park,' I'd say.

'Oh, you support the Arsenal then?'

'Sort of,' I'd say.

Silence.

'You go up the North bank then?' he'd ask.

'No, I don't like football.'

Silence. Silence. Silence.

But after I'd had a few sips of barley wine in the pub and he'd had a pint of light and bitter, I could ask . . . 'So Bobby, where do you work then?' And look interested when he told me that he worked a machine in a greetings-card factory.

'You know all those cards with the little pink and blue bears on?' he said.

'What, the ones with the big eyes?' I said.

'Yeah, the cute ones, and they're always holding balloons,' he said.

'Oh yeah,' I said.

'Well, I folded all of them,' he said with definite pride.

Then one night I was walking home with Lenny and Carol. She held his arm and he bowled along in his green Harrington jacket and trilby hat. I felt a bit of a gooseberry but I didn't really care. I was staying at Carol's, I had no choice. We passed an Indian man in the street and Lenny said, 'Put, put, put,' really loudly in an Indian accent. The man looked at him sheepishly and Lenny went 'Boo,' into his face and laughed. Carol laughed too. But I'd had enough barley wine to say, 'Leave him alone.'

Lenny and Carol looked at me, still smiling.

'It's only a Paki,' Lenny said.

'So,' I said.

'I fucking hate 'em,' he said.

'Why?' I asked.

Lenny looked at me with a frown. 'Cause they shouldn't be here,' he said. I began to get nervous. Lenny's mouth curled into a snarl. 'They deserve what they get.'

'What, they deserve to get beaten up,' I said, although I didn't really want to.

'If they don't like it they should go back to where they came from,' Lenny said, looking at Carol. Carol was looking at me.

'There's our bus, Viv,' she said.

'You're stupid,' I said to Lenny and wished Olive was there to see me.

'What, are you a Paki-lover?' Lenny grinned, and turned to Carol, who let go of his arm.

'Come on, let's get the bus, Viv,' she said, grabbing me. She kissed Lenny quickly on the mouth. We jumped on to the bus and I watched Lenny getting smaller as it pulled away.

Carol packed Lenny in a few days later. 'He's thick,' she said. 'He don't even know what procrastinate means.' When we went to the Oak, Lenny spent all night staring at Carol, looking over at where we sat. He nodded 'Al'right,' to her when she saw him, but she only smiled a little.

The Oak became our nights out. Carol and me would sit at the bar tapping our legs to the music – looking around. We had a cigarette every now and then and sang along to the Four Tops. And we'd have a laugh.

'Ooh, look at that arse, Viv – you could crack walnuts in that.'

'Nice, Carol, but look at the mush.'

'But Viv, as my mum always says, you don't look at the mantelpiece whilst stoking the fire.'

'Or, Carol, my mum always recommends the clever use of a paper bag,'

'Ah yes, for wrapping round the meat and two veg?'

'Comes in very handy, Carol.'

We giggled and talked to people who walked by us. The black boy from the Sporran came in one night with a white girl hanging on his arm. As he passed me he said 'Hello sister,' and Carol and me laughed. I didn't mind that I hadn't been out with a boy – away from Pam and Linda it didn't seem to matter. There were other things in life.

One night Gary came in.

'Al'right,' he said to me and Carol. 'You want a drink?'

Carol looked surprised but said, 'I'll have a rum and pep and Viv'll have a port and lemon.' Gary flinched a little but then caught the barman's eye and ordered the drinks. Carol looked at me and winked. We always ordered big when someone else was paying.

He handed us the drinks and stood holding a pint beer-jug.

'Do you still go up the Sporran?' he asked Carol, although he looked at me.

'No,' we both said together.

'Do you go up the Sporran?' Carol asked.

'No,' Gary said, 'too much aggro. I'm fed up with all that stuff.' He took a long sip of his beer and wiped his hand across his face.

'You don't go down the club any more?' he asked Carol.

'No – it's a bit babyish. Do you?' Carol said.

'Yeah, well, no, well sometimes, but not really,' he said. 'I have to see Ted though.'

'Why?' Carol asked.

'Oh, he's helping me do—' Gary looked embarrassed and flicked his fringe out of his face. He had deep grey eyes.

'What, table tennis?' Carol laughed.

'Get off,' Gary said, waving his hand at her and smiling so two dimples appeared in his cheeks. 'No, he's . . . well, I'm going to college soon. You know.'

'What you doing?' Carol said, raising herself up in her seat.

'Oh, just City and Guilds in electric stuff, you know, wiring and that.'

Carol and me looked at him, waiting to hear more, but he took another sip of his drink and looked around.

'How long d'you have to go a college for?' Carol asked.

'Well, it takes a long time. It's worth it though – I want to get a qualification, get on a bit, you know,' he said. We both nodded.

'I like wiring,' he added. We nodded again.

He stood by us for most of the night, even when girls who obviously fancied him came up and tried to tempt him away. He just talked to them but stayed on his spot. Carol kept catching my eye and pointing at Gary behind his back, rolling her eyes and holding her nose. Or doing a wanker sign and pretending to grab his bum, all when he wasn't looking. She really fancied him – I could tell.

Lenny came smiling over to Carol.

'Give us a fag, Carol,' he said. She looked at him like she'd just found him on the bottom of her shoe. 'I wouldn't give you the steam off my piss,' she snarled, and turned her back on him. Lenny's smile faded and his eyes squinted. He walked back across the pub but kept looking over at us, his lips moving in curses. But Carol didn't notice, she didn't seem to care, sipping her drink and laughing with Gary. She started to show Gary a mole on her back. She pulled her T-shirt down off her shoulder.

'Go on, can you see it?' she was saying as Gary was looking hard at the spot. Lenny came back and pushed past Gary. Gary's beer spilt on Carol and Gary said, 'Oi.' Lenny puffed himself up and out.

'Yeah, what!' he said.

Gary looked at Lenny but didn't say anything. Lenny pushed himself forward. 'You wanna make something of it?' he said. Gary put his hands up in the air, palms out, but Lenny pushed him in the shoulder. All this happened in a flash. Carol didn't really know what was going on. She was brushing beer off her lap, until Lenny took a swing with his fist at Gary. It missed and made Lenny lose his balance. I got pushed off my stool by Carol who was trying to avoid the punch.

'Stop it!' she shouted. 'Stop it, you stupid bastard.'

Gary pushed his body into Lenny who was trying to punch him again. Gary pinned Lenny against the bar and hit him in the stomach. The barman started shouting, 'Break it up – break it up!' He tried to get through the gap in the bar, but it was blocked with people come to stare. Someone screamed. Lenny was pushed up against the bar and Gary had him by a ruffle of clothes at the throat. He couldn't move, and Gary was shouting, 'Fuck off – fuck off,' into Lenny's face. Then he let go his grip a bit. Lenny picked up a beer-glass at his side and smashed it against the bar. He pushed the jagged stump of the broken glass hard into Gary's face and twisted it. Right there in front of me – right in front of Carol. He crunched the glass into his face, then dropped it and ran out of the pub, with the barman chasing him.

Gary held his hands up over his face but didn't say anything. For a moment it was silent and everyone stared.

Blood started dripping through his fingers and suddenly he howled. He let his hands down and looked at them. His face was blood. He screamed and began to fall forward on to me. I caught him but he was too heavy for me and he slid his face down the front of my cream satin blouse. He landed on the floor in graceful faint. I screamed. And people turned their faces away from the sight.

Carol shouted 'Get an ambulance!' She knelt down by Gary but didn't touch him. A piece of glass stuck glistening out of his cheek. He didn't move.

'He's still breathing,' Carol said, and I bent down with her.

'D'you know him?' someone asked.

'Of course I fucking know him,' Carol snapped. 'Get an ambulance.'

Gary began to moan and then to yell out, 'Shit, shit.' He tried to cover his face again but it obviously hurt him. Carol and me flinched together and shouted, 'Don't!'

'The ambulance is coming, Gary,' Carol said, as she patted at Gary's back. He began to cry.

The barman came back puffing and saying, 'I know him – I know him,' to himself. Then he looked at the scene. 'Christ almighty,' he said. He started pulling people away from around us. 'Come on, break it up – out, everyone out – there's nothing to look at. Out.' Carol and me stayed by Gary, tapping his back and trying not to look at the mess of blood, glass and tears that was his face. We were pathetic.

Two ambulancemen came in. One carried a bag and momentarily rolled his eyes when he saw Gary on the ground. They pushed Carol and me away and looked at Gary's face.

'Can you walk?' one of them shouted. Gary nodded.

'You're a bit of a mess,' one of them said. They helped Gary stand up. We grabbed Gary's coat and handed it to him but one of the ambulancemen took it instead. We followed them out and the crowd outside round the ambulance all seemed to say 'Ugh,' together when they saw Gary.

Carol had her foot on the ambulance step ready to get in,

but was stopped by the man pushing her gently back. 'All right – we'll deal with it now,' he said.

Gary looked small and scared in the white light of the ambulance.

'If you want to see him he'll be at the Whittington,' the driver said as he closed Gary in.

We stood with the crowd listening to whispers of 'A glass . . . a fight . . . only young . . .' as the blue light disappeared. It was then I started to cry, and Carol put her arm round me.

'He'll be scarred for life,' Carol said to me as we walked down the road away from the pub. We could hear sirens all around us. And every person coming towards us or moving away seemed to menace. I held on to Carol's arm tight and shivered. I was so scared.

'I hate Lenny – I fucking hate Lenny. I'll tell the police – I'll tell them anything,' Carol kept saying over and over.

'I hate them all,' I said, but she didn't hear me. Carol noticed the blood on my hands that I'd smeared on to my cheek. We bent down by the kerb and I washed my hands in a puddle and Carol wet a tissue and rubbed at my face.

We got to the main road and found we were suddenly standing outside a pub. Music was playing, I could see the live band clearly, standing on a stage. In front of them people were dancing round. Women with long hair flying this way and that, men in T-shirts waving their arms in the air; singing, clapping, laughing. A load of hippies we'd have called them a year ago, and pulled faces. But me and Carol watched. Creatures from another planet watching humans having fun.

Olive

Peter started getting ideas about bringing up children. He went on about how I shouldn't say 'no' to Amy. How I should try and explain things to her instead. 'She can't speak yet,' I told him, but he said it didn't matter. He said that children learn by experience. He got annoyed with me when I shouted at her as she was about to touch Vivien's heated rollers that were plugged in and on the floor of the front room. He said, 'If she touches them, she'll know they're hot and next time she won't do it again.' And I said, 'She won't do it again because I won't let her.' He didn't like that – he didn't like me arguing with him.

One night I put Amy to bed in her cot at about eight. She was lying down when I left her. She looked so peaceful asleep, I wished it was me in there. Peter was watching the telly and my mum was knitting. I could see the noise of her needles clacking was annoying Peter. He kept looking at her, but she didn't take any notice. I was in the kitchen washing clothes when Amy started crying. She just whimpered at first but then she started really bawling.

'Pete, could you get her?' I shouted.

'No, leave her,' he said.

I went in the room and stood in front of him. 'Could you get her – I'm busy.' He pushed me a little to get out of his view of the telly and said, 'Let her cry, babies need to cry, it's good for their lungs.' My mum sucked her teeth but carried on knitting as if nothing was happening. And Amy was still crying. 'Please go to the baby, Peter.' I was very reasonable. He looked at me and started to give me one of his lectures.

'You shouldn't go to babies every time they cry, it spoils them. If you just let her cry, she'll cry it all out and settle down eventually.' He said it in the same way as he did when he was explaining his stupid political ideas. Like he'd just read it in a book.

'She's only little!' I shouted, and went to go to her. But suddenly Peter sprang off the settee and grabbed me back. He started shouting down my ear, 'Leave her! Leave her! You're spoiling her – you don't have to go to her all the time. Leave her.' I was really shocked.

'She might have got out of her cot – she's big now,' I yelled at him. I tried to push him off and I was surprised how he held on to me. 'I said leave her,' he said, slowly, right into my face.

'That's not what you say in the middle of the night – then you can't wait for me to shut her up,' I told him. And he said 'Don't disobey me.' Like I was a kid, like he was my mother. I didn't know what to say. I held my breath, then I said 'Fuck off.'

My mum got up from her seat and said, 'I'm going to the child.' She walked out through the other door in the room. Peter let go of me and ran round to stop her. He stood outside our bedroom door and wouldn't my mum go in.

'Leave her, Mrs C.!' he shouted. My mum smiled a little, as if they were having one of their other rows.

She tried to reason with him: 'But Peter, the child is crying, we need to see what's wrong nuh.'

'I don't want anyone going in there – she'll be all right, she'll stop in a minute.'

'But Peter—' my mum started saying, when he suddenly yelled, 'Stop interfering, it's none of your business.' And Amy screamed louder.

'It is my business when you live in my house,' she shouted loud. She wasn't trying to be nice now. This was my old mum, my hopping-mad mum. 'What you know about children – you too young. I have two girls, I know what to do. Let me see that child.'

113

I got scared, everyone outside Amy's room screaming and shouting. 'Shut up – shut up both of you.'

Peter started pointing his finger at my mum, 'I'll bring up my kids my way!'

And she pointed back. 'You're a man, you know nothing about children. The child could be choking, anything, in there.' She pushed at his arm and he pushed her hand away.

'Leave us, Mum,' I said.

She took no notice of me. 'You're a fool, Peter, a fool,' she spat out.

Peter held up his hands in the air and said, 'All right – all right – I'll go in, I'll make sure she's all right.'

We stood looking at each other. All of us breathing hard. Peter went in and shut the door behind him, leaving me and my mum outside. I hated him. Amy stopped crying after a few seconds and he came out again.

He looked so smug. 'See, I told you there was nothing wrong, she's going back to sleep. We could have just left her and she'd have cried herself out. And tomorrow night she'd have known not to bother crying. That's how babies learn.' My mum gave him one of her dirtiest looks.

'Let me see her,' I said. I didn't trust him. He might have killed her. He opened the door a tiny little bit so I could just see in. I could see her lying in her cot, not asleep, but quite happy. Then he slammed the door shut again.

We went back to the front room, with him still going on about how his mum was always running to his little brothers and how spoilt they were. But neither of us spoke to him.

I didn't speak to him for days. He kept trying to be nice, saying he only did these things for Amy's own good. But I still didn't speak to him. And during the day when he wasn't there, I'd run to her every time she called out or cried. I'd go to her and hug her in my arms, tight.

After that Peter changed his shift at work. It meant that he didn't come home until really late some evenings, although he still went out early every morning.

Vivien

'Oh yes, that's nice,' Mum said, when I told her I'd passed five GCE's. But she seemed more interested in the ones I'd failed. 'You fail History, Vivien,' she said, looking at the little bit of paper that the exam results came on. 'You must try harder. You spend too much time with your rough friends. You must study, Vivien. You're a clever girl, but you must study hard if you want to be a teacher or a nurse.'

I was surprised that I hadn't passed History. I'd spent hours the night before the exam copying down all the relevant dates on a little piece of paper. I slipped the paper under my legs as I sat down at the exam desk. And when I looked deep in concentration, head bowed, I was in fact reading off my list – the dates for the repeal of the corn laws or the rise of the Chartist movement. But I still didn't pass. And I did pass Geography, when I had spent the last two years in geography lessons perfecting my technique of sleeping on one side of my face, which was covered by my hand, while the other side stayed awake. I didn't know anything and just answered the questions with the abandon of pure ignorance. I got a C.

Carol only got two O-levels, both in English, and a grade one CSE in Sociology. We both got grade four CSE Maths; 'That's for getting your name right on the top of the page,' Carol said.

'Are you still going back, though?' I asked her.

'Oh yeah – I have to,' she proclaimed.

Being in the sixth form was different to being in the lower school. We had a common room, not a classroom. It had soft chairs that had no arms; you could push them together and lounge about on them. There were no desks, just a few tables that were put away when not needed and posters on the walls of Salvador Dali paintings and Marlon Brando on a bike. At the side of the room was a small kitchen which had a kettle and a toaster. In the sixth form everything was meant to be relaxed and informal because, as our form mistress Miss Adams said, 'We were there because we wanted to be.' Miss Adams was supposed to let us call her by her first name, Elizabeth, but when someone did she flinched and smiled such a pained smile that nobody tried it again.

We didn't have to wear a uniform in the sixth form. The theory was that you could come in your own clothes, except that they insisted we wear dark-coloured trousers and definitely no jeans. Carol and me didn't have anything suitable and had to go to Kensington market just to get something we thought would fit in. Brown and navy loon pants with twenty-six-inch flares. We bought one pair and stole the other because we didn't have enough money. Carol laughed at my flares, which completely covered my shoes. 'You look like you're standing in a hole in the ground,' she said. I took them up, but was conscious of them flapping round my ankles.

We were the only girls from the B-stream in the sixth form. Carol and me sat in a corner on the first day, not talking but trying to look big and confident by putting our feet up on the chairs. We watched the clique of A-stream girls sitting on the tables laughing, pointing and joking together.

I only knew one A-stream girl. She used to get the same bus to school as me. At first I ignored her, but we were always late together and sometimes we'd be the only ones on the bus.

'My name's Georgina,' she said to me one day, in a voice that needed the corners of your mouth to be stitched up to get the accent right. I said 'I'm Vivien,' as posh as I could, but I knew she knew.

We used to line up in the late line together and she'd wink at me as she pleaded with the teacher on duty.

'My mother's very ill and I had to take my small brother to school.' And when the teacher told her that she'd been late every day for the past six weeks, Georgina looked at her and with a dead serious face said, 'Well, my mother's very ill, very ill indeed.' The teacher let her go. When it came to my turn I got the usual detention.

Georgina passed me outside the youth club one night when I was waiting with everyone to go in. She approached us in a flowing velvet maxi-coat and hippie beads.

'Hello,' she said, in her way, and everyone turned and stared at her like she'd been sent from outer space to embarrass us. I said hello back and hoped she'd go away, but she asked, 'What are you doing?' and smiled, showing the gap in her front teeth. I could hear everyone sniggering.

'Just hanging around,' I said.

She looked around at us all, then walked on saying, 'I'll see you tomorrow.'

We watched her walk up the street and Arthur shouted, 'I'll see you tomorrow,' trying to imitate her poshness but failing.

Georgina was in the middle of the group sitting on the desks, screeching when she laughed. All the A-stream girls seemed to have long fair hair that covered their eyes. They all wore tight cotton T-shirts with bell sleeves and scoop necks. Everyone had on rows of beads except me and Carol. Georgina waved when she saw me but none of them spoke to us.

We were summoned to the headmistress's office on the first day. We all lined up outside her room at the end of a long corridor. Carol and me stood picking our nails, trying not to look scared. The only reason I'd ever been to the headmistress's office before was so that she could give me a lecture on why I must not talk in assembly or why chewing gum makes you look vulgar. But Miss Adams said the Head wanted to see her new sixth form for a 'chat'. I was in front of Carol and when my turn came and I heard Fat Bag Baker shout 'Next' I nearly wet myself.

She was sitting behind a huge desk in an office that seemed

117

a bit grand for a headmistress. It was full of antiques, little African statues and books lined up on shelves. I walked slowly down the stretch of carpet towards her, my instincts screaming 'danger!'

She looked up at me briefly and said 'Ahh yes,' as if my appearance had confirmed something for her.

'Olive – come along,' she beckoned.

'Vivien, miss,' I whispered, but she didn't hear. There was a chair but I didn't sit down.

'Now, what A-levels do you want to do?' she said, looking at the paper on her desk.

'Uhmm,' I started.

'Yes, yes,' she said. She looked at me, waiting for an answer.

I couldn't remember. Mrs Baker rolled her eyes a little, then looked at the papers again. 'Oh yes, here it is: Art, English and History,' she said.

'Now, what did you get at O-level?' she went on, in a manner that made it a question that didn't need an answer. She flicked ash off a cigarette that was lying in an ashtray and put it to her lips. She was smoking in school and that was strictly forbidden.

'You didn't get History?' she said, looking up at me and squinting her eyes so that cigarette smoke didn't get in them.

'No,' I confessed.

'Well, I can't let you do History A-level, then,' she said. She made a simple stroke with a pen. A stroke through History A-level.

'You can take the O-level again, and do English and Art – good,' she said to herself. Then she waved her hand for me to go. Our chat was over.

'Wait a minute, Olive,' she said.

'Vivien,' I repeated.

'Are you doing typing?'

'No.'

'Well, I think it would be useful for you if you learned to type. I'll put you down for typing,' she said, this time putting a simple tick. She looked at me briefly and pulled her face into a smile, then let it snap back into ogre position.

Carol came out of the office swearing and smiling at the same time. Only from where I stood was it obvious she was calling Mrs Baker a fat cunt. Mrs Baker no doubt thought she was a very pleasant child.

'She won't let me do three A-levels,' Carol said, close to tears.

'Nor me.'

'I told her my mum wants me to so I can do law, but she didn't care. She said she don't think I'm capable of doing it. What does she know?'

We'd gone into the sixth-form toilets which were different from the toilets in the rest of the school because they had soft toilet paper.

'Bitch!' Carol said. She blew her nose on the roller towel, 'Just English and Sociology, and she says I've got to learn to type.'

'Me too!' I shouted. We looked at each other, then laughed. 'She thinks we're thick as shit, just 'cause we don't talk like that lot,' I said. Carol grunted like an ape and scratched her head.

We left school early that day. In the sixth form you could come and go as you pleased. You didn't have to get permission or bring a note, although they did like you to go to the lessons.

We walked down the road and saw two first-years looking crisp and neat in their new uniforms. In the sixth form we were all prefects, which meant you got to boss the little kids about.

'I'm a prefect,' Carol said. 'Where are you going?' They looked frightened, like two little spaniels, wide-eyed and shaky-legged.

'You should be in school,' Carol went on with authority. 'Who said you could come out?' She frowned very convincingly and so did I. One of the girls produced a note from her pocket which she handed to Carol. Carol flicked the note open while still looking at the girls. Then she looked at the paper and moved her head slightly as she read. She folded up the note and handed it back in one gesture.

'Well, that's all right then, but see I don't catch you again,' she said, pointing a finger which the two girls cowered from.

We walked off and ducked down behind a car and I wet my knickers laughing.

'What did the note say?' I asked with tearful eyes.

'Fuck knows – just a load of scribble,' she shrieked.

Carol was going out with Gary. His face had healed quite well, with only a faint trace of a scar. He had to have four stitches in his cheek and the doctor said he was lucky the glass missed his eye or he could have been blinded. He didn't even have to stay in hospital overnight. 'It looked worse than it was,' he said when Carol phoned him the next day. He couldn't speak properly because he couldn't move his mouth. Carol kept thinking up jokes to tell him. She said she liked to see him squirm because it hurt him to laugh. She visited him a lot. I didn't go with her – I knew I'd be a gooseberry.

Gary didn't want to go to pubs anymore. The police wanted him to press charges against Lenny, and we said he should. But he didn't. He said it would get him into more bother from Lenny's mates, and he wouldn't be able to go anywhere. 'I just wanna forget it,' he said. And when he smiled now his dimple pointed to the beginning of his scar. But he was still gorgeous.

'What you doing tonight?' I'd ask Carol, and more often than not she'd say 'I'm going round Gary's' or 'He's coming round mine.'

So I stayed in a lot more. I stayed home with my mum, Olive and Peter. When Amy was awake it was fun. I loved reading to her. I'd sit her on my lap and she'd point at the pictures in the books and try and say the word. She'd pull the pages back to her favourite bit and laugh. Or she'd play with my hair and give me wet kisses on my cheek. When Amy was around she seemed to cast a spell on the whole room.

But after she'd gone to bed the flat fell into a strained silence. My mum didn't talk to Peter any more. She rolled her eyes and sucked her teeth at his every move and gesture. And he would lay sprawled out on the settee, taking up three people's places. Or he'd put the record-player on really loud in the kitchen when we were all watching television. Nobody would ask him to turn it down, Olive would just get up and turn the television up. Olive used to skip round him, ruffling his hair or lying with him on the settee. But Peter didn't take any notice of her. She tried to make out that they were still happy. But I could hear them at night having whispered rows.

'You never take me out any more,' she'd say.

'I'll do what I like, when I like,' he'd reply.

Only when Peter wasn't there would everyone breathe out again. It was horrible.

I met Georgina on the bus nearly every morning. She was doing English and Art like me, but they let her do History as well. She said she lived off the Seven Sisters Road near Holloway. I didn't tell her where I lived.

We had art lessons together, and one day Georgina had to set up a still life for us both to paint. She brought some black velvet fabric and dismembered plastic arm and legs off old dolls. We dripped blood-red paint on the limbs. Our teacher, Mr Roach, looked at it, held his chin and asked, 'So what is this saying, girls?'

And Georgina said, 'It's our comment on the futility of existence, sir. Isn't it, Vivien?' She grinned at me and I laughed. We sat together and painted while we sucked, chewed and crunched our way through bags of sweets.

Then she asked me if I'd like to go out with her one night. 'Helena and me are going to the King's Arms on Upper Street – do you want to come?' she said.

Olive

'Do you want a cup of tea?' I asked Peter.
'No,' he said.
'I'm making one.'
'So what, I don't want one.'
'I was only asking.'
'That wasn't asking, that was nagging.'
'I wasn't nagging – why should I nag you about a cup of tea?'
'Because you nag me about everything.'
'I was just asking – anything I ask you, you say I'm nagging.'
'Because that's what you do, you just go on.'
'I only asked you if you want a cup of tea – you're the one going on.'
'Nag, nag, nag.'
'I'm not nagging, I'm trying to talk.'
'Nag, nag, nag, yap, yap, yap, all the bloody time.'
'I can't talk to you any more, Peter.'
'You can't talk to me?'
'Yeah, I can't talk to you.'
'That's a joke. When did you ever talk about anything except nappies anyway?'
'I don't only talk about nappies.'
'No, I'm sorry, I forget – you like to moan as well. "I want a washing-machine. I want some saucepans of me own. I want some towels." I'm sick of it.'
'Well, I'm sick of being here all the time.'
'Oh God, here we go.'
'Well, when are we getting our own place?'

'Oh yes, that's something else you talk about. "When are we getting our own flat, Peter? Peter, have you seen any flats? Peter, there are some flats in the paper – go and see them." Change the record, Olive.'

'It was you who said we wouldn't have to live here long. We've been here for over a year!'

'I know how long I've lived in this dump, Olive. You don't have to remind me.'

'I want us to get our own place.'

'Oh really. I didn't realize. I didn't realize what you meant when you kept saying "I want my own flat".'

'Stop being clever.'

'Fortunately for you, Olive, I can't stop being clever.'

'You think you know everything.'

'No, not quite everything. Like I don't know why you keep going on about getting a flat when I keep telling you there aren't any we can afford.'

'You haven't looked in ages.'

'Because, and I'll say it slowly for you so you'll understand, there aren't any flats.'

'How do you know if you don't look?'

'Why's it always up to me? Why don't *you* look? Why should I do all the looking?'

'I went down the council.'

'Big deal – once. You went down the council once. Do you know how many flats I've seen?'

'Well, I've got the baby.'

'I've seen hundreds of stinking holes. Do you want to live in a stinking hole? No, you want a nice flat, with a kitchen you can sit in.'

'I'd go if it weren't for the baby – I'd look every day.'

'Yeah, of course you would. You wouldn't just sit on your arse all day at home, moaning, would you Olive? You'd be out finding us a flat, one like in the adverts. Of course you would.'

'I don't just sit on my arse – it's hard looking after a baby.'

'Oh I know, all that playing, reading books to her. All that watching the telly.'

'That's what you do with her – it's not what I do. I have to do everything, all the washing and—'

'Oh, not the washing again.'

'It's not only that, I have to feed her.'

'Feed her, yes, that sounds hard.'

'It is. And I have to make sure she's all right.'

'Sort of, stop her falling off chairs – that must take a lot of doing.'

'Its all right for you, it seems easy to you, all you have to do is play with her in the evening. It's hard during the day.'

'What, when you've got nothing else you have to do except look after her?'

'It's not like that!'

'Don't shout Olive, you'll wake that evil mother of yours.'

'I'm not shouting.'

'I think you'll find you are; on a decibel rating, I think you'll find you're very high.'

'Oh shut up! You make me sick – you think you're so clever.'

'Now, now, Olive, calm down. You wouldn't want Amy to wake up and then you'd have the terrible task of getting her back to sleep again. A task, I might add, that takes me three seconds and you at least an hour.'

'Oh shut up!'

'Make up your mind Olive – a minute ago you said I didn't talk to you, now you want me to shut up.'

'You think you're so clever.'

'Yeah, yeah, you said that before. And I am clever actually.'

'Then why can't you find us somewhere to live – why can't you get us all our own place?'

'Because I'm at work all day, dearest, sweating my bollocks off with a sack on my back.'

'So, you could look in the afternoons. You just don't bother, you don't care. It's all talk with you. You just go on, say all these things, but you don't do any of it. What have you ever done?'

'I do plenty.'

'What? What? What have you ever done?'

'Calm down, Olive.'

'I am calm.'

'Well, stop shouting then – you're getting hysterical.'

'I'm not getting hysterical! I just want you to listen or talk like you used to!'

'Well, which do you want me to do, listen or talk. Make up your mind.'

'God, I hate you. I hate you!'

'You're definitely hysterical.'

'I'm not!'

'You are. You know what you look like to me? You look like a stupid hysterical black cow to me.'

That's when I went for him. I had had enough. I made a grab for his throat. It was like an instinct. He looked surprised. Then he pushed my hands off and I came back at him and started hitting him round the head. I just couldn't stop myself. I wanted to hurt him. He held my hands up and I stopped struggling for a bit. We looked each other in the face, in the eyes. Then he said, 'That's done it.' He smiled, let go of my hands, walked out of the flat and slammed the door behind him.

I was so angry, I ran out after him. I was in my dressing-gown but I didn't care. I started crying, and the stairwell looked all watery and fuzzy. There were people coming up the stairs but I just ran straight past them. I could feel them looking at me. But I didn't care. Bastard! Bastard! He never listened to me, never.

I could see him getting in the car, so I ran across the grass and grabbed the handle of the door. But he wouldn't let me in. So I banged on the window. 'Let me in, let me in, you bastard.' But he still wouldn't open the door. And he was smiling – looking at me and smiling. Then he put two fingers up at me and started the engine.

I wasn't going to let him get away with that – he'd got away with too much already. I ran round in front of the car, right in the headlights, and I pushed myself up against the bonnet. 'Run me over then, you bastard,' I shouted, and clung on to the car. I wasn't going to let him get away. I wanted to talk. And the car started moving slowly but I didn't budge. I could feel my legs being lifted off the ground. I let go of the bonnet and ran round to the door again and grabbed at the handle. I was yelling at him, but he didn't take any notice. The car started moving faster but I was still hanging on to the handle. And it got faster and faster and I had to run with it. I kept banging on the window and shouting, but he didn't even look at me. I ran with the car and I was tripping up on my dressing-gown which was getting all muddy and ripped. But he didn't stop. Eventually I had to let go and I watched the car drive away until it was a little speck that vanished. I thought he'd come back. I sat down in the road. But he didn't come.

Vivien

'Sorry I'm a bit late,' Georgina said. She walked towards me with her black coat billowing out around her. It was seven-thirty and she was meant to meet me at seven. I had been standing outside Highbury and Islington tube station for over half an hour, and had had two offers – one from a middle-aged man who wanted to buy me a drink, and the other from a grubby-faced boy of about twelve, who wondered if I fancied a bunk-up.

'Have you been here long?' she asked.

'Not really,' I lied.

She looked into my face and smiled. She stared at me for such a long time that I had to look away. She had blue eyes that seemed to penetrate your skull, like she was looking at something inside you.

'We'll meet Helena in the pub,' she said, grabbing at my arm. She looked at my face again and I began to wonder if I had a bogey hanging out of my nose. I put my hand up to wipe it, just in case. She didn't have any make-up on. Her face was bare, scrubbed and rosy-cheeked, just like when she was at school. I suddenly felt like a painted doll beside her with my eyelashes heavy and sticky with mascara.

'You look different,' she said. 'You look really pretty – you've got such long eyelashes.' She put her finger up to try and touch my face. I backed away and she laughed. 'Take no notice of me – I always envy people who can wear make-up. I can't, I just look stupid, like a courtesan.'

'Well, you look good without it,' I said, wondering what a courtesan was.

She grinned, and I noticed how wide the gap was in her front teeth.

'I can get a two-shilling bit in this,' she said, when she saw me looking. 'Horrible, isn't it?' I didn't know what to say so I shook my head.

Georgina walked very fast, I had to run every few steps to keep up with her. The metal clasp on her shoulder-bag kept clinking and tinkling but she made no attempt to stop the noise.

'You used to go to that youth club, didn't you?' she asked. I nodded.

'Isn't it a bit rough there?' she said.

'A bit. Not as bad as the pubs.'

'Really, do you go to rough pubs?' Every time she asked a question she stopped walking as if she couldn't do the two things at once. I had to keep turning round and waiting for her. Then she'd start walking again and I'd have to run to keep up. I missed Carol.

'What pub did you go to?'

'Oh, the Sporran, the Oak . . .'

'The Sporran! That's really rough.' She stood still, looking impressed and slightly scared. 'Did you see any fights?' She began walking again, looking into my face.

'Yeah, a few.'

'What, with blood?' I wasn't sure if she really wanted me to answer that. I stared at her. But she looked so keen that I said 'Yeah, loads of it.'

'Tell me.'

'What?'

'About the fights. Was it skinheads?' She was a little girl wanting to hear a story.

'Well, they had long hair most of them – that's crombie, really.'

'Are you a skinhead?'

'Me, no.'

'Were you though, before, you know, when you were in the other class?'

128

'No.'

'Because those other two girls were that you and Carol hung round with.' I realized she meant Pam and Linda and that she must have watched us, noticed us. I thought no one ever did.

'Not really,' I said.

'But you saw fights.'

'I saw a boy get a glass smashed in his face once,' I said matter-of-factly.

'You're kidding!' She was so impressed I wanted to elaborate.

'Yeah, I got blood all over me. Carol was there – she'll tell you. We had to help him, stay with him.'

'Carol's quite rough, isn't she?' she said.

'Not really. Haven't you ever seen a fight?' I asked, wanting to change the subject.

'No,' she said. Then remembered. 'Nick, this bloke we know, he . . . Well, it was nothing really. He sort of pushed a guy off his bike once, because the guy had called him a name.'

'Oh,' I said, trying to sound impressed.

'It was nothing though, the guy just got up and walked up the road. He didn't do anything.' I nodded.

'Do you still go to the Sporran?'

'No, I don't like all that stuff – it's horrible.'

'Well, I wouldn't go into one of those pubs,' she admitted. 'Although it sounds exciting.' I didn't say anything.

'Nothing ever happens in here,' she said, pulling open the door of the King's Arms.

The pub was yellow-bright inside, like it was lit by a bare lightbulb. It made everything look grubby. The posters on the walls for films, bands and dance companies had turned-up edges and crease marks. And the floor was polka-dotted with cigarette burns and little flattened crushed stubs. Some of the seats were the kind you find in cinemas, but old and shabby with the stuffing hanging out. Everyone in there had long straight hair that fell on shoulders and backs that were covered in gaudy velvet or cotton tops which hung over bright flared trousers.

My hair was short – still growing out of a long crop style. I'd borrowed a yellow and brown smock top from Olive. She wore it during her pregnancy and her protruding belly button had worn a hole in the fabric which I had to sew up. But it was the only thing I could think of to wear to make me look enough of a hippie. There was no music playing in the pub, just people chattering, moving their hair slowly out of their eyes and taking long slow drags on hand-rolled cigarettes.

Georgina slung her bag over a chair at a table and walked to the bar. I followed her.

'I'll get the first one, you can get the next one, OK,' she said. She contorted herself so she could slide her hand down the front pocket of her skin-tight jeans. She pulled out some change and looked at it, then dug her hand down deeper. 'I've lost my purse,' she said as she pulled out a crumpled-up pound note. She began to straighten it out. 'What do you want?' she asked.

'Barley wine,' I said.

'Half or pint?'

'It comes in a bottle.'

'I don't think I've ever had that. Is it nice?'

I thought of Pam: *It's cheap, it lasts for ages, and it makes you really pissed.*

'It's all right,' I said.

Georgina ordered and the barman pushed my drink to me. When she turned round Georgina was holding a pint of lager. In the Oak it was an unwritten rule that only men drank pints – a woman with a pint was always a 'whoops how's yer father'.

Georgina took a tiny sip from the beer and put the glass on the bar. 'Helena,' she shrieked, and waved her arms in the air. Everyone looked round, everyone heard, everyone stared but Georgina didn't seem to care. She ran up to Helena as if she hadn't seen her in a hundred years, not like she'd just left her at school a few hours earlier. They met in the middle of the pub and Georgina kissed Helena on the cheek. Helena didn't look embarrassed.

'Hi, Vivien,' Helena said, putting both her hands on my shoulders and pulling me to her a little. Her tits stuck out in front of her like a huge padded shelf. I resisted and she let go.

Helena was a bit of a legend at our school. She was the only girl doing four A-levels – three of them in science. At prize days she spent most of the time on the stage, collecting prizes for nearly every subject she took. She was Greek. Carol called her 'the wop swot'.

'Is Carol here?' I shook my head and wished she was. Helena had a pretty face with round dark eyes, but the black hair on her top lip was beginning to break through the thick pan-stick she'd used to conceal it.

'I asked him,' Helena said to Georgina, obviously carrying on a conversation they'd been having before.

'And,' Georgina prompted.

Helena took a deep breath. 'Well, he said I can stay out until nine-thirty during the week but ten-thirty at the weekend.' Helena smiled triumphantly.

'Well done,' Georgina said, kissing her friend again. They both giggled together, then saw me looking confused.

'Isn't it great, Vivien, Helena can stay out until ten-thirty at weekends now.' My smile was so weak that Helena tried to explain.

'My dad wouldn't let me go out at all in the week – he's really strict but I managed to talk to him, and now I can stay out until half-past nine.'

'Oh right,' I said. Big deal, I thought.

Helena looked over my head at the barman. 'Pint of lager, please,' she called out.

'Let's sit down,' Georgina said, moving to where she'd left her bag.

My chair was rickety. It kept swaying underneath me like I was sitting on a drunk's lap. I was scared it was going to collapse and leave me splayed on the floor, so I sat dead still, hardly turning my head to the left or right.

'Ciggie?' Georgina asked. She rummaged in her bag and pulled out a packet of ten Number Six. I didn't think A-stream girls smoked. You never saw any of them in the toilets at school, sitting four to a cubicle, sending smoke-ring messages and flushing stubs down the lav.

'Have you got a light?' Georgina asked Helena, who bounced on her chair and said, 'No but I've got a striking figure.' She threw a pose – her arms outstretched, her breasts jutted forward and wobbling dangerously. Georgina laughed and I wanted to go home.

'Have you got one, Vivien?' Georgina asked. I shook my head carefully and the chair bounced me back and forward.

'I'll get one,' Georgina said, getting up.

'No, wait,' Helena grinned. 'Just see how long it takes for someone to offer us one.' She held her cigarette up high in the air and scanned around her with a wide-eyed, slightly helpless look. 'I've always wanted to try this. They do it in those black and white films and someone always offers the woman a light after a while.'

Georgina laughed and held up her cigarette too. I rolled my eyes to myself. If Carol could see me, I thought.

'Come on, Vivien.' Helena nudged my arm and I held my cigarette up too. No one came. We sat there for ages, like three pathetic starlets.

'I'll go and get one from the bar,' Georgina said eventually.

'No, wait, wait,' Helena ordered. She threw her head back and flicked her hair around her. A man appeared.

'Do you need a light, ladies?' he asked. He struck at a lighter which didn't light until the third attempt. Then he lit my cigarette first. He had on a brown leather cowboy hat and his long straggly hair flopped down into my drink as he stretched across to reach Georgina.

'Thank you,' Helena said. She winked at the man, and puffed smoke into his face.

'My pleasure, ladies,' he said, nodding and looking at us in turn. He smiled. 'Mind if I join you?'

'Feel free,' Georgina said, and pulled a chair up beside her using only her foot to drag it along. The man sat down and beckoned to someone at the bar. I turned round and saw a man in a beige raincoat shaking his head and taking a sip of his drink.

'He's shy,' the man in the hat said when he saw me looking. 'Not like me. My friends call me Eddie, amongst other things.' He tipped his hat at us. 'What are your names, then?'

We all said our names in turn while taking long, elegant drags on our Number Sixes.

'Vivien,' Eddie said, studying my face. 'My sister's called Vivien. Does everyone call you Viv?'

'Sometimes,' I said. I took a sip of my drink and had to hold on to the table to steady the chair.

'Having trouble with the old chair there?' Eddie asked. 'Let's have a look.' He held my hand and pulled me out of my seat. Then he got down on the floor and waggled each leg of the chair in turn. 'Gor blimey,' he said. 'Look at this.' He held the chair up and showed us all the shaky leg. He put it back down. 'You have mine, Vivien,' he said, pointing to his chair. 'I'll sit on this – I'm used to things wobbling about.' He smiled and we sat down in our new places. 'Now, excuse what I'm going to say next.' Eddie put his hand on his heart. 'It may sound like a cliché to you. You may have heard it before but I really do want to know. Right, here goes. Do you come here often?' We all laughed as Eddie was saying, 'Honest, I want to know.'

'Do you?' Georgina said.

'Now, now,' Eddie said, pointing a finger. 'I asked first. Because I haven't seen you in here before, and I would have remembered, because I never forget a pretty face.' He was looking at me, and I turned away and flicked ash on to the floor.

Helena looked up at the door. 'There's Nick,' she said to Georgina. She grabbed her drink and stood up.

'Leave him,' Georgina said, waving her hand.

'I'll just go and say hello,' Helena said. Georgina looked at me and rolled her eyes as if I knew what was going on. Helena walked across the pub into a fug of smoke on the other side.

'Was it something I said?' Eddie joked. 'I'm not that bad, am I?' He sniffed under both his armpits and laughed, then asked, 'Can I get anyone a drink?'

I was about to say I'll have a port and lemon, when Georgina said 'No, we've just got one,' and pointed at our glasses. I had much less left than she did in her pint jug, but I didn't say anything.

Georgina offered Eddie a cigarette. 'No, I can't,' he said, holding up his hands, 'its bad for my voice.' He looked round, waiting for one of us to ask more, but we didn't. 'It makes me go all hoarse,' he went on, 'all croaky, and I can't sing.'

'Are you a singer?' Georgina asked.

'Well, I sing sometimes in a band,' Eddie said.

'Oh, are you in a group?'

'Yeah, well, yeah . . .' Eddie made a gesture like he didn't want too much fuss made of him.

'What group – would I have heard of them?' Georgina said.

'You might have.' Eddie leant back shakily on the chair. 'Anyway, you'll see me play tonight.'

'Oh, are you in this band?' Georgina said, pointing towards the tiny makeshift stage in a corner of the pub.

'I'm just jamming with them tonight, they asked me to – you know,' he said, like it was nothing.

'What do you play?' she asked.

Eddie waggled his fingers around in front of his chest, miming a guitar.

'Guitar,' Georgina cleverly guessed.

'You got it. Lead usually, but I'm just doing rhythm tonight.'

'What did you say the name of your band was?' Georgina asked again.

Eddie leant forward, resting his elbows in a pool of beer of the table. 'Well, as it happens, I'm sort of between bands at the moment.'

'What sort of music do you play?' Georgina persisted.

'Rock,' Eddie said emphatically.

'Heavy rock or folk rock?'

'There's only one real rock,' Eddie said with one arm outstretched, miming guitar again. His hat fell off his head and he bent down to pick it up. 'I'm a pure rock musician,' he said, getting up from the floor. 'A gladiator of rock.' He looked at us both and grinned with all his teeth.

He had a strange face, like a caveman. Heavy-boned brows that sat close to his eyes, and a wide flat nose. He had long straight dark hair and sideburns that curled over his pink cheeks. And when he smiled he had a glint in his dark eyes that sent a little beam directly to you.

'You don't talk much, Vivien,' he said, turning his gaze on me alone.

'Nothing to say,' I smiled.

'My sister's shy too – must be something to do with the name. Does it mean Shy One?'

'No, I don't think so,' I said.

'What does it mean then?'

'I'm not sure . . . something . . . Alive, or something . . . Life . . . something like that.'

'That's nice. Mine means the Keeper of Riches. Well, Edward does, but nobody calls me that except my dear old mum.'

Georgina leant forward. 'Mine means . . .' she started, but then stopped as Eddie looked away and beckoned to his friend at the bar again. He pulled a face when his friend still refused to move.

Eddie tapped Georgina on the arm. 'I think your friend wants you.' Georgina looked across the pub and saw Helena with her arm straight up in the air, signalling for her to come. Georgina rolled her eyes and sighed. 'I won't be a minute,' she said, getting out of her seat and laying her hand lightly on my arm. I watched her winding her way through the now crowded bar.

'Just me and you then, Vivien,' Eddie smiled. He took a sip of my drink.

'Where you from?' he asked, not changing his expression or tone at all.

I sighed to myself. I wanted to be from somewhere he would be interested in, not just prejudiced against. 'Mauritius,' I said.

'Oh yeah,' he said, frowning a little. 'Doesn't that mean you speak French?' I hadn't thought of that.

'Well, I don't,' I invented fast. 'But my parents do . . . my grandparents did.'

'Is it nice there?'

'I haven't been.'

'Sounds nice, sounds exotic, full of girls in grass skirts. Where is it, then?'

I didn't know. 'Oh I'm not sure . . . somewhere . . . it's been a long time, you know.'

'Well I wish I was from somewhere,' he laughed. And I said, 'I was born in this country.'

'Oh well, you're a Londoner then, like me.' He took another sip of my drink, and saw me staring at it.

'Oh sorry, it's yours, isn't it?' he said. 'Take no notice of me . . . the manners of a pig. Where's my drink? Sorry, I'll get you another one. What do you want?'

'I'll have a port and lemon,' I said.

I watched the band setting up their equipment on the tiny stage. Amplifiers, mike stands and little boxes with dials and foot pedals. They seemed to be having trouble fitting it all on. They taped down wires to the floor with wide brown Sellotape.

'Did you miss me?' Eddie said, putting a drink down in front of me. He tipped his hat at me again as he sat down. 'Can't stay long – my public awaits.' He put his pint of beer to his lips and seemed to drink half the contents in one gulp. 'Nectar,' he said, as he breathed out. 'I usually have a bottle of whisky as well so I can use the neck as a slide on my guitar.' He mimed moving the bottle up and down, and shook his head to imaginary music. 'But I'm only rhythm tonight,' he said, with a serious expression.

Someone on the stage caught his attention and he nodded to them and finished the rest of his beer with a gulp.

'I'm going to have to leave you, Vivien.' He cracked the knuckles on one of his hands. 'Vivien's a lovely name,' he said, cracking the other hand. 'You've got lovely eyes.' I looked away from him, embarrassed. 'I love black eyes – they're mysterious.' I could feel myself getting hot. 'I'll play well tonight, knowing you're watching.' He stretched his arms in the air. 'You look all shy,' he said, and I smiled at him. 'Look after this for me, till I get back.'

He took off his hat and pushed it down on my head. It was warm and smelt of leather and patchouli oil. 'Wear it for luck,' he said, and walked off.

I watched him get his guitar out of its case and lovingly wipe it down with what looked like a bit of old curtain. He wrapped the strap from the guitar round his shoulder and hung the instrument from it, low down, over his crotch. He saw me staring and winked. Some people looked around to see who had caught his eye.

Georgina came back and sat down.

'Helena's staying with Nick,' she said, in an annoyed way. 'It's a long story. I'll tell you one day.' I nodded and tried to look concerned.

'Oh, you've got his hat – I think he fancies you,' she laughed.

'Get off,' I said, hoping he did.

'What do you think of him?'

I watched him walk on to the stage into the lights as a few people started clapping . For a moment he looked like Mick Jagger.

'He's different,' I said.

'Oh,' Georgina sang. She looked closely into my face. I sipped my drink, pretending not to notice her. But she stayed staring.

'Get off,' I said.

'You do fancy him, don't you?' she teased, and the band started to play.

The music was incredibly loud. Everyone seemed to jump at once as the place suddenly shook with the vibrations of it. The drummer started whacking the drums, pumping them with enough sound to fill a stadium. People who stood near the speakers put their fingers in their ears and pulled faces like they were being strangled.

The singer started singing – something about love. Eddie looked deep in concentration, listening to the lead guitar and drums in turn. He walked round the stage tapping his head up and down like a real professional.

As the first song ended Eddie jumped in the air on the final beat and landed down hard. The force of the jump rocked everything on the stage and the singer had to grab the mike stand to stop it falling over.

Eddie counted the next song in with 'a-one, a-two, a-one-two-three-four', and jumped again on the opening chord. The lead guitarist stepped out of his way and stared at Eddie as he twisted his legs round in the air like Pete Townshend of the Who. Then Eddie stood still, legs apart, bent double, flapping his head up and down and swinging his hair around. He jumped once more. A glass of beer that was sitting on the edge of the stage fell off on to a woman's legs. She leapt up and her chair fell over, catching someone on the shin as it landed. But Eddie was oblivious. He started to strut up and down the stage but it only took two steps each way before he came to a stop. He accidentally bashed the singer in the back with the neck of his guitar as he rushed past him. The singer's voice quivered momentarily and his eyes rolled but he carried on. Eddie jumped at the end of the song and carried on strumming his last chord long after everyone else had finished playing.

When he stopped he smiled a 'job well done' smile. Then he walked to the back of the stage and picked up a towel which he wiped over his forehead. 'It's loud,' Georgina said into my ear. I nodded, but was busy watching the drummer talking to Eddie. I could see him saying, 'Just cool it – there's not enough room,' as Eddie wiped his face and neck like a superstar.

Eddie was almost in a trance for the next numbers. He sprang about the stage like an ape. The drummer looked annoyed, rolling his eyes and mouthing curses to himself. But he smiled when Eddie accidentally landed in a painful-looking split – one leg off the stage and one leg on – with his tight trousers slicing his balls. The lead guitarist stood motionless, pressed up against the amplifier at the back of the stage, and the singer began to push Eddie out of his way as he pranced by him.

Eddie was on his knees at the end of the last number, striking the strings on his guitar like he was trying to kill it. The other members of the band finished playing and stared at him in disbelief. Eddie bowed to the applause and waved a little at the audience. He looked flushed and spent.

'He's funny, don't you think?' Georgina said, leaning towards me and laughing. I laughed too. Eddie undid his guitar strap as the drummer and singer were talking furiously to him. Eddie looked serious as he put his guitar in its case. He moved his hands to try and calm the two men down. 'All right – all right,' I heard him say. The drummer snarled 'Wanker,' as he watched Eddie walk away.

'What did you think?' Eddie grinned at Georgina and me. We both nodded enthusiastically but didn't say anything.

'They're crap, really,' Eddie went on, sitting down. 'I only played with them to help out. It's not really my sort of music.' He waved to his friend at the bar who was still standing in the same place.

'It's very loud,' Georgina said.

'Rock is loud, baby,' Eddie laughed. He grabbed his hat from my head. 'Thank you for looking after her.'

Helena walked to our table. 'I've got to go, George, are you coming?'

Georgina looked at her watch. 'It's only quarter past nine – it's Friday.'

'I have to be in at nine-thirty on Friday,' Helena said.

'But I thought it was ten-thirty at the weekend,' Georgina said.

'My dad says the weekend is Saturday and Sunday.'

'But that's stupid!'

'It's what he said,' Helena insisted. 'Just come on – I've got to go.' Helena began to cry. She turned away from us and ran for the door. Georgina sighed. 'Are you coming, Viv? We'd better go.'

'You're not leaving me, are you?' Eddie asked me. 'I was just going to get you a drink.'

Georgina picked up her bag. 'Nice to meet you, Eddie,' she said, putting on her coat.

'The pleasure was all mine,' he replied with a bow, then turned back to me. 'Don't go – the night is young.'

'I have to,' I said. 'I can get the bus with them.'

'Don't go,' he pleaded, grabbing my hand. 'Stay and keep me company.' I looked at Georgina who shrugged her shoulders. 'I'd better go with her – her dad'll kill her if she's late,' she said.

'I'll walk you home later,' Eddie said. I looked at him and he winked at me. 'Stay with me – I'll show you the stars.'

So I stayed.

Olive

Peter didn't come home for days. I was pleased. I couldn't have cared less. It was peaceful without him. I liked it. It was better. I didn't care if he was dead down some alley or smashed up in the car. So badly crushed that nobody would recognize him to find out where he lived. I didn't care. It didn't matter to me. I didn't give it a thought.

My mum asked me where he was. She wanted to know when he was coming home. I didn't know why, she hadn't spoken to him for months. He just got on her nerves. But she started asking me and I just shrugged.

'What do you mean?' she said, all annoyed. I shrugged. She rolled her eyes and sucked her teeth as usual, but she didn't ask me again. She kept looking at me, staring at me, as if the answers to all her unasked questions were in my face. But I didn't care. I carried on as usual.

Vivien didn't notice. She didn't notice anything. Amy missed him, I could tell. She kept looking at the door every time someone came in. Poor Amy. She didn't know her 'dada' was a bastard.

Then one afternoon he came back. He brought me a bunch of flowers. Roses. I hated roses. They smell so nice and look so pretty but they'll tear you to bits with their horrible spikes. Amy cuddled up to him and wanted him to look at this and play with that. He was pleased to see her. He was pleased to see her, but not to see me.

Vivien was in when he came. She said 'Hello, Peter.' Then she looked at me, and then at him, then back at me, and said she'd take Amy to the park. I didn't look at him. I just sat in a chair. I didn't want to make up.

'Olive, I'm leaving,' he said. I shrugged. So what, I wanted to say. So bloody what. What's it got to do with me? I lit a cigarette, as calm as anything. I think that annoyed him. I think he wanted me to break down and cry – fall to my knees on the carpet and beg him not to go. I think that's what he wanted. Joke.

Then he said he'd met some other woman, that he'd been seeing her for months. Well, I wanted to laugh. I mean it was funny. He'd met some other poor cow. He said he was moving into her flat. That she had a flat and two children and he was moving in straight away. I took another drag on the cigarette. I looked out the window.

'Aren't you going to say something?' he said. I could tell I was getting on his nerves because I wouldn't say anything. He wanted me to get upset. He thought I would. But I honestly didn't care. Why should I?

I looked out of the window. There was a man washing a car. It had soap suds all over it and he was soaked in water. He was making a right mess of it. He kept slipping in the suds. Idiot.

Peter started going on about how Amy could come and stay with him in his flat – in his new flat, with his new girlfriend, and her two children. Oh what a happy family. I lit another cigarette but it was making me feel sick. He tried to get me to look at him. To look into his beady blue eyes, but I just stared at the man washing his car, lifting up the windscreen wipers and rubbing down the windscreen.

'Do you want a cup of tea?' Peter asked me. Don't nag me. Don't nag me, I wanted to say. It would have been funny if I'd said don't nag me. I wondered if she'd nag him, his new girlfriend in his new flat. I didn't look at him. I didn't want to.

He said he'd leave the record-player. He called out from the kitchen, 'I'll leave the record-player for you and Amy.' I nearly said take it. I didn't want his things. I didn't want anything from him. Take it, take it. I expect she'd got one, his new girlfriend, in his new flat, with her two children. But I didn't care. Leave it – take it. I didn't care.

He started packing up his things. I could hear him in the bedroom, huffing and puffing about. He came into the room with three carrier bags stuffed with clothes and a box of records. But no record-player. She must have one, in his new flat. He came over to me and held out a twenty-pound note. What was that for – the sex? I just looked at it.

'Don't be childish, Olive,' he said. He shook the note in front of my face. I turned and looked out the window. The man had finished the car, it was all shiny. Peter put the money down on the table.

'It's better all round,' he said. 'It'll be better in the long run.' He went on, talking and talking. I didn't know what about: I wasn't listening. He wanted us to be friends. I noticed he was balding. He'll be bald as anything soon. She'll have a bald boyfriend, in her new flat, with her two kids. It made me smile. He thought I was smiling at him. I wasn't smiling at him. I was laughing because he was going bald. I didn't care, I didn't care less. And he thought I was smiling at him.

One of his plastic bags broke and all his clothes spilled out. He wanted me to help him pick them up. He looked at me. He wanted me to help him. I leant forward and lit another cigarette.

'For God's sake say something, Olive – don't be so childish, we need to talk,' he said. I was really annoying him. He couldn't stand it that I didn't care. He wanted me to cry. You must be joking.

He slammed the door when he went. It made me jump. I watched him walk with his bags to the car – my car. He bought that car for me. It was my car. I watched him walk to my car. He looked so stupid, trying to carry three bags and a box of records. He was wobbling about, spilling things and picking things up. He looked so funny and small. Funny, small, boring, balding bastard – I just had to laugh. I laughed.

Vivien

Georgina had to organize an election at school, and Carol and me had to become communists.

'I'm not doing that,' Carol protested. 'I'll be a Conservative, like my dad.'

'No,' Georgina said. 'It's only pretend. I've got no one else who'll do it.' She'd had trouble getting anyone interested in taking part at all, but Fat Bag Baker insisted a mock election would be good for our education.

Georgina was very keen on politics, but no one else seemed to be. Except Gillian Roberts, who didn't really count because she was fat and believed that there should be no parliaments or leaders, but that people should govern themselves in small communities. She wanted to stand as an anarchist, but Georgina said nobody would take her seriously. Gillian stormed out of the sixth-form room when Georgina suggested she could stand as a Monster Raving Loony instead.

Georgina and Helena were Labour and wanted nationalized industries and workers' rights. Lindsay and Catherine were Conservative and wanted better law and order and everyone to go to private schools. Gretchen Wild was Liberal and wanted everything, as far as I could see. And Carol and me, we were, well . . . Red.

I made Carol come to the library with me and I read books on Karl Marx and Lenin. I read out loud to her about dialectical materialism. And she looked at me and said, 'I know, I know all that stuff.'

Carol didn't want to do it. 'It's stupid,' she said.

144

'It's important to know what's going on in the world,' I told her.

'It's not the world, Vivien, it's only this crap little school.'

We had to walk round the school campaigning – wearing badges with our political parties on so the lower school could approach us and ask questions. A second-year came up to Carol. 'Why should I vote for you?' she said, all cocky with her hands on her hips. Carol looked down at her and said: 'Because if you don't I'll have you killed.' The second-year ran off and Carol laughed.

'You shouldn't say that,' I said. 'You should take it seriously.'

'I am serious,' she said. 'That's what they do.'

'But you're supposed to act like you believe in it.'

Carol looked at me for a long time. 'Since when have you been interested in all this crap?'

'Well, I am interested,' I protested.

'Only since you started hanging around with that gap-toothed prat,' she muttered.

'Well, at least she knows about things,' I shouted.

And Carol said, 'Fuck off, Vivien.'

We campaigned separately after that. Although Carol just sat in the classroom and if anyone asked her about communism she said she'd just defected, and that they should ask me. Labour won.

Carol didn't ask me anything about Eddie. She didn't seem interested that I, at last, had a boyfriend. I tried to get her to come to the King's Arms with me and meet him.

'It's full of hippies,' she said. 'I hate hippies.'

'It's not.'

'I like to wash – they'll all wonder what the smell is.'

'You could meet Eddie – you'll like him.'

'I'll feel like a gooseberry.'

'Bring Gary.'

'Skinny – he'd think I'd gone mad.'

'Well, come with Georgina and Helena.'

Carol looked at me like I'd just slapped her across the face.

'You'll like them – honest, they're not like you think,' I said.

'You can say that again – that wop swot has to shave a moustache off every day.'

'Don't be so horrible, Carol.'

'Don't be such a snob, Vivien.'

I didn't bother after that. Carol started taking days off school – sometimes weeks. Miss Adams said her dad was ill. So I phoned her.

'How are you?' I asked.

'All right.'

'When are you coming back to school?'

'Don't know.'

'How's your dad?'

Silence.

'I heard he's ill.'

Silence.

'Is he ill?'

'Yes.'

'Do you want to come out?'

'No.'

'Shall I come and see you?'

'No.'

Georgina wanted to know everything about Eddie. 'Did he kiss you?'

'Oh yes,' I told her. 'It was my first kiss.'

'Really! I don't believe you.'

'It's true – honest.'

'Well, what did you think?'

'It just sort of happened – I didn't have time to think. I was just kissing him all of a sudden – sort of came naturally really.'

Georgina always listened to me with her eyes firmly fixed on mine. I had to find things to do with my hands and places to stare at so I couldn't see her gaze.

'I'm not boring you, am I?' I'd ask.

'Oh no,' she'd say. 'I really like listening to people. Tell me more.'

I started spending a lot of time at Georgina's house. We sat in the kitchen at a large pine table and drank coffee with hot milk which she warmed on a big cooker thing.

'It's an Aga,' she explained. 'My mum always wanted one. It's what they have in country cottages.'

Georgina's house was old. From the outside it looked run-down, with peeling paint and planks of wood in the garden. But inside it was big. Georgina showed me round, into every room, up every flight of stairs, starting at the top and working our way down. Some rooms were beautiful. Tall and airy like classrooms, only with a bed with brass fittings or a huge sofa and chairs. They had fitted carpets and cushions scattered around with books on bookshelves. And everywhere was painted white, so any colour stood out. But some rooms were bare with old-fashioned light-fittings that were hanging off the ceiling and walls. And old, patterned wallpaper that was half stripped-off and dark floor boards spattered with paint. In those rooms Georgina would say, 'This is going to be a study,' or 'This is going to be a play room,' and then go on to explain what was going where and who was going to use it. I lost track of how many rooms there were and always had to ask where the toilet was.

Georgina had her own bathroom. 'Nobody else can use it,' she said. It was attached to her bedroom. 'It's called *en suite*.' It was painted white. 'My dad paints everything white – he's an architect,' she said, as if that explained it.

Her bedroom had a double bed and stereo, with speakers high up on the wall. She played me 'The Boxer' by Simon and Garfunkel, and made me lie down next to her on the bed. 'You can really hear the stereo effect from here,' she explained. 'Hear the banging – they're church doors – see how one comes from one side, and one comes from the other.'

Georgina had a brother, her 'little baby brother', she called him, although he was only a few years younger than she. She used to cuddle him when she saw him and he would wriggle away from her and run out.

Her dad was mythical to me – someone everyone talked about. 'My dad'll fix it – I made it for your dad – Daddy'll bring one home,' but who I never saw.

Her mum wore jeans and T-shirts like Georgina. She was young with long hair that she kept pulled back under a band. 'Hi,' she would say, and join us round the kitchen table. 'How's your day been, Georgie?' or 'How's tricks, Vivien?' Sometimes she would stay and talk. She'd offer us white wine which she'd get from the fridge, where there was always a bottle open. She'd sit sipping, wanting to know what we thought about the Vietnam war or the state of the economy. I didn't say very much. I didn't know very much, but she and Georgina would chatter away. Once she asked me, as bold as anything, if I was still a virgin. 'Don't be shy,' she said when she saw me blush. 'We don't have an secrets at this table.' She was a counsellor for the Marriage Guidance Council and Georgina told me she could talk to her about anything. 'My mum is my best friend,' she announced.

I began to hate going back to my house – to my flat – to my council flat. Since Peter left nobody spoke. Olive sat in a chair and smoked cigarettes and would growl at you if you asked her anything. My mum went on as usual but without talking to Olive. Amy played on the floor but if anyone went out of the front door she would sit down and stare at it crying, until someone picked her up.

'Is Peter coming back to see Amy?' I asked one day. Olive's eyes darted around in her head and she looked over at my mum, who turned away quickly. And another secret was formed. Nobody was allowed to mention that he'd left: we had to believe that he'd never existed.

Olive

No. It was as simple as that. That's what I told him. No. He should have thought of that before he left. Why should I let him see Amy?

'I'm her dad,' he shouted down the phone. What a cheek! I couldn't believe it. He'd been gone for weeks. He'd been gone for weeks, and he never contacted Amy. Nothing.

'Well, I'm asking now – I'm settled now. I want to see her. Take her out.' He wanted to take her to the park, or the swimming pool, or somewhere fun. Something to make her think he was nice. Probably buy her sweets or a toy. And she'd think he was great. She'd start to miss him.

But he didn't even say goodbye to her, he was so keen to get to his new flat. To his new girlfriend.

Why should I? What had he ever done for her? What had he ever done for me?

He said I was being unreasonable. But I was only thinking of Amy. It was for her sake. I didn't want her to get confused. She was only young. She might have got confused. She might have thought his new girlfriend was her mother. She might have thought anything. Because she was only young. It's easy to confuse children when they're young.

She'd had enough upsets. We were happy without him. We didn't need him. Everything was getting back to normal. It was for her sake. I was thinking of Amy. I had to think of Amy – I was her mother. It was me she needed.

He said he was going to get a solicitor. I said I didn't care who he got, I still wasn't going to let her go with him. He said he had a right to see her, and I slammed the phone down.

Vivien

'Was that your mum? She don't sound French,' Eddie said to me on the phone.

'She's got a cold,' I offered.

'Oh well, wish her better from me. I'll come and pick you up, shall I? Where do you abode?'

A horrible vision went through my head of Eddie tipping his hat to my sister who would snarl at him, ready to bite. Then Eddie turning to my mum and asking her all about the far-off land of Mauritius, as she stood, open-mouthed, looking at his long hair and wondering why I couldn't find a decent man.

'No,' I said.

'I'll meet you in the pub then – eight o'clock?'

Or in a pub on my own, standing at the bar trying to get the barman's attention while everyone stared at me, convinced I was on the game. Before I had time to think I'd said, 'I'll come and call for you if you like.'

'Oh! You're not one of them women's libbers, are you?' Eddie laughed, then gave me his address.

Eddie lived near the Angel in a posh tree-lined street with a canal running close by. There were lots of tall, elegant old houses with front doors, black and shiny, like number ten Downing Street. Then there was a block of flats made of pale grey concrete slabs. Just one block on its own, angular and ugly, looking like the council had left it there to upset architects. De Beauvoir House. Eddie and his family lived at number twenty-seven.

I could hear laughing as I approached the glass-fronted door. I rang the doorbell and the first few bars of the American national anthem chimed. I heard feet running down stairs, and then saw the unmistakable outline of Eddie on the glass.

'You found it,' he said, opening the door wide. He stood there silhouetted against orange and black swirly patterned wallpaper that seemed to be moving.

'I like your bell,' I said.

He rolled his eyes. 'Nothing to do with me.' Eddie looked clean and scrubbed pink, and his hair was wispy in a just-washed way. He had on a white collarless shirt and blue denim waistcoat and jeans. He pulled me in the door and kissed me on the mouth, wrapping his arms round me. He tasted of beer. I didn't have time to catch my breath and had to breathe in hard after he'd finished, and pat my hair back into place.

'Now don't say I didn't warn you,' he said, pulling me through the hall and up a flight of stairs. 'My family are all mad.' He laughed and opened the door to the front room.

The room was thick with cigarette smoke and smelt of alcohol and fried food. It was small and oblong and was packed full of people and furniture – there were two settees and two dining-tables. The orange and black swirly wallpaper actually seemed to take up space, except for where green velvet curtains ran down a wall. A man was standing with his back to us in the small patch of empty space that was the middle of the room. He turned round swaying and dancing and singing 'Oh, you beautiful doll, you great big beautiful doll,' along to a Max Bygraves record. He had on a sailor's peaked cap with 'Captain' written in gold letters.

'This is Vivien,' Eddie announced to the room. The man in the hat didn't say hello, but came up to me still singing and swaying. He held my arms and pulled me into the centre of the room, trying to get me to dance with him. I smiled. I laughed. I went weak with embarrassment.

'Put her down, Dad,' Eddie said, grabbing me back. I sat down on a settee. 'This is my mum,' Eddie said, talking to a woman who was sitting on a chair by a table. She looked pregnant, although I knew she couldn't be at her age.

'Oh, Vivien,' she laughed. She had a cigarette stuck to her bottom lip that didn't move as her mouth opened. 'Here look, Viv, that's your name as well,' she shouted, pointing to a young woman sitting on the other settee. 'There's two Viviens – we'll have to call them Vivien One and Vivien Two.'

'Yeah, yeah,' Eddie's dad said, trying to get her to shut up.

'Or Big Vivien and Little Vivien,' she went on, oblivious.

'Take that cigarette out of your mouth, woman,' Eddie's dad shouted.

'You can be Little Vivien,' she laughed again, and the cigarette quivered on her lip. 'You're littler than my Vivien. 'Ere, stand up Viv.'

'Get off, Mum,' the young woman said from the corner. She was small and blonde and knitted quickly without looking at her needles.

'That's my sister,' Eddie said, and she smiled at me.

'Or Dark Vivien and Blonde Vivien,' Eddie's mum was saying.

'Oh shut up, woman,' his dad said, now dancing with an imaginary partner.

'You shut up Frank,' his mum laughed. Eddie's dad laughed, a deep-throated cackle, like a machine-gun firing off.

'This is my uncle Des, say hello, Des,' Eddie carried on.

Des was laying out cards on the tabletop – playing patience. He took his cigarette out of his mouth using his thumb and index finger.

'Hello Vivien – that's a nice name. Where have I heard that before?' A curl fell out of his immaculately greased hair on to his forehead. He smoothed it back and I smiled at him.

'He's not my real uncle,' Eddie explained. 'What are you, Des?'

'He's your fairy godmother,' Eddie's dad interrupted.

'Yeah, I'm your fairy godmother,' Des repeated, and

laughed: a sound that made me want to cough for him.

'Who's left,' Eddie said, turning round. There was a young, fair-haired man lying on the floor in front of the television which was on, but had the sound turned down.

'This is Pat, my sister's fiancé.'

Pat glanced up at me, smiled quickly, then went back to looking at the telly.

'Turn that thing off,' Eddie's dad shouted at Pat.

'I'm watching it,' Pat said.

'You can't hear it.'

'So, I can watch the picture.'

The television showed racing cars whizzing silently round a track.

'We're meant to be having a party,' Eddie's dad said.

'I'll turn it off in a minute.'

'Everyone wants it off.'

'In a minute,' Pat snarled.

'Here Reenie – turn up that record,' Eddie's dad commanded. His mum went to the small red box-turntable that was on the floor. She turned up the volume so loud that the noise distorted and Max Bygraves singing 'Who Wants to be a Millionaire,' became unbearable.

'Not that loud,' his dad yelled.

His mum laughed and the cigarette on her lip bobbed up and down and deposited ash on her chest. She brushed it off and turned the volume down at the same time.

''Ere, you ain't introduced her to me – to yer old dad,' he said, dancing towards me again.

'And this,' Eddie said, like a grand finale, 'is my mad dad.'

Eddie's dad grabbed him round the shoulders and pulled him close, squeezing his cheek and saying, 'Ohh, this is my son – ain't he lovely?' He shook him and tried to kiss Eddie's cheek as Eddie struggled away from him saying, 'Get off, you silly sod.' His dad let go. 'He's lovely, my son, ain't he?' he said, nudging me. I nodded.

His dad had obviously lost a few teeth which made his

lower jaw come up higher on his face than it should – like an amateur girner. When he smiled it created a lipless gash from one side of his face to the other.

'D'you want a drink?' Eddie asked. Then whispered, 'Take no notice of him,' nodding towards his dad. He screwed his finger into his temple.

''Ere, I saw that,' his dad said, pointing. His mum laughed and then began to cough. 'Take that bloody thing out of your mouth,' Eddie's dad shouted. She immediately obeyed, flicked ash into an ashtray and placed the cigarette back on her lip.

'What do you want to drink?' Eddie asked again.

'What have you got?' I whispered.

'We've got everything,' Eddie's dad butted in. 'Gin, whisky, vodka, beer – you name it, we've got it.'

'I'll have a white wine please,' I said.

'Have you got any wine, Dad?' Eddie asked.

'Wine?' his dad repeated. 'I don't know. 'Ere Des, have we got any wine?'

'What's that, Frank?'

'Wine – the lady wants wine. Have we got any?'

Des looked in the air, thinking.

'We ain't got wine,' Eddie's mum added. 'Pat, did you get any wine?'

'Wine, what, barley wine?' Pat asked, without moving his head.

'Not barley wine – wine wine. The white and red stuff,' Eddie's dad said.

'It doesn't matter,' I said.

'I think we have got a bottle somewhere,' Des finally added.

'Have we?' Eddie's dad asked. He went over to a bar in the corner of the room. It was shaped like the front of a boat. I watched him through the little glass portholes – bending down, rummaging around. He stuck his head up over the top.

'Was it in here, Des?'

'Yeah, Frank – at the bottom.'

'I can't see any.'

'It doesn't matter, I'll have something else,' I offered. Nobody took any notice. 'Eddie, go and look in that box in the kitchen.'

Eddie got up from his seat to obey. I grabbed his arm. 'I'll have a port and lemon, if you've got that.'

Eddie patted my hand. 'Change of plan, Dad – port and lemon,' Eddie said.

'What's that?' His dad was standing up and straightening his hat.

'She'll have a port and lemon.'

'You don't want a wine?' his dad asked me.

'We haven't got any wine,' his mum said.

'I'm sure we had some somewhere,' Des said.

'Port and lemon will be fine, thank you,' I said. Everyone was staring at me and my smile got stuck on my face.

'Port and lemon coming up,' Eddie's dad sang.

'D'you want anything to eat?' Eddie asked.

'No!' I said, a little too quickly to be polite.

Eddie's dad bent down to give me the drink. He belched a loud two-note burp. I smelt fish digesting. 'Excuse my French,' he said, thumping his chest with his fist.

'Oh, charming,' Eddie said.

'You're a lovely one,' Eddie's dad said, looking into my face. 'You're not English, are you?'

'I was born here,' I said as I sipped my drink.

'She's from Mauritius,' Eddie said.

'Oh . . . 'Ere, Des, that coloured fella at work, where was he from?'

'What coloured fella's that, Frank?'

'You know, the one with the limp – lovely fella.'

'Oh, I know – lovely bloke – never any trouble.'

'Where was he from?'

'He was Indian, weren't he?'

'Not him!' Eddie's dad shouted. 'Not the Indian one. That other darkie.'

Des looked blankly into the air to think.

'Where's your dad work?' Eddie's dad asked.

'He's dead,' I said.

'Well, where did he work before he died?' he went on without hesitation.

'Dad! Excuse him, Vivien, he's got the manners of a pig,' Eddie apologized.

'I only wanna know – I might have known him. What's his name?'

'Newton Charles.'

'Oh, no, it wasn't that, was it, Des?'

'Abdul,' Des suddenly shouted.

'Abdul,' Eddie's dad agreed. 'That's right – lovely bloke. We used to call him the Sheik of Araby. Remember, Des?'

'That's right, Frank – the Sheik of Araby.'

'Do you know that song, Vivien?' He began to sing loud and everyone except me shouted 'Shut up.'

'You working then, Vivien?' Vivien asked me. Her knitting-needles moved at such a speed that they became a blur.

'No, I'm at school.'

'School!' Eddie's dad shouted. 'Cradle-snatching now, Eddie?' He ran over and grabbed his son and squeezed him.

'She's in the sixth form,' Eddie protested.

'What you doing?' Vivien asked.

'A-levels.'

'Ohhh,' Eddie's dad said. 'We've got a brain-box here – we'd better watch what we say.'

'Drink up.' Eddie nudged. 'We'd better be going.'

'What you going to do when you leave?' Eddie's mum asked.

'We're going to the pub,' I said.

'No,' Eddie's mum laughed. 'Not now – when you leave school.' She started muttering 'We're going to the pub' to herself and giggling.

'Oh,' I said, hoping no one else had heard. 'I might go to college, I don't know . . .'

'A college girl,' Eddie's dad shouted, and winked at Eddie.

'Are you clever?' his mum asked.

156

'Of course she's clever – she goes out with me, don't she,' Eddie said.

'Ohh, listen to him. How d'you like my son?' Eddie's dad said, grinning.

''Ere – we can call them Clever Vivien and Stupid Vivien,' his mum laughed.

'Thanks a lot, Mum,' Vivien said. Pat looked away from the telly for the first time and smiled. Eddie's mum began to cough.

'Can't you give them bleedin' coffin-nails a rest?' Eddie's dad said. He burped again. 'God, those prawns are repeating on me. Where d'you get those prawns, Des?' Des didn't reply, he just carried on with his card-game.

'We're going out now,' Eddie said, standing up.

'She ain't finished her drink. Let her finish her drink,' Eddie's dad said. Max Bygraves started singing 'Tea for Two,' and Eddie's dad looked into my face, grinning and pretending to tap-dance.

'Can you do this, Vivien?' he asked. I smiled and gulped my drink in one mouthful. I put my glass on one of the tables and Eddie's dad grabbed my hands and pulled me up to dance. 'Come on,' Eddie said, taking my arm.

'Oh, it's just getting good – stay here!' his dad pleaded.

'No, we're going out,' Eddie said.

'You coming back later?' his dad said to me. I looked at Eddie and shook my head.

'We'll see you another time, then.'

'It was nice to meet you all,' I said, looking around.

'Hear that! She's got some manners,' Eddie's dad shouted. He walked over to the television and turned it off.

'Oi – I was watching that,' Pat moaned, from the floor.

'Say ta-ta,' Eddie's dad said to him.

As Eddie and me walked out of the room, I could hear his dad: 'Come on, let's have a bit of a dance – it's meant to be a party – what's the matter with everyone?' He clapped his hands and began singing the Lambeth Walk along with Mr Bygraves. And everyone groaned.

Olive

I couldn't sleep. It was Amy: it wasn't her fault, but she kept scratching herself in her sleep. All night it would go on, or it seemed like it. There was no reason why she did it. There was nothing wrong with her – she just liked to scratch – her head, her arms, her legs. But only at night. Or she'd suck her thumb with loud slapping and slurping noises. It kept me awake.

I'd lie there in bed looking at the walls. Every night. Every single night. I thought I'd get something to help me sleep, some pills. So I went to see the doctor.

I left Amy with Vivien. I had to run out when Amy wasn't looking, but I could hear her screaming when she realized I'd gone. Vivien held her up to the window so she could see me walking across the car park. I waved to her, but she was just crying and banging her hands on the glass. She didn't like me to go anywhere.

My doctor was old, too old to be working. He looked like an old man who should be sitting in a wheelchair in a home somewhere, dribbling down a bib and pissing into a nappy. But he asked me what he could do for me. I told him I wanted some sleeping-pills.

'What do you want those for, young lady? A girl like you should be able to sleep,' he said. So I explained about Amy. And he kept nodding his head and saying 'I see.' He asked me if I was anxious about anything. I said I wasn't, but I told him that my husband had just left me. 'That must have been very difficult for you,' he said. And I don't know why, but I started to cry.

He pulled out a handkerchief from the top pocket of his jacket and handed it to me. He asked me if I had been married long, where I lived, and all sorts of questions. And he kept writing things down on the little cards they keep. He was being so nice.

Then he said, 'What contraception are you using?' I'd just told him my husband had left me, so I said, 'None.' And he started going on about how I should make an appointment to get a coil fitted. He said the coil would be the best form of contraception for a woman like me – a woman in my position. What position? I didn't know what he was talking about; I never wanted to have sex again. So I told him I wasn't having sex. And he said, 'Just in case.' He said how the whole procedure was quick and easy and how there were hardly any side-effects. He said how he wouldn't like me to get pregnant again, as I was obviously having trouble looking after one child. 'But I'm not having sex,' I repeated.

'Just a precaution,' he added.

He went on, but I didn't listen. I looked at the height chart on the wall and blew my nose into his hanky until it was soggy with snot and tears.

'And I can give you a prescription for five sleeping-pills,' he said. 'If you need any more, come back and I'll give you another five. I'm sure you understand why I have to do that, Mrs Flynn?'

I just wished I hadn't cried. That's all I could think: I wished I hadn't cried. I threw his hanky at him, took his prescription and left. I screwed it up and put it in the bin when I got outside. Fuck him.

When I got home Vivien was drinking tea. She was sitting on the settee with her legs folded up around her, dunking digestive biscuits into a mug and watching something on the television. She didn't look up at me.

'Where's Amy?' I asked.

And she said, as calm as anything, 'Peter came and took her.'

Vivien

'What!' Olive screamed at me. She made me spill my mug of tea down my jeans. The hot liquid quickly went cold and clammy on my legs. I tried to hold the fabric away from my skin but Olive came and pushed my shoulders. I thought she was going to hit me. I backed away from her and fell down on to the settee. Olive stood over me, blocking out the light.

'Peter came to take her out,' I tried to explain quickly. 'It's all right, she's with Peter.'

'Why did you let him take her, you stupid little cow!' She whacked at the air above my head and I put my arms up over my face to protect myself.

'She'll be back soon – he's only taken her out!' I yelled through the fabric of my jumper.

Peter had come just after Olive had left the flat to go to the doctor. I was sitting with Amy trying to get her to stop crying. I was singing 'Brown girl in the ring', and jiggling her up and down on my knees. I'd repeated it about six times and she was, by then, only sniffing and wiping snot round her face with the back of her hand. Peter used his key. I heard the key in the front door and thought it was Olive come back. I was surprised to see him standing in the doorway.

'Hello, Titch,' he said, as if he'd just come back from a day at work. As if this was nothing unusual. He'd shaved his beard off and looked different – young and clean.

Amy put her arms out to him immediately and I could feel her straining to get off me and on to him. He ran to her, sinking down on his knees on the floor to be at her height. Then he cuddled her tight and she grabbed his hair. He stood up with her and did a whirling dance round the room.

They both looked so happy, it made me smile. It made a change to see someone happy in that room.

'Do you want a cup of tea?' I asked him.

'No thanks, Titch,' he said, 'I'd better be going.'

'You only just got here,' I said. 'Amy'll start crying again if you go straight away.'

'I'm taking her with me,' he said.

'Oh – does Olive know?' I asked.

'I told her I'd come and see her. I told her on the phone.'

I didn't think anything of it. He looked around for Amy's coat and a few other things. He went to the bedroom and came back with a carrier bag, stuffed full. 'I'll leave this note for Olive,' he said, showing me an envelope then putting it down on the table.

'She'll be back soon,' I said. 'You could wait.'

'I don't think Olive wants to see me, do you?' he said. I suddenly felt stupid. I went to Amy, who was still in Peter's arms. 'You going with your daddy?' I said in baby tones. 'Have a nice time – see you soon.' As I leant and kissed her on the cheek, I could smell Peter sweating.

'What time will you be back?' I called out as they left. But there was no reply. I shuddered when I heard the front door slam. The flat felt desolate. So I put on the television.

Olive pulled my arms apart and pushed her face into mine. 'What did he say?' she yelled. I smiled – it seemed funny. Like the games we played when we were young, where I was Cinderella and she was the ugly sister. I could see the little dangly bit at the back of her throat. I tried to hide my face again, but she kept pulling at me.

'Get off! Get off!' I shouted. I started punching at the air with my arms and legs to get her away from me, but she held on to my leg tight.

'What did he say, you stupid cow!'

She pulled my leg so I landed on the floor with a thump. It

hurt. I looked at her face – it was distorted with real rage. I started to cry.

'He left a note,' I screamed.

'Where, where?' she shouted, pulling me round by my leg. I pointed quickly at the table. Olive threw my leg down and snatched up the note.

She opened the letter quickly, ripping the envelope into pieces. She read the note and looked slowly up into the air. Then she leant forward gracefully on her toes and vomited on to the floor. It landed with a watery splatter and seemed to surprise her as much as it did me. We both looked at the patch of yellowy slime sitting neat and round on the carpet. The acrid smell began to hit the air and I felt sick too. But Olive just stared. Quiet and still. 'I'll get a cloth,' I said.

When I came back in the room Olive was still standing in the same spot. I pushed the cloth at her. 'I'm not clearing it up,' I said. She didn't take any notice. I waved the cloth in front of her eyes, but she didn't see. So I knelt down and started wiping at the sick which kept rolling away from me as I tried to mop it up. 'Oh God, this is disgusting, Olive,' I said. But she didn't say anything.

I went back to the kitchen with the cloth. When I came back Olive was crumpled up on the floor, like someone had just screwed her up and thrown her away. And she was crying. Quietly at first, but then her body started to shake as loud sobs retched out of her. She had the letter in her hand, held tight in her grip. I watched her for a while, not knowing what to do. I knelt down beside her and just looked.

'What did the letter say, Olive?' I said, after what seemed like hours. She didn't reply. 'What did it say?'

Olive slowly turned her head to me. Her eyes were red jelly, and her cheeks were streaked with black mascara. She looked helpless. Not like my older sister at all. Not like Olive. Then her mouth turned vicious.

'It says – you stupid cow . . .' she began. I backed away from her but she came closer towards me. 'It says that he's taken Amy to live with him.'

'He can't do that!' I said, standing up.

'He can, thanks to you,' she said. She stood up, looking in my face.

'It's not my fault,' I said feebly.

'Well whose fault is it then? You let him take her.'

'He said you knew – he said he told you he'd come for her.'

'I didn't want him to see her,' she screamed.

'Well I didn't know,' I shouted, 'nobody tells me anything.'

'God, you're so stupid, Vivien. You don't know anything, do you, you don't know anything that happens in this house!'

She was following me round the room, wanting to keep her face in mine. I could smell her bitter breath. She pushed my shoulder.

'You're meant to be the clever one, aren't you?' She pushed my shoulder again, harder. 'But you don't know the first thing about anything. You just live your spoilt-brat little life.'

'I'm not spoilt,' I whined.

'You've had it so easy – so bloody easy – all your bloody life. You've never had to put up with anything.'

'I have,' I protested.

'No one ever hit you – never – not their precious Vivien, not their precious, spoilt Vivien. You never got chased round – nobody thinks you're a whore. You haven't had any of it.' Olive pulled off her shoe and held it in the air. I flinched away. She tried to hit me with it, holding it up like a hammer with the heel pointing at me. I grabbed it and pulled it out of her hand.

'Get off – it's not my fault!' I shouted, pushing her away from me.

'Oh, nothing's your fault, is it Vivien? You just carry on with your perfect life and all your friends. You don't know what's going on – you're spoilt – you're a spoilt brat!'

Olive grabbed my hair and pulled it hard. I had to bend double to stop the ripping pain. I reached up and grabbed a handful of her hair and ear. We staggered round the room, panting hard, locked in the violent clinch.

'It's not my fault!'

'Stupid bitch – you stupid, spoilt bitch!'

Olive started crying again and I felt her let go of my hair. I ran to the bathroom and locked the door. But she came and started kicking and banging at it. 'Stupid little cow – where's my baby, you stupid, spoilt bitch!' I sat on the toilet, shaking and crying and watching the door pulse in and out with every blow.

Olive

I was very calm. Peter left me a letter. It said that he wanted Amy to live with him and Karen and Karen's children, for a while. It said that he was forced to do this because I was so unreasonable. It said that he would take good care of Amy and that I wasn't to worry. It said he hoped that one day we could all be friends and that I should realize how much better it would be for Amy if she lived in a happy family environment with him.

Vivien was in a state. When she realized she shouldn't have let Amy go with Peter she was almost hysterical. When she knew that he'd kidnapped her she just kept screaming that it wasn't her fault. Just kept shouting it over and over. She locked herself in the toilet and cried. I could hear her. She wouldn't come out.

I was really good. I rang Peter's work. They said he hadn't been in for a few days. They said he was on annual leave. I asked if I could have his home number, but they wouldn't let me. I said I had a right to know – that I was his wife and they had to tell me. But the bastard just slammed the phone down. When I rang back this official-sounding woman came on, trying to be all understanding. But she wasn't really interested in Amy. She said it was a domestic matter and didn't have anything to do with them. She said it wasn't helping anyone to keep ringing them. She said that if I was that worried I should ring the police, so I slammed the phoned down.

When Mum came in I told her straight. I told her that Peter had taken Amy and that she'd probably live with him for a bit. I saw her shudder like she felt a sudden chill. Then she turned her back to me. I could see her shoulders going up and down. She was crying. I knew she was crying but she didn't make a sound. It made me want to cry. I went to put my arm around her. I walked across the room, but before I got to her she said, 'Oh God, oh God, what a mess you make now child. Oh, God.' She turned round and looked at me. 'Why you let the child go? Why you don't call the police? He might harm the child. A child needs a mother. A girl needs a good mother. Why you bring that man in this house? It's not natural for a man to take the child. Everything you do turn bad. Amy is your responsibility and you let her go. When will you see poor little Amy? Oh God, what a mess. I knew this would happen. I knew something like this would happen . . .'

I told her to shut up and mind her own business. I went to my bedroom and shut the door. But all I could see in there was Amy's empty cot. Even when I shut my eyes – even with the blankets over my head and my fingers in my ears. I went to the front room. It was empty. My mum and Vivien were in their rooms. I sat on the settee and watched the room get darker and darker.

The phone rang at about eleven o'clock. I knew it was him.

'Amy won't stop crying,' he said to me. 'She wants you.' I smiled.

'Well, bring her home then,' I said.

'I can't leave here – Karen's at work and I've got the other kids as well.' I could hear Amy crying – no, screaming. He wanted me to feel sorry for him.

'Can you come and get her?' he asked me.

'Where d'you live? Where is she?' I shouted.

'Streatham,' he said.

And I just screamed, 'You bastard – you fucking, fucking bastard – bring her back. Bring my daughter back, you fucking bastard.' I couldn't help myself. 'There's no need to be like that . . .' I could hear him saying. But my legs went under me and I was suddenly sitting on the floor. Vivien grabbed the phone and I could hear her taking down the address.

Then Vivien rang her boyfriend.

Vivien

'Super Ed to the rescue,' Eddie said, as I put down the phone. It made me smile until I looked at Olive slumped on the floor, shaking and crying. She was muttering Streatham to herself, although I don't think she knew she was doing it.

'Eddie'll take us down there, he's got a van,' I said to her. I put my hand on her shoulder and she straightened herself up.

'Good – when's he coming?' she asked.

'Now. He's coming right over here.'

Olive kept reading the little bit of paper I'd written Peter's address on, like she was trying to memorize it. Mum came out of her room and stood over Olive, looking at me.

'What's all this fuss now?' she said.

'We're going to get Amy,' I said.

'Now?' she said, surprised. She looked down at Olive. 'Where's the child?'

'Streatham,' Olive said.

'Where in God's name is Streatham?'

'South London,' I informed her, 'near Brixton.' I knew she knew where that was – her Sodom and Gomorrah.

'Brixton! How you going to get all the way to down there – it's the middle of the night?'

'Eddie's coming to take us,' I said.

'Who's Eddie?' she asked.

'My boyfriend.'

'What? Wait – you have a boyfriend now, Vivien – since when?'

It seemed a stupid time to go into it but she stared at me so intensely that I had to.

'I've been going out with him for a few weeks now.'

'A few weeks!' she shrieked. 'A few weeks – and the man is coming in the middle of the night to take you all the way across London?'

'It's all right, Mum,' I said.

'No it's not all right. You don't even know this man.'

'I do know him, I've been to his house and everything.' This knowledge didn't help my mum, who looked even more horrified. Her face contorted so much it made her hair curlers move independently. 'You've been to his house!' she screamed.

Olive stood up and looked her in the face. 'Oh shut up, Mum,' she spat out. 'Don't make such a fuss.'

'Fuss, who's making fuss. It's not me that cause all the trouble in this house.'

Olive and me both breathed out hard. Our mum looked at me, then at Olive, speechless. She went to the kitchen muttering, 'All this foolishness . . . you two girls . . . if your dad was here . . . I have the trouble.'

When Eddie rang the doorbell Mum came out of the kitchen to look.

'Your carriage awaits,' Eddie laughed, as I opened the door. My mum looked at Eddie, standing in his army greatcoat with his hair straggling round his shoulders and a good day's stubble on his chin, and said 'Oh God,' and went back to the kitchen.

'This!' Olive said, when she saw Eddie's van. Even in the glow of the street lamps you could see the small van had seen better days. It was white – once – but now it was pitted with rust.

'It goes really well,' Eddie said, fiddling with the lock on the back doors. He leant against the doors. 'They're a bit stiff,' he said. Olive rolled her eyes and I gave her a dirty look. Eddie climbed in the driver's door and crawled through the van until his face appeared at the little windows at the back.

'Right – you pull, I'll push,' Eddie shouted through the glass.

'Oh, for Christ's sake,' Olive said.

'Don't be so rotten, Olive,' I snapped. I wasn't sure what to be more embarrassed about – Eddie meeting Olive for the first time, or Olive meeting my boyfriend.

'Come on ladies,' Eddie's little voice pleaded. I tugged at the door, it opened and Olive climbed inside.

I sat in the front with Eddie. He leant over and kissed me, then rummaged through the glove compartment and pulled out several pages of what was once an *A to Z*.

'Are you all right there, Olive?' Eddie asked, turning round. Olive was curled up small on a cushion in the dark of the van. She didn't answer.

'Where are we off to, ladies?' Eddie smiled.

'Streatham,' I said.

'Right, you look it up, Viv. I'll get us to Streatham High Street – and you can sing us a song, Olive,' Eddie chirped. 'Only joking,' he added quickly. I didn't hear, but I could feel Olive groan.

Eddie turned the key in the ignition and looked a bit surprised when the engine started first time. 'That's my baby,' he said, patting the dashboard. 'Wagons roll – next stop Streatham.' He looked at me and winked.

I tried to make the *A to Z* fit together, straining my eyes as I tried to read the tiny print.

'So who we going to rescue, then?' Eddie asked over his shoulder to Olive. I wanted him to shut up but I hadn't known him long enough to know how to do it discreetly.

Olive tutted. 'Didn't she tell you?' I had only told Eddie that we had to go to south London to get someone.

'She said we had to rescue someone,' Eddie said.

'I did not. I said we had to pick someone up,' I protested.

'It's my daughter, Amy. Her father kidnapped her while Vivien was looking after her.' I rolled my eyes, although Olive couldn't see.

'When did that happen?' Eddie asked, concerned.

'This morning.'

'Oh well, she's not been gone long then,' Eddie said, smiling at me.

'Long enough,' Olive snapped.

'Was it your husband who took her?' Eddie went on. 'How long you been married? You look too young to be married.'

'I am too young.'

'Well – don't take this the wrong way, Olive – but was it a shotgun wedding?'

'A what?' Olive said.

'Did you have to, you know?' Eddie asked.

'No,' Olive said emphatically.

'Oh, you liar,' I said.

'I didn't have to get married – I wanted to,' she said. There was silence, and I hoped it would stay like that, but then Eddie said: 'What's his name, then, your husband?'

'My ex-husband,' Olive corrected. 'Peter – Peter Flynn.'

'So you're Mrs Flynn, are you?'

Olive didn't answer.

'Is he Irish? That sounds like an Irish name ' Eddie asked.

'His parents are, but he was born here.'

'Like you and Viv – your parents are Mauritian but you were born here,' Eddie said. I wanted to get out of the car and walk. I hoped Olive hadn't heard.

'Mauritian!' she screeched from the back of the van. She leant her head forward so it popped in between Eddie and me. 'Did she say Mauritian?'

'Yeah. Viv told me your mum's from Mauritius,' Eddie said, sounding slightly doubtful.

'She's not from Mauritius, she's from Jamaica, and so's our dad for that matter.' Olive laughed. 'She's ashamed – she's ashamed we're from Jamaica.'

'I am not.'

'You are. Why did you say they were from Mauritius then, wherever that is?' Olive poked me in the back with her finger. 'She don't want anyone to know we're black.'

'Shut up, Olive,' I snapped. I'd never heard her use that word before. I mean I knew we weren't wogs or coons but I never thought we were black.

'You might have said Jamaica, actually, Viv – I can never remember these things,' Eddie said, hitting his head with his hand.

'No, she's ashamed – aren't you, Vivien?' Olive said, leaning closer to me.

'Oh, shut your face.'

Olive started sniggering. 'What's the matter, Vivien, don't you want your boyfriend to know?'

'Shut up,' I yelled.

'Jamaica's a nice place,' Eddie was saying. 'All those beaches.'

'Scared he'll go off you?'

'Shut up Olive – I mean it.'

'Reggae – that's where reggae comes from,' Eddie mused.

'Jamaica not good enough for you?'

'Just shut up, Olive, just shut your stupid face.' I wanted to punch her. She was so embarrassing.

'Now, now girls,' Eddie said. 'Sisters, eh,' he tutted, then began singing 'Sisters, sisters, there were never such devoted sisters . . .'

Olive settled down in the back of the van. I could hear her muttering 'Mauritius – you're so stupid, Vivien.'

Eddie started to hum his 'Sisters' tune when he finally ran out of words. I looked out of the window at night-time London rushing past in dark, bright, dirty bursts. I found the page with the street we needed on and kept my finger pointed at the spot as we drove, in silence, for what seemed like hours. 'Streatham High Street up ahead,' Eddie said eventually. 'Beautiful, ain't she? Where do I go, navigator?'

I read the map and said left and right in the hope that it corresponded with the direction in some way. Eddie turned the wheel whichever way I said without question. 'You'll never be a rally driver,' was his only complaint, as I took him up dead-end streets and round industrial estates.

We finally found the house. It was a big Victorian house, but run-down. 'My car,' Olive pointed. Peter's car was in the front garden and I could just make out that it was propped up on bricks.

Eddie let Olive out of the back of the van.

'I've got pins and needles,' she complained. Eddie offered her his arm and Olive leant heavily on it.

We all went up to the huge stained-glass-fronted door. There were a lot of bells but only one was lit up. It said Karen in typewriting and Peter in a hand-written scrawl beside it. I pressed it. Olive looked nervous, although she patted her hair, tutted and rolled her eyes at the broken bottles and mattress in the front garden.

'Bit of a dump,' Eddie said, as feet started running down the stairs. Peter opened the door. He had no shoes on.

'Where is she?' Olive said, stepping forward into the light.

'Come in,' Peter smiled. He looked past Olive to Eddie and me and nodded.

'Just get her,' Olive commanded.

'She's sleeping. I'll just have to . . .'

'Just bring her here, you bastard,' Olive said, raising her voice.

'All right,' Peter said, trying to quiet Olive with his hands.

'We'll wait here,' I added, as clipped and angry as I could.

Peter left the door open as he went back up the stairs. Eddie nudged Olive. 'Never trust a man whose eyebrows meet in the middle, Olive,' he said, tapping the side of his nose. I could tell that Olive wanted to smile but had to stay angry instead. She pushed at the door and looked in at the hallway which was littered with bikes and cardboard boxes spilling over on the black and white tiled floor. Peter came back slowly down the stairs. Amy was in his arms. He held her little red coat over her and she rubbed her eyes and blinked around her. Peter passed her to Olive and Amy went back to sleep on her shoulder. Olive breathed in – smelling Amy. She shut her eyes and held her daughter tight.

'I'll come and see her soon,' Peter said, straightening out Amy's coat on Olive's shoulder.

'You stay away from us,' Olive shouted. Amy began to wake up.

'I'm going to see her, Olive, whether you like it or not,' Peter said.

'No, you're fucking not, you bastard,' Olive screeched. I grabbed Amy from Olive and Olive hardly noticed. 'You're lucky I didn't get the police on to you. You leave her alone.'

'She's my daughter,' Peter said, trying to sound calm.

'You left her. You just stay away or I'll—'

'You'll what? You let me see her else I'll do it again.'

Olive was frantic; her voice faltered and croaked as she shouted, 'You stay away – I'll kill you – you just stay away.'

Eddie stepped forward. 'Come on, Olive,' he said, taking hold of her elbow. She shook him off and stepped closer to Peter.

'Is that your new boyfriend, Olive? You always were quick,' Peter laughed. I pulled Eddie back.

'Shut your mouth,' Olive yelled.

'Oh, charming – still as charming as ever,' Peter goaded.

Olive stepped back a little, then with the full force of her body she whacked Peter on the side of his face with her fist. Peter lost his balance as the crack of the blow filled up the night air. She went to hit him again, but Peter caught her hand and held it. She started kicking at him and yelling 'Bastard, bastard.' Amy began to cry. Eddie grabbed Olive round the waist and pulled her back. She kept kicking out and struggling away from Eddie, but he held her firm. 'Stay away, you bastard – I'll kill you. I fucking hate you – you just stay away.'

Peter held on to the front door looking shocked at first, but then he began to smile. His lips moved. 'Silly cow,' they said, and he shut the door.

Olive struggled and yelled all the way to the van.

'What's all this noise?' a man shouted from the front door of a house.

'Mind your own bloody business,' Olive screamed out. Eddie put his hand over Olive's mouth.

'It's nothing, mate,' Eddie called.

'Silly bitch – give her one from me,' the man replied.

Eddie got Olive to the van doors. She stopped struggling and began to cry. He hugged her and she put her arms round him and cried into his shoulder. After a few minutes he opened the back doors of the van and Olive climbed in, wiping her face and nose on the sleeve of her jacket. I passed Amy over to her and she got herself comfortable on the cushion. Olive cuddled Amy on her lap and started humming 'Brown girl in the ring' as she rocked her.

Olive

'I can't look after you, Olive, I don't have the money. You're not a child any more. You have to stand on your own two feet. You must get off your backside. You can't just sit around all day, you must help yourself. It's up to you now.'

I had to put up with my mum going on all the time. She didn't care what I'd been through. She was pleased to have Amy back. When I brought her home she was cuddling her and promising her this and that. But she just looked at me like it was my fault: my fault Peter left me, my fault he was a bastard. Like I should have known. On and on she went. I'd just be sitting down or watching the telly and she'd start. I didn't say anything to her – it just went in one ear and out the other. Like water off a duck's back.

'I knew he'd be no good,' she said. 'With all his big ideas – you should have found yourself a decent man like your father. Mark you, he had his bad points, but he would never have left me. But no, Olive, you wanted to get married and have a baby and you were too young, but you never listen to me. So now you've made your bed and you must lie in it. The Bible says, As ye sow so shall ye reap. You hear me, Olive . . . Olive, you listening to me . . .'

I phoned Peter. I thought, why should I have to have all this trouble? He should take care of me and Amy. Just because he'd left me didn't mean he hadn't got responsibilities. I was still his wife. She wasn't – never would be. I said I wanted him to give me some money every week, like he used to. I said I wasn't going to go away and that he had to take care of us. He said if I let him see Amy he'd give me some money. I told him that Amy didn't want to see him. And he said that I should stop ringing him because it was upsetting Karen.

So I rang him every morning at about seven and I just said, 'Hello, it's your wife and child – I need some money.' That really got on his nerves. It was so funny. He started leaving the phone off the hook, but I'd keep ringing until I got through. She came on the phone once, shouting and telling me that Peter didn't want to speak to me, to leave them alone or else she'd make me sorry. I told her that Peter would do the same to her as he did to me. I told her not to trust him, that he was all mouth. She said he only married me because I tricked him and got pregnant. And I said he only wanted her because she had a flat. She said that as soon as she found out I was coloured she knew I'd be trouble because all wogs were the same. And I told her she was a stupid white cow.

In the end I had to go down the dole. I took Amy with me because I didn't like leaving her. But when I opened the door at the unemployment office I wished she'd stayed at home. It was foggy in there – everyone was smoking. There were windows around but they had glass in them that you couldn't see out of and bars over every one. The place was stuffed with ugly people with big noses or yellow teeth or craggy, lined skin. They were all standing in long lines, shuffling their way down to a long counter. It was horrible. It didn't look real in there – it looked like something you'd see on the telly about the olden days and workhouses. They'd come in the door, join a line and just stand there, moving slowly forward until they got their turn. So I went and joined a line.

I had to carry Amy – there was nowhere to sit. I held her for ages, but then she started struggling, wanting to get down. I put her down and she ran off. I had to go and get her, then get back in the queue. People started tutting like I was pushing in, but I didn't take any notice. I tried to hold

Amy beside me, but there was nothing for her to look at, nothing for her to do. After a while she wanted to go and play again and started screaming. People gave me dirty looks. So I let her go and I had to keep watching her. I could see her weaving her way through people and smiling at them. She was like the only bit of colour in the grey room.

Then this big fat white man came in and stood at the back of my queue and started shouting. 'We're always queuing up 'cause of those fucking wogs over there.' Right at the top of his voice he shouted. People turned round to look at him. He pointed to two black people who were serving behind the counter, taking cards and getting people to sign things. 'What's a matter with everyone? People are fucking scared of 'em. Fucking coons. I wouldn't be in here if it weren't for those fucking wogs, and nobody does anything – they're fucking scared of 'em.'

Then people just turned back, uninterested. Nobody said anything to him, not even the people behind the counter, who looked up when he started but then carried on like they'd heard it all before.

He was looking round the room. 'Fucking scared of 'em – fucking wogs.' His face all screwed up like it was ready to explode. Amy started to run up to him. She was smiling and running with her arms out. She grabbed hold of his trousers. He looked down at her and shook her off. She thought it was a game and went to grab his trousers again. I hurried over to pick her up. As I stood up I looked at the man and he looked at me. 'What you looking at, fucking coon bitch?' he said. I walked back to my place in the queue and he was shouting after me, 'They're fucking everywhere – I ain't fucking scared of 'em.' I looked around me, but no one was taking any notice. It was like it was just me and him in the room. I kept thinking of all the things I should have said to him. I should have said, 'I don't know what I'm looking at, but it's making me feel sick.' I should have said, 'Shut up, you ignorant pus-faced fat git.' I should have said . . . but there isn't anything you can say to a white man that's as bad as *coon bitch*.

* * *

When I got to the counter the man behind it said I was in the wrong queue. He pointed to the sign that was hanging up above my head. He said that this was the queue for signing on surnames from A to D. He said I should go and register at Inquiries, which was at the other end of the room.

I carried Amy through the lines of people to Inquiries. And there was a queue, longer than the one I'd just left. I went to the back. Amy had wet her nappy and it began to smell. People pulled faces and held their noses when she ran past them. But I had to stay in the queue, so what could I do?

When it was finally my turn a black woman gave me forms to fill out – read that, sign here, declare this. I just did what she said.

'So when will I get some money?' I asked her. She looked at the forms, took them away to a little office, showed them to a man who was sitting at another desk, came back and said, 'You're not entitled to unemployment benefit because you haven't got enough stamps.' I didn't know what she was talking about – not enough, I didn't know I had any!

'Well where can I get some more?' I asked her. She laughed. Then she said I could only get them if I was working.

So I told her I was a mother with a small child and that I couldn't work. But that Amy needed some new shoes. I picked Amy up and showed the woman the old ones. I made her feel how Amy's toes were right up against the end. And I said that I had a husband, but that he had just left me for a white woman and didn't give me any money, and child benefit wasn't enough. And how although I lived with my mum, she didn't have the money to look after me and my child as I had a younger sister who still went to school and lived at home. And how I'd been waiting in this stinking, disgusting office for over two hours and there were no seats and Amy needed her nappy changing. And that I only stayed because I thought I'd get some bloody money . . .

The woman behind the counter told me to calm down. She gave me another form to fill in and a letter that she sealed up in a brown envelope. She wrote a telephone number on the letter. 'You'll have to try Social Security,' she said. 'Phone this number for an appointment.' She slapped the letter in my hand then shouted, 'Next.'

Vivien

The moment Eddie opened the door of the clubhouse a voice screeched from inside: 'Viv!' Eddie's dad ran towards us.

'You found her then,' his dad said, knocking Eddie with his shoulder. 'He was worried you'd got lost.'

I had got lost. I'd been wandering round the Caledonian Road for nearly an hour looking for the street. I was about to go home when I saw Eddie waiting outside what I had thought was a derelict building. Eddie wanted to show me a working-men's club. 'We go every Sunday – me, me dad and Des,' Eddie admitted. Eddie said I needed cheering up. 'All those exams. Bring Olive if you like. She could do with a bit of a laugh – my dad would soon make her smile.' I thought of Olive and Eddie's dad, shuddered, and decided to go on my own.

I usually only met Eddie on Wednesday and Saturday nights. We'd go down the King's Arms and listen to a band, which Eddie never thought was any good, and sip drinks until it was time to go home. Then we'd walk through Islington. We always walked no matter what the weather – Eddie would never drink and drive. We'd walk and we'd talk – through Highbury Corner and Highbury Grove. Past my old youth club in Eddie's old school.

'I hated school,' Eddie told me. 'They hated me an' all. When I left, my English teacher – what a sadist. He used to throw the chalk rubber at me. It would hit me on the head and I'd get chalk dust all over me. I got the name Chalky 'cause I was always covered in white dust. Anyway, he said,

'Cooke, you're finally leaving, thank God. That's five years of taxpayers' money wasted on your education."'

We'd carry on through Highbury Fields. 'Did you know, Vivien, that these fields were once a burial-ground for plague victims? They'd collect up the bodies in carts. They'd sing "Bring out your dead" and people would load up all the corpses and bring them here. When it was full up, they filled it in. And late at night you can hear owls hooting and see their eyes in the trees. Look there! Oh, too late, you missed it.'

Then along down Blackstock Road. 'I hate working – if it weren't for the money I wouldn't do it. I work at this whisky merchants', in the City. I'm a clerk, you know, filing and that sort of thing. It's not that bad, we get free samples and some not so free, if you get my meaning. We have a laugh sometimes. But I just wanna play music, that's my real love. I'm getting a band together with some blokes in my office. We're going to make a demo to take round the record companies. We've started collecting the egg boxes. We're gonna paste them on the wall in my mate's sitting room to soundproof it out, because he lives in a block of flats. But once you've got egg boxes on the wall you can't hear a thing next door. His wife won't mind, as long as we paint them white.' We'd talk until we hit dingy Finsbury Park and my flats. Then up along the balcony to my front door. And after a long goodnight kiss, he'd walk all the way back again.

'This is a genuine working-men's club, Viv,' Eddie said, moving his arm around like he was showing me a beautiful view.

'It's not posh like you're used to, Viv – ehh – ehhh,' Eddie's dad added, nudging my arm with his elbow.

It was like a pub, but one that was down on its luck. There was no carpet – just wooden tables and chairs, with wood-look Formica halfway up the yellowing walls which were peeling and cracked. There were at least three dartboards around the room, with men who looked nine months' pregnant with beer guts leaning towards them and stabbing them with flying darts. The room vibrated with talk and laughter bubbling from the tables and bar. And Max Bygraves singing 'Show me the Way to Go Home' was playing from somewhere.

'Come and have a game,' Eddie's dad insisted, pulling my arm.

'I'll get you a drink,' Eddie said. 'Port and lemon all right?' I nodded as Eddie's dad pulled me over to a table.

'Vivien,' Eddie's mum shouted. She looked different, dressed in a yellow satin blouse, pink lipstick and her hair in neat waves on her head and no cigarette. 'This is my sister,' she said, nodding her head to the woman sitting next to her. Her sister looked like her, but had the permanent expression of having a nasty smell just under her nose. Eddie's mum leant over to an ashtray on the table, retrieved a cigarette and placed it on her bottom lip.

'Here's a chair, Viv,' Eddie's dad said, crashing a chair into the back of my knees so I had no option but to sit down.

'Al'right, Vivien,' Uncle Des said from the other side of the table. He was playing cards. I looked over to Eddie at the bar, engrossed in conversation with a man who kept heading an imaginary ball.

'Can you play cribbage, Vivien?' Uncle Des asked.

'No,' I admitted.

'No – no!' Eddie's dad imitated as he sat down beside me. 'What do they teach you in those schools?' He picked up his hand of cards and held them up in front of my face. He started pointing to the cards, telling me the rules of the game. Something about fifteens. I kept nodding and tried to look particularly interested when he showed me a little block of wood with pegs in that Uncle Des kept fiddling with.

'It's how you score,' Eddie's dad explained.

Eddie came back and handed me a drink and perched on the chair with me. 'Is he boring you?' he said with a smile, nodding to his dad.

'I'm teaching her to play cribbage – she can't even play cribbage,' Eddie's dad said. 'Right now, Viv, what's this lot add up to?'

I looked at him. I had no idea what he was talking about.

'Come on, I'll give you a game of darts,' Eddie said, getting up.

'No, she's learning to play crib, ain't you, Viv?'

'D'you wanna stay here, then?' Eddie asked.

"Course she does, don't you, Viv? She wants to stay with yer old dad – we're having a good time here. Go on, you go.'

Eddie got up, squeezed my hand and went over to a dartboard before I had time to shout 'Oh God, please take me with you.' Eddie was immediately joined by two other men who began to rub chalk marks off a little blackboard. They didn't speak to one another but performed their tasks and took aim with their darts in a well-rehearsed ritual. Eddie's dad held another batch of cards to my face.

'So what should I put down now, Viv?' he ordered. And I wished I was with Eddie, trying to hit the little round board and laughing as he showed me where to aim for next time.

'Come on, Viv, stop dreaming,' Eddie's dad said. His face was right in mine, creased like an ageing apple and grinning. And I wished, for the first time in my life, that I knew how to head-butt.

'Look, I'll put this and this, see,' Eddie's dad carried on. 'Right, now we'll have to add up what's left – so that's fifteen-four, two for his pair of sevens and one for his nob – you got that, Viv?' I nodded. 'Well you move the pins then – Des, let her move the pins.'

'Oh all right Frank,' Des obeyed.

'Right, that's fifteen-four . . .' Eddie's dad said again, slowly.

'I don't know how to do it,' I admitted. I took a sip of my drink.

'Come on, I just showed you.' He knocked me in the back with his elbow and I had to cough.

He tutted. 'Gor blimey, all that education – what's the point if you can't even score a game of cribbage, eh, Des, eh, Des?'

'That's right, Frank,' Des agreed.

184

'Here Vivien,' Eddie's mum called out. I was pleased to hear her – she'd come to my rescue. I turned right round to her and smiled attentively. 'What country is it you said you were from?' she asked.

It was then that I noticed everyone in the club was white. I felt the room suddenly stop. Like in old Western movies when the baddy walks in. Men with glasses of beer halfway to their mouths, women mid-sentence, darts mid-flight. The place went quiet – you could have heard a silent fart. Everyone looking at me, waiting to hear.

'I was born here,' I tried.

'Yeah – but your mum and dad.'

Everyone strained in closer. I swallowed.

'They're from Mauritius,' Eddie's voice said behind me. He picked up his pint of beer and took a long mouthful.

'Where's that?' his aunt asked.

'It's in Jamaica,' Eddie said, winking at me, then going back to his dartboard.

'Yeah, Mauritius in Jamaica,' Eddie's mum repeated to her sister, who nodded whilst staring and smirking at me.

'Look at the time, woman!' Eddie's dad suddenly shouted.

'Oh my God – come on, Joanie, the dinner.' The two women got up, collecting handbags, cigarettes and lighters.

'Eddie,' his mum called across the club. 'Come on, your dinner'll be ruined.' Eddie nodded but carried on having his throw.

'You coming back, Viv?' his mum asked.

'I don't think—' I began.

'Of course she is. Of course you're coming back – you can't miss a Sunday dinner. Skinny thing like you needs feeding up – come on.' Eddie's dad took my arm. 'Oi, boy, I've got your woman here, I'm keeping her my prisoner.' He laughed. I didn't.

Sunday dinner at Eddie's house made up for everything. Roast beef, roast pork, roast potatoes, boiled potatoes, Yorkshire pudding, peas, carrots, Brussels sprouts – for those that liked them – all covered in rich gravy. It was wonderful. We ate it on our laps, watching football on the telly. And nobody spoke as we slurped, crunched and chewed our way through the heaped platefuls of food. One by one as people finished they'd comment. 'That was a nice bit of beef, Reenie,' or 'Any more spuds going?' or 'That filled an 'ole.' Even I managed to say 'Thank you very much, Mrs Cooke, that was very nice.'

'Yeah, my Reenie does a lovely bit of grub,' Eddie's dad replied. 'I bet you can't cook like that, Vivien, can ya – they don't teach you that at fancy schools.'

After apple crumble and hot custard, at least five cups of tea and the washing-up, everyone disappeared except me and Eddie. 'Where they gone?' I asked him.

'They always have a nap after Sunday dinner,' Eddie explained. 'They've gone to lie down.'

We sat in the empty room and Eddie yawned every two seconds.

'Do you wanna lie down?' I asked him.

'Well only if you want to.'

'All right,' I said. And Eddie led me through the flat to his bedroom.

Eddie's bedroom was small. The main items of furniture were a single bed along one wall under the window and a huge speaker and amplifier along another wall. His clothes were hung up on a tiny rail which was squashed in the corner of the room next to the bed. Under them was a stereo and a collection of records. When Eddie shut the door behind him, it felt like we were in a crowded cupboard. There was nowhere to go but on the bed.

'Sit down,' Eddie said, picking up a red guitar from the bed. He held it up to show me. 'What do you think of her?' he said, turning it round in the air. 'See the flame on the wood?' He twisted it round some more. I nodded. 'What a baby – Les Paul copy – Jimi Hendrix played one of these. Best there is.' He turned it round again for me to appreciate it, then pulled out a case from under the bed and put it away. I recognized the cloth he covered it with from the first night we met in the King's Arms.

'Aren't you going to give me a tune?' I joked.

'Later, when everyone's awake – it's a bit loud now,' he replied seriously.

He pushed the guitar case back under the bed, then stood on the bed and drew the curtains across the window: they were the same fabric the guitar was wrapped in. Then he clicked a light at the side of his bed and the room lit up with coloured shapes moving about across the walls.

'It's an oil light,' Eddie explained, 'the heat from the lamp makes the oil move.'

I'd seen the lights before, but only at discos and pubs.

'It's nice,' I said, as I watched colours and shapes slowly merging into one another.

'I use it sometimes when I do my mobile disco.'

'I didn't know you did that.'

'I haven't done it for ages – my double deck broke.' He pulled out an old deck from behind the amplifier and showed me some wires coming from it. 'Des said he knows a man who can fix it, but the bloke's waiting for the part from somewhere – anyway, I'm concentrating on me music at the moment, so I don't mind.'

Eddie looked through his records. 'I'll play you some real music,' he said. He put on a record, then sat beside me on the bed. 'My Brother Jake,' started playing out of the speaker. The sound filled up the tiny room although it wasn't playing loud. 'I love Free, don't you?' Eddie said. 'And Bad Company.'

'What's that?' I said.

'What's that – what's that,' he imitated, sounding too much like his dad. 'Only the greatest group ever.'

'I've never heard of them.'

'Never heard of Bad Company.' He started singing a song: 'Bad company until the day I die . . .' and playing an imaginary guitar. 'You never heard of that?' I shook my head. 'I can see I've got a lot to teach you,' he smiled.

'I like Tamla Motown,' I said.

'Yeah, well, that's all right. Marvin Gaye . . .'

'Four Tops, the Temptations, Diana Ross, the Jackson Five.'

'Oh don't, no, the pain, the Jackson Five. You listen to this – you'll never want to hear that squeaky little kid again,' Eddie said. He laughed and lay down on the bed beside me. 'Make yourself comfortable,' he said, pulling my arm for me to lie down with him.

We lay there listening to the record as the colours in the room changed – red, green, gold, blue. I could smell him beside me – patchouli oil and roast beef – and feel his leg tapping to the beat. I put my arm over him and rested my head on his shoulder. He wrapped me up tight in a cuddle. I felt so safe. He kissed me on the mouth quickly and I kissed him back. Then he kissed me again, longer. I moved into him and pressed myself against him as we kissed using our tongues. I began to get hot. I slipped my hand in his shirt and felt the spiky hair on his chest. He put his hand on my breast, but I didn't feel it there. I felt it between my legs – a warm pulsating. I wanted him to touch me all over, anywhere, everywhere. I kissed his neck and bit it gently. He squeezed me tighter and pressed his legs hard into me.

'Shall we get in the bed?' Eddie said breathlessly into my ear.

I nodded. Eddie jumped up and I stood up too. In a few movements he had taken off all his clothes, and in a flash of flesh he was back under the covers. He held the covers open for me.

'Don't look then,' I said.

'Oh, spoilsport,' Eddie said shutting his eyes.

I took my clothes off, hiding my soggy knickers under the pile of clothes on the floor. I thought of my mum – folding her arms, sucking her teeth, shaking her head. 'What you think you doing, Vivien. Decent girls don't do this sort of thing. You want to end up like your sister?' But it felt too good, too right. I cuddled up to his body and felt his unclothed penis, hard as a nose, against my leg.

'Have you done this before?' I asked him.

'Yeah,' he said reluctantly.

'How many times?'

He looked at me and smiled. 'Why d'you wanna know? It doesn't matter.'

'Tell me.'

'I don't know – once or twice.'

'You're lying.'

'Well, what about you? How many times have you done it?'

'Never,' I said.

He looked at me disbelievingly.

'And I don't want to actually do it now,' I said, looking into his face.

'No,' he said without a hint of disappointment. 'We'll just lie here.' He held up the covers and looked at my body. I tried to cover myself up.

'You're beautiful,' he said. 'All golden and lovely. You shouldn't be ashamed of—'

Suddenly the door opened and Eddie's dad stood in the doorway. 'You coming down the pub?'

Eddie quickly put the covers down and I hid my face in his chest. I felt like a whore.

'Oops – sorry,' Eddie's dad said closing the door. He tapped on it. 'Eddie, you decent in there – you coming down the pub?'

'Hang on, Dad.' Eddie lifted my head from his chest. 'D'you wanna go down the pub?'

'When?' I said.

'Now.'

'Now!'

Eddie looked at his watch. 'I always go down the pub with me dad and Des on Sunday nights. You know, for a game of darts and that.'

'We only just got back from there.'

'Well it's . . .' Eddie looked at his watch again, 'it's half six – we always have a few pints on a Sunday night.'

I kissed him on the lips. 'Can't you miss it tonight – just for me?' I whispered. I rubbed myself against him. Eddie grinned like a little boy who'd just found a shiny conker.

'Dad,' he called out.

'Yes, son,' Eddie's dad said. He was obviously waiting by the door.

'We're staying here.'

There was silence.

'What, you not coming?' his dad eventually asked.

'No, we're staying here.'

'It's bingo – down the club – bring Vivien, she'll like that. You like a bit bingo, don't you, Viv?' he shouted through the door. Eddie looked at me waiting for me to answer his dad. I didn't know what to say. Piss off was far too impolite. 'You wanna play bingo, have a drink, don't you Viv?' his dad shouted again.

'No thank you, Mr Cooke,' I said tentatively.

'Suit yourself,' Eddie's dad replied, stomping away from the door.

'He's upset now,' Eddie said.

'Why, just because you won't go?'

'I always go on Sunday nights – he likes it, you know.'

'Well I'm here now,' I said, rolling on top of him.

The doctor at the clinic looked surprised when Eddie walked into the consulting room with me.

'Oh, there's two of you,' he said looking around the room for another chair. The advert on the bus said young people could go along to the clinic for a 'chat' and ask questions about contraception in complete privacy.

'I don't want sex to ruin my life,' I'd told Georgina. 'I want it to be pleasurable.'

'I don't want to end up like Olive,' I'd told Eddie. 'I don't want to get pregnant. I want to be prepared.'

Eddie said he'd come with me, 'See what they've got to say.' But he wondered if they'd still consider him a young person at twenty-two.

The doctor's room was like all doctors' rooms, with a bed with a paper sheet on it and a desk covered with bits of paper and pens. It wasn't trying to be for 'young people' like the reception area, with its posters of the Osmonds, *Jackie* magazines and Radio One blaring in the corner.

'We don't often get to see the young man,' the doctor laughed. Eddie shifted around on his seat.

The doctor looked at my notes and clicked open his ballpoint pen.

'Now let's see,' he started, 'are your parents both alive?' he asked without looking up. Eddie said yes, and the doctor looked at him. 'Umm – not you,' he said smiling, 'I was addressing the young lady.'

Eddie sat back and rolled his eyes at me. The doctor looked back down and started asking me questions about my mum, dad, blood pressure, measles, mumps, headaches and lumps. Firing questions as fast as an automatic tennis-ball server. I didn't really know all the answers, but said yes or no as the doctor ticked them off with business-like efficiency.

'Right,' he said, clicking his pen off again, 'I've given you three months' supply of pills. If you hand these notes to the nurse, she'll explain how you take them and I'll see you in three months and we'll take a smear then.' He held out the brown envelope of notes for me to take and smiled first at me, then at Eddie.

I looked at him. 'I'm not sure I want pills,' I said tentatively.

'What?' the doctor said.

'We came to talk about the different options,' I said, looking at Eddie who was nodding.

'Oh,' the doctor said, pausing for a minute. 'Well, the pill's your best option,' he added.

'What about the side-effects? I read in a magazine that you can get side-effects,' I said.

The doctor nodded, then blew out his breath. 'Well, there are fewer side-effects when taking the contraceptive pill than there are with, say, an aspirin.'

Eddie and me stared at him. 'Does that answer your

question?' the doctor said smiling. We both nodded and I took the notes.

'Miserable bastard,' Eddie muttered as we left the room.

The woman at the dispensary asked me what borough I lived in, then gave me three shiny packets of pills. 'You're not covered for the first two weeks, so I'll give you some condoms to cover that time,' she said.

'There are seventy-two condoms in here,' Eddie laughed when we got outside. We went and sat on a bench in a nearby park. 'For two weeks – that's fourteen days. That's . . . umm . . . a lot a day,' he said turning the packets round in the air. 'We better get started.'

'Put them down,' I snapped, looking around me. 'It's not funny.' I looked at the packets of pills. It had all happened too fast. I could feel tears coming into my eyes.

'What's the matter?' Eddie said, putting his arm around me.

'I wanted to go and talk. Ask them what was best to do and that. I wanted us to decide. Now look – I'm just on the pill. I feel . . . I feel dirty,' I explained.

'Look, we don't have to do it,' Eddie said. 'We'll throw them away.' He grabbed the pills from my hand and stuffed them in the bag with the condoms, then looked round for a bin. But I stopped him.

Olive

'Are you sure your husband has left you for good?' I just looked at this woman. Her face was all distorted because it was behind really thick glass. If I moved my head her face began to look squashed like in the fairground mirrors. I'd waited three hours in the social security office (not to mention the hours I'd spent waiting on the phone) and then when it got to my turn she asked me that bloody stupid question. It was then I understood why she was behind glass and why everything in the room, like the chairs and the ashtrays, was attached to the floor.

They wanted to know the ins and outs of a cat's arse. Everything about me. Was I looking for a job? Did I get any money from my husband? Everything about Amy. Was she living with me all the time? Everything about my mum. Was she a tenant or did she own her own house? And everything about Peter.

They said that he should be paying maintenance to me. They said he should be giving me money every week. I smiled to myself when they said they'd be asking him to pay something. Good I thought. I would have loved to have seen his face when he was told – officially – that he should give me money. No, *had* to give me money.

I gave them his phone number, his address, I told them where he worked. Everything. I told them that he was living with another woman who had two kids. The woman behind the glass said 'Oh' when I said that. Then she asked me if the person he was living with was working. 'I don't bloody know!' I shouted. She said she was only trying to do her job.

Four to six weeks, she said, before I would get any money from them. I could starve by then, I told her, and she said that was how long it would take to process me and that it was the same for everyone.

My mum kept going on that she couldn't look after me – that she didn't have the money. But she always had the money to buy things for Amy. I told her I was getting social security soon. 'When – when's it coming?' she'd scream in my face. I tried to stay out of her way, but it wasn't easy.

Amy was getting really difficult. It wasn't her fault: it was just that she was interested in everything. Wanted to look at everything. All day she just walked round the flat picking things up, putting things in her mouth, throwing things down. I couldn't leave her for a minute. Not one minute. I had to watch her all the time. I tried putting everything up high so she couldn't reach. But she'd climb on chairs or stand on tables to get at things. She didn't seem to care. It wasn't like when she was a baby, when you could just put her down and she'd stay put.

I was running her a bath one day when I heard a thud. I ran out of the bathroom and saw her in the kitchen, standing on the sink, pulling things out of the food cupboard and throwing them on the floor. There was flour and jam over everything: the walls, the sink, the cupboard. It was in her hair and sliding down her face. I yelled at her and pulled her off the sink. She started screaming and kicking and punching me. I put her down in the other room and she threw herself on the floor and was screaming and thrashing about like she was having an epileptic fit. She was raging red. I shouted at her to stop it but she wouldn't. I didn't hit her hard. Just a little tap, just to shut her up.

I was clearing up the kitchen on my hands and knees, getting everything into the bin, when I heard my mum come in and shout 'Olive!' really loudly.

I ran out of the kitchen. I thought something had happened to Amy. But she was sitting on the settee whimpering. I went into the bathroom. The bath had overflowed; there were great sloshing puddles of water everywhere. My mum was trying to mop it up with towels.

'Stupid child,' she shouted. 'Stupid, stupid child.' I tried to help her. I handed her some toilet paper and another towel. But she just kept shouting, 'You can't do anything, you stupid child, look at the place and the water probably go through to her downstairs. I have enough trouble without you.'

'It was Amy's fault—' I started to say, when she turned on me. She took off her shoe and lifted it up in the air. I pushed her away – hard. She slid backward on the water and fell on the floor. She hit her head on the side of the bath with a crack that tipped her head into an odd angle. For a moment I thought I'd hurt her. But it was her fault. I wasn't going to take any of that any more. I was a mother now.

She looked so pathetic sprawled out on the floor. I leant forward to her and held out my hand. But she pushed it out of her way and started getting up by herself.

She stood up in front of me and pushed her face about two inches from mine. 'I want you out of this house – you hear me nuh – out.' She sort of whispered it, then went to her bedroom and locked the door.

Vivien

Olive made it sound like she was doing me a favour.
'I'll come out with you tonight,' she said.

'I'm only going down the pub.'

'Yeah, well, that's all right, I'll come.'

'What about Amy?'

'You'll have to ask Mum if she'll babysit.'

'Me! Why can't you?'

'She won't do anything for me. You ask her if you want me
to come.'

My mum said 'Yes – good – get that child out of the house,
give me some peace. A whole night where I don't have to
look at that long face. That miserable long face. It make me
feel sick, every night looking at her. Leave little Amy with
me. She better off with me.'

And Olive said, 'I bet Mum moaned, didn't she, when you
asked her to babysit? I bet she said, "Olive shouldn't go out,
she has responsibilities. She should stay here with me and
look after her child." I bet she went on like that, didn't she?'

I nodded.

'Who's that?' Olive whispered to me, as Georgina held her
arm up in the air whilst shouting, 'Vivien – over here.'

'It's Georgina,' I said, waving back.

'Is she a friend of yours?'

'Yeah, it's who I've come to meet.'

'I thought you were meeting Eddie,' Olive said.

I looked at her. 'No, it's Friday, he's started playing darts
with his dad on Fridays.'

'That Carol isn't coming, is she?' Olive sneered.

'No, I don't see her any more.'

'Good.'

I gave Olive a dirty look and began to wish she hadn't come. I only let her for Amy's sake. When I'd come home from school a few days before, Amy was encased in chairs. She was sitting in the middle of six kitchen chairs that were all propped up so they wouldn't move. It was like a prison. She was playing with her building bricks and dolls but she couldn't get out. And Olive was asleep on the settee in her dressing-gown at half past four.

'She likes it,' Olive said, 'it's her little house.'

But when I asked Amy if she'd like to come out, she nodded hard and held on tight to me for ages. I suggested to Olive that if she wanted to go out with her friends one evening I'd babysit for her. She hadn't really left the flat for years, not since Amy was born. She said, 'Yeah – I could do with a night out.' Then she 'offered' to come out with me.

Olive looked shocked when Georgina kissed me on the cheek and I kissed her back.

'This is my sister Olive,' I said to Georgina.

Olive had started fumbling in her bag for her packet of cigarettes. She didn't take any notice of my introduction. 'Olive,' I said. She looked up. 'This is Georgina.' Olive smiled the briefest of smiles, then carried on looking in her bag.

'Nice to meet you, Olive,' Georgina said. But Olive didn't take any notice.

'Sit, sit,' Georgina carried on, 'I've bagged these two tables.' There were about eight chairs round the tables all with bits of Georgina on them – her bag, jacket, sunglasses. Olive removed a row of green beads from a chair, placed them on the table and sat down.

'What do you want to drink? I'll get the first ones,' Georgina said.

'Half a lager,' I said, and Olive nodded too.

As Georgina walked to the bar Olive said, 'Can you tell

your friend that I've only got enough money for one drink – I won't be able to buy a round.'

'You tell her,' I said.

'She's your friend and I didn't realize I'd have to buy drinks for everyone.'

'All right,' I groaned.

'It's a bit of a dump here,' Olive commented, looking around.

'Yeah, but it's got a nice atmosphere, don't you think. And nice people.'

Olive moved her top lip slowly into a sneer.

'There are live bands sometimes,' I said.

'Ooh wee,' Olive said, totally unimpressed.

'Well, go home then,' I snapped.

'Touchy,' she said with a sarcastic smile.

Georgina handed us our drinks and sat down, tucking her legs under her on the chair.

'Have you been here before, Olive?' she asked, taking a sip of her drink.

'No, I don't like pubs.'

'Oh – where do you go, then?' Georgina said.

'I used to go to clubs up in the West End when I was young – your age. But now I've got a baby all that sort of stuff seems childish.'

'Oh yeah. Vivien told me you had a kid – what was her name?'

'Amy,' I said.

'That's a nice name,' Georgina said smiling at Olive. Olive looked away from Georgina as she pulled the ashtray closer to her. She lit a cigarette without offering them around, then took a long drag on it and blew the smoke out into my face.

'I suppose it's quite good to be living at home,' Georgina went on, 'if you've got a kid on your own.' Georgina took out her cigarettes and offered me one. I refused. Olive looked at Georgina.

'What do you mean?' she said.

Georgina looked a bit puzzled. 'Well, I mean, there's always someone to babysit. Vivien told me your husband didn't live with you any more. Peter, was it? Was it Peter, Vivien?'

Olive looked a dagger at me. I felt it pierce my skin.

'Oh look, there's Helena,' I said pointing to the door.

Georgina carried on, oblivious to the family secrets she was trampling over. 'She said he left you for someone else. All men are bastards,' she laughed.

She took a sip of her drink. Helena was waiting by the door, looking out and waving at someone.

'She's not coming in,' I said to Georgina, who swallowed her drink and said, 'I expect your mother is babysitting, isn't she? It must be good. Who needs men? Women should just stick together, don't you think, Olive?'

Olive shrugged her shoulders and said, 'I'm getting a place of my own as soon as I can.'

'Oh – why?' Georgina asked.

'I don't get on with my mum, she's a bitch. And I need a room for Amy.'

'Are you renting a place then?'

'No, the council are getting me one.'

'Really – where?'

'I haven't had an offer yet but it won't be long now – I've been on the list for ages.'

'How long?'

'Nearly two years.'

'That's not very long,' Georgina said. 'Not for the council. Some people have been on it for twenty, thirty years.'

'Yeah, but I've got a child – I'm a priority.' Olive gave me another dirty look as she stubbed out her cigarette.

'Hey, Olive, you know what you should do?' Georgina said excitedly. 'You should get your mum to say she's throwing you out because you don't get on – then you'll get a place quicker because you'll be homeless and they have to house you then.' Georgina looked at me, then at Olive, pleased with her suggestion. She opened her eyes wide. 'People do it all the time.'

Olive looked at her seriously, then said: 'I know that – but

I don't have to do that because I'm a priority already.'

Olive sat back in her chair and turned her body away from Georgina. And Georgina pulled a face as she began to realize she may have offended my sister.

'I'm sorry, Olive, I didn't mean to upset you,' Georgina said.

'I'm not upset,' Olive snapped back. 'It's just that I don't think you know what you're talking about.'

Georgina leant back in her chair and looked to the door. 'Oh, there's Helena,' she said to me.

Helena came into the pub with two men.

'This is Nick and this is Laurence,' she said, grinning like a row of aunts were sitting in front of her. She looked overdressed for the pub in a blue flowery maxi-dress with a plunging neckline and frills.

'She's pissed,' Nick said, sitting down and pulling Helena on to a chair. Helena giggled. 'I'm not,' she said, then grabbed at Laurence and pulled him down to sit. Nick had a beard but no moustache. He looked like he'd just escaped from the *Old Grey Whistle Test*. His friend Laurence was like a little boy who'd put on his dad's clothes for the evening. A young man who was going to grow into a bank manager.

'We've been waiting outside Helena's house for hours,' Laurence said. His accent was so posh it made you want to imitate it immediately to see if you could do it. I found myself mouthing 'Helena's house' with hot, breathy aitches. Olive just stared at him.

'We thought she'd never come out – I was beginning to worry that we looked like we were loitering with intent.'

Georgina explained to me that Helena's dad was away and that she had to wait for her mother to go to bed before she could come out.

'She doesn't know I'm out, she thinks I'm in bed,' Helena said leaning forward and taking a sip of my drink. 'Nick, are you getting any drinks?'

'I think you've had enough,' Nick said to her. 'We've been on a bit of a pub crawl, I'm afraid. Laurence here doesn't get to go out much – he's a boarder.'

Georgina smiled and I said, 'A what?'

Laurence looked at me and smiled with a set of perfect white teeth. 'I board at school, for my sins. Nick here's a day-boy.'

I didn't really know what he was talking about.

'I'm sorry, I didn't really catch your name,' Laurence said to me.

'I'm Vivien and this is my sister Olive.'

Olive was busy looking around her and blowing out smoke.

'Oh, you're sisters – actually now you say . . .' Laurence said. 'And are you at school with Helena and Georgina, Vivien?' I nodded.

'A-levels?' he said. It took me a few seconds to realize it was a question.

'Oh, yes,' I said.

'Which ones?' he smiled.

'Just English and Art.'

'Art – I would have loved to have taken Art.'

'What are you doing?'

'Well,' he looked embarrassed, 'I'm doing Physics, Chemistry, Maths and English.' I didn't know what to say.

'I'm an awful swot I know – but I want to do Medicine,' he said. 'And what are you doing, Olive?'

Olive looked at him and said, 'Nothing.'

'Olive's left school,' I said quickly.

'Oh, are you at uni?' he said to Olive.

'No, Finsbury Park,' Olive answered. Laurence laughed and his face broke into a thousand tiny, slanting lines. He thought Olive had made a joke. But Olive rolled her eyes.

'So what Shakespeare are you doing, Vivien?' Laurence asked.

'*King Lear*,' I said.

'Same here. Georgina, are you doing *King Lear*?' Georgina nodded.

'Wait,' Laurence lifted up his head and held his hand in the air. '"Blow, winds, and crack your cheeks! rage! blow!

201

Till you have drenched our steeples, drowned the cocks."
Wonderful, my favourite lines. What are yours, Vivien?'

I thought long and hard and then said the only line I could
remember: '"Out, vile jelly!"'

Laurence laughed so much I thought he was going to fall
over. 'That's excellent – I wish I could have thought of that.'

'It's all I could remember.'

'Quite right. That's the trouble with public school: you get
to be such a little prig.'

'Do you like your school?' I asked.

'No, but my father went there and his father before him
and his father, so I have to go. It's awful, and I have to board
because my father did and his father . . . well, you get the
idea. I'd much rather be normal like Nick.'

'Nick's not normal,' Helena giggled.

'Who's talking about me?' Nick said, putting some drinks
on the table. He put a glass of water in front of Laurence and
Laurence took a sip.

'What time are you going home?' Olive whispered to me.

'Not yet,' I said.

She sucked her teeth like mum and sat back on her chair.

'Are you drinking water?' I asked Laurence.

'Yes, 'fraid so – I've got a bit of a stomach ulcer – can't take
too much booze.'

'Yes, he's a miserable bastard,' Nick said. 'Don't know
why I put up with him.'

'He's lovely,' Helena said, putting her arm round Laurence.

'Unhand that man,' Nick said, pulling her off.

Olive leant over to me. 'Is there a band tonight?' she
whispered.

Laurence looked at her and she dropped her eyes and
stared at the floor. She leant back on her chair.

'I think your sister wants to know if there's a band – is that
right Olive?' Olive shrugged and turned away.

'Is she a bit shy, your sister?' Laurence asked me.
Apparently, I thought, and shrugged my shoulders too.

'Oh, don't be so stupid Nick,' Georgina shouted.

'I'm not being stupid, Georgina, it's absolutely true,' Nick insisted. They were watching a man in an old overcoat weaving his way through the crowds in the bar, asking people for money. The barman grabbed the man by the arm and led him out.

'I bet he'll go down the road and get into a Jag. They make tons of money, those people,' Nick went on.

'Don't you think you'd have to be in a pretty bad state to have to do that? It must be humiliating,' Georgina said.

'Rubbish – it's a con,' Nick said. Georgina blew out an exasperated breath.

'Oh, you've not started him off, have you?' Laurence said.

'It's true!' Nick said loudly. 'Anyway, you shouldn't encourage people like that.'

'What do you mean?' Georgina said.

'I'm afraid he means,' Laurence started, 'that he doesn't believe in the welfare state, he doesn't believe in free education, he doesn't believe in social security. Stop me if I'm wrong, Nick, or if I've left anything out. He thinks everyone should be middle-class and live in Hampstead.' Nick laughed.

'Basically, Georgina,' Laurence went on, 'Nick is a raving Conservative, with too much money and not enough brain.'

'And Laurence here is an insane socialist,' Nick said, putting his arm round his friend. 'All I think is that if you give people money then it encourages them not to work. They don't have to – it's simple logic.'

'That's crap!' Georgina shouted. 'What about people who can't find jobs?'

'I think Nick would shoot them, wouldn't you Nick? Involuntary euthanasia,' Laurence said.

'Everyone could find a job if they wanted one – they could do something,' Nick said.

'You wouldn't work on the buses,' Georgina said to him.

'Of course I would. If I had to feed my family.'

Georgina and Laurence laughed. Helena leant forward and put her head on her hand.

'I can see Nick as a bus conductor living in a council house, can't you, Georgina?' Laurence sniggered.

'Most people living in council houses don't work at all – I'd be the odd one out,' Nick said. 'They just scrounge off the state.' Everyone groaned.

'Tell him, Olive,' Georgina said. 'Tell him what it's like.'

Olive looked up at everyone and swallowed hard. She took a drag of her cigarette and scanned round her like she was looking for escape. I quickly said, 'My mum works and so did my dad and we live on a council estate. So you're talking absolute crap.' I was surprised at my sweating palms, my thudding heart.

'Well, present company excepted, of course,' Nick said, a little embarrassed.

Olive looked down at her feet. I nudged her elbow. I wanted her to tell him. To blow him away with a lash of her tongue, like only Olive could. But she sat there like a little girl scolded.

'I'm not saying everyone is like that,' Nick said, as Laurence and Georgina jeered.

Helena banged her glass on the table. 'I think I need another drink,' she said. 'Whose round is it?' Georgina looked at Olive.

'Olive hasn't got the money for a round,' I whispered to Georgina but Laurence heard.

'Allow me,' he said getting up. 'If I can't drink them, at least I can buy them.'

Helena downed her drink in one go and shouted 'Next,' and giggled. She stood up quickly. 'I'll get them this time,' she said. She wobbled about and then fell back on her seat, hard, and slipped on to the floor, catching Olive's arm and making her spill her drink which splattered all over the front of her clothes.

'Oops,' Helena giggled, as Olive slid her chair back away from her. Nick bent down to pull Helena up. 'Oh, for God's sake, Helena.'

'Sorry, Olive,' Helena said, patting at Olive's lap. Olive

stood up and turned away from the table, brushing down her skirt with her hand.

'I'll get a cloth,' Georgina said.

'I'm sorry, Olive,' Helena said again, sounding like she might cry.

'Let me get you another one, Olive,' Laurence said.

Olive looked round but didn't look anyone in the eye. 'No, it's all right, I have to go now.' She looked at her wrist, but there was no watch on it.

'Don't go,' I whispered. Olive gave me a look that I knew from when I was young. A look that said 'If you say one more thing, Vivien, I'll kill you.' She started collecting her bag.

'Would you like me to walk with you, Olive?' Laurence said. 'It's very rough out there.' I nearly laughed out loud at the thought of Laurence, the boarding-school boy in man's clothing, wanting to protect my sister. She didn't answer him as she ran out of the pub. My bossy big sister was gone without even looking back.

'Will she be all right?' Laurence asked me.

'Probably,' I replied.

'I feel a bit sick,' Helena said.

'Oh, bloody hell, it's up-chuck time,' Nick groaned.

Georgina and me had to walk Helena home.

'You take her,' Nick had said, 'I've got to go with Laurence here and get him back through halls.'

'I'll go on my own,' Laurence had said. But Nick told him he was a cretin and that he'd get them both in the shit without his expert guidance.

Helena had been sick twice. Once in the toilet and once just in front of the toilet door. And both times Georgina and me held on to her as she leant over and emptied the contents of her stomach with a splat.

'Nick, Nick, where are you going?' she called out down Upper Street, as Nick and Laurence ran to catch a bus. She started to cry.

'I love Nick,' she said, looking at me then Georgina. 'He's lovely, don't you think he's lovely?'

'Actually, Helena, I think he's a bastard,' Georgina said.

'Oh don't say that,' Helena drooled. 'He's lovely he's so clever and he's . . . he's . . .'

'A snob,' I offered.

'A wanker,' Georgina said.

'A prat.'

'A moron.'

'Oh don't say that he's . . .'

'Oh, for God's sake, Helena,' Georgina said, irritated. 'He treats you like shit, why do you put up with it? I mean, why isn't *he* taking you home? He doesn't care about you.'

'He does, he loves me, he does, he does. He does, Georgie, he does . . .'

'All right, he does.'

'He doesn't know my dad owns the old café though.' Helena chuckled. 'But he wouldn't care. I just haven't told him.' She started to cry. 'I love him, though – he's gorgeous. I love him.'

Helena stopped to be sick four times as we led her home through Highbury Fields.

'Have you got your keys?' Georgina asked her. Helena dangled her bag in front of Georgina and Georgina rummaged through it and pulled out the bunch of keys.

'What are we going to do with her? She can't even stand up,' I asked. 'Her mum'll go mad; she doesn't even know she's out '

'We'll just stick her in the door and close it and hope for the best. It's what I always do.'

'You've done it before?'

'Loads of times – she always gets in such a state. She goes mad when she goes out.' I looked at our school swot who grinned back at me with damp, heavy-lidded rolling eyes.

'She usually sobers up before her mum wakes up,' Georgina went on with a shrug, 'then she gets to her bedroom somehow. Well, usually anyway.'

Helena's house was in complete darkness. We pulled her up the path, feeling our way as we went. Georgina turned the key quietly in the lock of the door and I carefully pushed it open. Then Georgina levered Helena in. She threw her handbag in after her and we shut the door and left.

My mum was waiting by the front door when I got in. 'What time you call this, Vivien?' she said.

'It's not late,' I replied.

'Olive got in hours ago – I thought you two went out together.'

'We did but she left early.' I tried to get into the bathroom but my mum stood, arms folded, in my path.

'What you been doing out so late? You been with that rough boy. What you been doing with that boy?'

'Who?'

'That boyfriend of yours,' she spat out.

'Eddie? No, I've been with friends.'

'What friends? I don't like you out so late, you hear me,' she shouted. 'I have the trouble. I don't want you starting all this funny business too – I have enough trouble. You see you get in at a decent time.'

'I'm nearly eighteen—'

'Don't give me any big lip – I don't want any cheek, you hear me nuh. I'm your mother and you do as I say. I don't want you ending up like—' she stopped herself as Olive stuck her head out of the living-room door and then shut it again quickly. My mum sucked her teeth. 'Don't start giving me trouble, Vivien,' she said pointing her finger. 'And you find yourself a decent boy, you hear me?' She went into her room.

'What is she talking about? God, I don't believe it. Did you hear her, Olive? I can't believe it, I'm nearly eighteen,' I ranted as I went into the front room. Olive was sitting on the settee with a smirk on her face.

'I mean did you hear her, I can't believe it. I'll be going to college soon and she's going on about me getting in late. I'm eighteen, I can do what I want, I'm an adult.'

I looked at Olive who slowly tilted her head to one side and said, 'I hope you don't want me to feel sorry for you, Vivien, because I don't. It's about time she had a go at you. You've had it too easy.' She got off the settee and as she walked out of the room she said, 'And I don't like your stupid bloody friends. They're so childish, I couldn't believe it. I just couldn't wait to get out of there. I don't know how you can hang round with people like that. Don't ask me to come out with you again, Vivien, because I won't!'

Olive

I smiled at first. I smiled a sort of 'what a cheek he's got' smile.

'I saw Peter today.' That's how she started, like she was telling me about the weather. 'And you know what, Olive?' That's when I smiled. 'He says he want to see Amy. He says I'm to try and talk some sense into you. He says he didn't want all this trouble to happen, and that if you could just see a little sense then you would realize that all this trouble is not necessary. He said that he's had people coming to him wanting money, but he says he hasn't got any money. And I said well, they can't get blood out of stone, Peter, and he agreed. Because you know, he's lost his job. He say he lost it because of all the worry he has. This new woman of his she give him too much responsibility. Wanting him to look after her children, they're not even his, but she expect him to take care of them. And all he want to do is see little Amy. But he can't. He want to get her things and look after her, but he can't pay money to you. He doesn't have money to give. And he had to tell these people this and it humiliate him to have to say it. He said he would look for another job but he want to get training. He doesn't want to be in dead-end jobs all his life. He has ambition. He want to get training and learn a proper skill, then he can earn more money and look to his responsibilities. But he says it going to take time, and that I must make you see that it's difficult for him.'

I stopped smiling. 'Don't look at me like that, Olive. You should have seen him. He look rough. Rough. I tell him he should get more sleep and he says he can't sleep with all the worry he have. I felt sorry for him. He's not that bad. Not many men would care if they saw their children. They just have children all over the place and don't give it a thought. But he's an English man, he's decent. He want to see little Amy. And, Olive, you know what? You know what I think? I think if you fix yourself up a bit, get your hair done nice and put on some good clothes, I think he might come back to you. That's what I think. You should fix yourself up nice – I can lend you money to get some good clothes. Then fix yourself up and I'm sure he'll change his mind and come back. Don't give me lip, Olive. What I'm saying is for your own good. All men stray, Olive. They have big ideas and women turn their head. They're weak. But he's your husband Olive, whether you like it or not. He's your husband and you have a duty—'

'Shut up!'

'Stop screaming, child, everyone will hear.'

'Shut up!'

'You being stupid, Olive, stop this stupidness.'

'Shut up! Shut up! Shut up!'

She slapped me round the face. It didn't sting until I looked into her two furious eyes.

I ran to my room. I packed everything I could get my hands on. I stuffed things down into carrier bags. Anything I touched. I got Amy's toys and her bedclothes and shoes. I had to get out. I had to get away from there, from her. I didn't care, I had to go. Anywhere.

I walked into the front room. She was calming Amy. She had her sitting on her lap and she was patting her and telling her it was all going to be all right.

'What are you doing, child?' she said when she saw me coming towards her. I grabbed Amy by the arm. She screamed out. But I didn't care, I had to get her away. My mum grabbed her other arm. 'Leave her – are you mad? What are you doing?' I pulled Amy and my mum pulled her back and she yelled in the middle. I didn't care. I pushed my mum hard in the chest – pushed her back on the settee. She let go and I picked Amy up and put her under my arm. She was kicking and screaming and shouting 'Nana! Nana!' But I didn't care. My mum tried to run out after us but I slammed the front door in her face and ran down the stairs. Suddenly I was standing at the bottom of the stairwell, with Amy under my arm crying, and three bulging carrier bags with my life spilling out of them. And I didn't know where to go.

It was four o'clock on a Wednesday afternoon and people stared at me until I asked them what they were looking at. Then they put their heads down and walked away. The world seemed such a big place but with no room in it for me.

I went to the council offices, the housing department. I needed somewhere to live. I walked in and left Amy sitting by the carrier bags near the door. She was still crying and wiping her eyes and rubbing snot all round her face. Poor Amy. I pushed past everyone and told anyone who got in my way to piss off. I just didn't care.

'I'm homeless,' I shouted to the man at the counter. 'You better house me now – I'm homeless and I've got a child.'

'You'll have to wait your turn,' he said.

'It is my turn.'

'Take a seat.'

'I don't want a seat, I want somewhere to live.' And then I started to cry. I couldn't stop. I sat on the floor. Amy came and put her arms round my neck and gently patted me. We sat there, the two of us, crying.

People kept coming up to me, wanting me to sit on a chair, wanting me to move, wanting me to be sensible, wanting me to be patient, wanting me to listen to them. Then a woman knelt down beside me and told me with a sympathetic whispered voice and tilted nodding head that if I stayed where I was, that if I didn't return home, then she would have no option but to take Amy away from me. She would have to put Amy into care.

Vivien

Eddie told me he loved me. He said it as we were getting into his van to go down and see the art college in Canterbury. He'd taken the day off work and washed the van. 'Waxed it too – well, the bits of metal left,' he said.

'Thanks for taking me,' I told him. And he had looked at me and said, 'I'd do anything for you, because I love you.'

I pretended I hadn't heard, and he got in the driver's seat and started fiddling about with something on the floor. But my stomach felt wobbly. Eddie loved me, and I supposed I loved him. Although I wasn't sure. In fact I wasn't sure what it felt like to love someone. I enjoyed making love – that was fun. I loved the rolling about and finding new places on my body that when he touched them made me want to sigh out loud. I enjoyed our afternoons in Eddie's room, feeling each other with oohhs and ahhs. The gradual sweating. The breathless panting and the sensations, like eating pink strawberry blancmange with every nerve in your body. Then the thumping, delicious pain of him inside me. I loved that. But I didn't say I love you back. I just looked in the glove compartment for the map.

My art teacher, Mr Roach, suggested I should apply to Canterbury Art College. 'You're good, Vivien,' he commented, 'your work has a naïve charm. I think you'd like it at Canterbury – it has one of the most varied foundation years. You won't get bored so easily.'

I looked out the prospectus in the library. I looked through it at the pictures of neat glass buildings in the middle of green fields, with light catching them in a romantic glow. I read about the different things you could do there – graphic design, textiles, fashion, ceramics, furniture-making, fine art, sculpture. *We aim for all our students to achieve success in art and design, gaining valuable qualifications which will enable them to move on to careers in their chosen field.* I looked at the photographs of happy young people wandering through idyllic settings with sketch books under their arms and easels on their backs. It looked so tantalizingly far from Finsbury Park. I knew that if I didn't go to college I'd have to get a job in Marks and Spencer and spend all my days stacking shelves on the food counter, pulling old food forward from the back and stuffing the new produce behind, or endlessly tidying assorted bras. And if I couldn't get a job, I would end up like Olive.

'I want to go to art college,' I said to my mum.

'Art college! Art college! Art college is for ruffians. Scruffy people go to art college. What good is art? You can't get a job drawing people. Nobody will want you if all you can do is draw people.'

'You do other things like graphic design, textiles, fashion, ceramics, furniture-making . . .'

'You want to go to university, Vivien. Clever people go to university. You'll meet a better class of person at university.'

'But—'

'Oh, do what you want, child! I don't know why you ask me – you children never listen to me anyway.'

Georgina was going to university in Edinburgh. She told me how she'd discussed it with her mum and dad, and how her dad had said that Scottish higher education was excellent. And how her mum had said that she thought English was a very good choice. Helena was going to university too. All the teachers at our school wanted her to try for Oxford or Cambridge. But Helena had looked on a map and measured the distance away from Highbury and her mum and dad using the nail of her thumb. She declared Oxford and Cambridge too close, and said that any university she went to would have to be at least ten thumbnails away.

213

But the decider for me was that I could walk into art college with my five O-levels and a portfolio of artistic work under my arm. I wouldn't have to pass my English A-level. They wouldn't want to know if I thought Dickens was the consummate social chronicler or whether I was intimate with any metaphysical poets. A-level English was hard. I had no one to talk to about books. The last book I had read because I wanted to was *The Runaway Echo* in primary school, and that was only ten pages long. My mum's idea of a good read was *Woman's Realm* and Olive's was a shampoo bottle. Everyone else in my class seemed to understand better than me. Georgina even went to see Shakespeare plays for fun with her mum. But I handed in essays and my English teacher would shake her head and tell me not to give up my typing lessons.

I had been studying typing for two years. Girls in my class had taken Pitman's this and Pitman's that while I was still struggling with ;,L,K,J. At every lesson for six months I had typed *Our group will meet at a quarter to six on Monday to plan the kind and size of project the club will do this year*. We had to type it correctly before we were allowed to move on. Every lesson I typed it, walked up to the teacher who put a red mark through something, then walked back to my typewriter to type it again. Helena wondered whether I may have discovered the secret of perpetual motion. Some days I cried. And my typing teacher encouraged me to keep up with my art.

Art. I spent days and days painting an umbrella with an orange. Sitting in the art room listening to James Taylor and David Bowie records as I dabbed on my paint and stood back to see the effect. I designed and made a six-foot-tall mouth with ceramic teeth and a cushion tongue which was obscenely poking out. When it was finished Mr Roach attached it to the wall and called it a masterpiece of defiance. And when Fat Bag Baker took it down saying it was one step away from a far ruder sign, Mr Roach stood up for my artistic integrity.

There was no real choice in it. Art was a doddle. It had to

be art college.

I was invited to attend an open day at the college, *where prospective students can view the facilities and have a chance to chat with staff.* Mr Roach said it would be a good idea to go. He said I needed to be sure about a place in which I was going to spend at least a year of my life. 'It's your choice now, Vivien – it's not the same as being at school,' he explained.

Eddie drove me down and walked through the college grounds and along corridors with me. We found the reception room where students were meant to *meet each other over a coffee.* The room was full of freshly scrubbed, wide-eyed, chirpy-looking young people all with paper cups in their hands, standing round chatting in small groups.

'I'll wait in the car,' Eddie said, kissing my cheek and turning to go.

'Come in, come in,' a woman's voice shrieked out above the chatter. Eddie took no notice, but the woman rushed past me in a waft of Rive Gauche and grabbed Eddie by the arm.

'Come back,' she said, pulling him into the room. 'I'm Ellen Schwarz, I'm one of the tutors here.' She had an American accent and large gestures. 'What are your names?' she said, looking from me to Eddie. Eddie looked at me and shrugged and I said, 'I'm Vivien and he's Eddie.' She pushed a cup of coffee into Eddie's hand. 'So, Eddie, you're interested in studying art?' she asked, tilting her head under the brim of his leather hat. He nodded. A woman with blonde hair and a black cameo choker smiled at me. I smiled and turned back to Eddie.

'Have you come a long way today?' Miss Schwarz drawled.

'London,' Eddie said.

'Fabulous – have you lived there long?'

'Born and bred.'

'Fantastic – what are you hoping to study, Eddie?'

I went over to a table and got a digestive biscuit. She didn't seem interested in me.

'So who is your favourite painter?' I heard her ask Eddie. And Eddie replied, 'My uncle Des.' Eddie looked so out of

215

place in the room, like a bohemian among a troop of boy scouts and brownies.

'Oh – your uncle paints?' she went on.

'Yeah, he painted the bathroom a few weeks ago.' I bit hard into the biscuit and crunched it round so the noise in my head was all I could hear. Miss Schwarz tipped her head back. I thought she was going to faint, but she brought it forward again and roared out a laugh that made the whole room suddenly go quiet and look at her. Eddie grinned and threw his shoulders back a little. He took a sip of his coffee.

'I can see you are an iconoclast, Eddie,' she laughed.

'No, I never touch the stuff,' Eddie said smiling. He was enjoying himself. Miss Schwarz laughed again and ran her fingers through her hair. 'I think you're teasing me now,' she said, looking into Eddie's eyes.

'Oh, I never tease a lady,' he said, looking directly back at her. My eyes rolled – I couldn't help it.

'Hello, I'm Clare.' The woman with the choker stood in front of me. She had freckles all over her face. I nodded at her.

'What's your name?' she asked.

'Vivien.'

'Are you thinking of coming here?'

'Yes,' I said with an inane grin.

'Me too.'

'Oh.'

There was silence enough for me to be able to hear Eddie saying, 'There's only one rock, Ellen.' Miss Schwarz nodded at Eddie with an interested frown. 'She's a foundation-year tutor,' Clare said, 'she's one of the people that will interview you.' My head began to ache.

Miss Schwarz clapped her hands and shouted, 'Can I have everyone's attention please?' Everyone looked at her except me. I was busy looking at Eddie.

'Why don't you go now?' I whispered.

'I might as well stay and look round.'

'It'll be boring for you.'

216

'That teacher,' he said nodding at Miss Schwarz, 'thinks I'll like it here.' He laughed and turned away without hearing my long tut.

Miss Schwarz was at the end of a speech about how the college expected their students to work hard and play hard, and how in return the college would reward them with a varied and stimulating foundation year. 'Mr Collins will be showing you around the facilities now. He is a technician in the furniture-making department. I hope you've enjoyed this morning and have had a chance to talk to one another. And I hope to see some of you here at the start of the year.' A titter rippled round the room and Miss Schwarz smiled at Eddie, who winked back at her.

We were taken round the college by a man in brown overalls who blew his nose and roughly wiped his hanky up each nostril about every two minutes. People stopped looking at him after a while. We were taken through paint-spattered rooms, rooms with desks, rooms with sawdust and industrial machinery, rooms with looms, silk-screen rooms, darkrooms. In each room Mr Collins wiped his nose and explained in a monotone: 'This is where you will, if you are accepted at the interview stage, be performing jewellery-making', or 'photographic processes', or 'the production of woven fabric'. And in every room Eddie stood at the back making comments: 'So how far's the bar from here?' or 'It could do with a bit of go-round with a damp rag', or 'Is this where you keep the hamsters?' which he thought were funny. People laughed at first. Then they only smiled, and by the last room I heard someone whisper 'Who's the oik?'

'Shut up, Eddie,' I snapped, but he just looked at me, grinning like his dad.

I didn't talk to Eddie on the way back to the van and only shrugged when he asked me what I thought of the college.

'What's the matter with you? You've got a face like a wet weekend,' Eddie said as we drove out of the college grounds.

'Why didn't you go?' I asked him.

'Go where?'

'Back to the van, to wait?'

'I tried to, but I think that teacher fancied me.'

'It was embarrassing.'

'I can't help it, it's the old Eddie charm. It works even when I'm not trying.'

I sucked my teeth. It was the first time I'd ever done it. It seemed the only thing to do.

'You're not jealous, are you?' Eddie grinned.

'No, I'm not jealous.'

'You are, you're jealous,' he said, nudging me as best he could while still trying to drive in a straight line.

'I'm not jealous.'

'You are, I can tell. There's nothing to be jealous about, she's not my type – too American.'

'I'm not jealous.'

'I don't like Americans, I prefer my women just like you.'

'I am not jealous,' I screamed.

'You can tell your old Eddie.'

'For Christ's sake Eddie, I am not bloody jealous, you stupid—'

'All right, keep your hair on.'

'Well, shut up then.'

'Didn't you like the college?'

I didn't answer.

'Cat got your tongue?' Eddie said.

I looked out of the window at the green blur of the countryside.

'It was a bit boring, I have to admit,' Eddie went on. 'But it's not my scene – I wouldn't like to go there.'

'Well, you won't be,' I snapped.

'Art doesn't grab me,' he carried on, oblivious, 'I'm a musician.'

'No you're not!' I shouted. Eddie looked at me. 'Don't look at me like that; you're not a musician. You haven't even got a band.'

'I'm between bands,' he protested.

'You've been between bands all the time I've known you. I've only ever seen you play once. Just because you've got a guitar that you get out and polish every night, that doesn't make you a musician.'

'I'm getting a band—'

'Yeah, sure, you're always saying that but you don't. You're twenty-two and you're still living at home with your mum.'

'I'm going to get my own place, I've just got to get this band together first. It's convenient at the moment but some of the blokes at work—'

'You always say the same things,' I interrupted. 'I mean . . . don't you want to do things, see things?'

'I do plenty of things.'

'Like what?'

'I can't think when you put it like that. Why are you having a go at me anyway?'

'All you do is drink beer, play darts and hang around with your dad.'

'What's my dad got to do with anything? You don't have to bring him into it.'

'I mean, do you ever read books? Can you recite any Shakespeare or—'

'What are you going on about?'

'Don't you want to do something with your life?'

Eddie turned his head to me slowly and bit his lips into a thin line, then turned back. We sat in a crisp silence for the rest of the journey.

Olive

I dreamt I was a jelly baby. A little black sugar-coated jelly baby that had been thrown away. I wasn't in a packet, I was on my own on the floor – on the pavement. And I couldn't move my arms and legs because jelly babies can't, they're solid. People started walking down the pavement, and because I was only the size of a jelly baby, their feet were enormous. Great big grey slabs of shoe soles pressing down and sharp heels digging in all around me. And they couldn't see me because they were big and I was just a jelly baby. I couldn't run away or hide – all I could do was roll out of their way. But there were lots of people walking: as soon as I rolled one way someone came from the other direction and I'd have to roll the other way. And I knew that if I didn't roll, I'd get squashed flat. Sometimes being asleep can be worse than being awake. Sometimes.

'Oh, you're back,' was all my mum said. But I saw her smile to herself as I took Amy into the bedroom.

I went to the council offices every day. I hated being in that flat. It was like being buried alive. Every morning I got Amy dressed and we went to the offices. And every day I walked up to the reception desk and said I needed somewhere to live. Then I sat on the seats and watched the other people coming in. Ugly people with their hair greasy or uncombed. People that smelt like the waft from a bin, trailing loads of kids who always had snot under their noses. All complaining – when you going to do this, when you going to do that. They looked so pathetic, so desperate.

'You don't have to come every day, Mrs Flynn, we're

sending someone round to see you,' they said to me. But I still went.

Amy enjoyed it. She liked the crisps we ate and all the other kids. She'd run up to them as they came in and make friends. She'd run round people's feet, climb on chairs, jump off, roll around on the floor. Scream, laugh, shout, cry, and I didn't have to tell her to stop.

Then a card came one morning saying that someone from the housing department would come to see me in the afternoon. Just before they were about to visit, Amy peed on the floor of the bedroom. She didn't have a nappy on and I was holding the potty, just about to put it in front of her. I watched the piss forming a little steaming puddle between her legs. She stepped in it, then jumped on my bed. I got a bowl of water to wipe it up. But I looked at the piss and the room in a state with clothes everywhere, and a mug of tea gone green and a plate with crusts of toast spilling jam and crumbs on to the bed, which was only a mattress on the floor, and the window that was so filthy with birdshit that you could hardly see out of it any more, and I thought, why bother. I picked up the bowl and chucked the water at the wall instead. The damp patch got gradually darker on the wallpaper.

When the woman came, her nostrils flared at the edges as she walked in. She asked me questions – who lived here, how long, how old, who, what, when, why, how. She sat down, this white woman, all prim and neat in patent shoes with gold buckles, looking around her, writing things down on a clipboard. And when I showed her my bedroom – where I sleep – where Amy sleeps, with the toast and the piss and the stain on the wall, she tutted. I bet she didn't live like that, with her tan tights and sculpted hair.

'See the rising damp,' I said and pointed to the wall where I'd thrown the water. She looked out of the window and felt the wall with her hand. 'On the third floor?' she said. I nodded and she wrote something else down.

Before she went I tried to explain that I had to get my own

place because my mum wanted me out, that the strain was making her violent and that really I was homeless and that I had to come back because they were going to take Amy away from me. But that there was nowhere for Amy to play and that I couldn't let her out because I couldn't keep an eye on her and so she had to stay in all day and how that wasn't good for her. And how there were too many of us living in this little flat and if I could just get a place of my own – somewhere, even if it was small – how everything would be all right then.

She smiled as I talked, then put her pen away in a patent bag that matched her shoes and said she'd be in touch. Then I watched her walk to her car: she flicked at her clothes with her hand, brushing off any trace of me before she got in it.

Vivien

The letter from the art college looked too thin and flimsy to be good news. I watched it float to the floor like a featherweight, landing feet from the door. Olive shouted 'Mind your own business' at Mum. And Mum ranted that it was her business, that it was her house. A door slammed and Amy started to cry.

'Now you made the child cry!' Mum shrieked.

'I didn't, you did. Shut up, Amy, for Christ's sake,' Olive yelled.

'Don't talk to the child like that,' came a reply.

And 'Tie a yellow ribbon round the old oak tree' was cheerily playing on the radio in the kitchen and Tony Blackburn and his dog wanted us all to have a nice day – woof! woof! I stuffed the letter in my bag and called out 'Bye' as I left, but no one replied.

At the interview at the art college, Miss Schwarz and a fat man called Mr Thompson had leafed through my portfolio making appreciative 'uhmm' noises. Mr Thompson sucked on a pipe all the way through and had to keep slapping ash off my work.

'So, Vivien, what do you like to do in your spare time?' they asked me. Going down the pub and watching telly, although the honest answer, didn't seem quite the right impression to make.

'I like to read,' I lied.

'Oh, who is your favourite author?'

'Dickens,' I said. 'I think he's the consummate social chronicler.'

I sat on the toilet at school and took the letter out. I'd gone through in my mind all the ways of telling everyone the bad news. A little laugh, and say how I didn't like Canterbury anyway. Or a firm jaw and a small speech about how they didn't understand my work and how there were lots of other colleges I could apply to. I opened the letter and saw the word 'pleased'.

'I got in!' I shouted, but there was no one around to hear me. I couldn't get my knickers up fast enough and I tripped over and fell out of the cubicle on to the floor. But I didn't feel a thing.

Georgina grabbed me tight and we jumped around the common-room, the two of us locked together, as everyone whispered my good news around.

'Let's see the letter,' she asked.

'I haven't read it properly yet,' I said, handing it to her. She read it and smiled at me. 'Well done, Vivien,' she said patting my back. 'Where are you going to live?'

'I don't know. I've got to talk to them about that.'

'I'm going into halls of residence for the first year.'

'I'll probably get a flat,' I said. I looked at Georgina and realized we were not the same two girls who used to stand in the late queue together. We had grown up. We were leaving school to go to college and I was going to get a flat.

'Great: I can come and visit you,' Georgina said and we both laughed.

Helena made a cup of tea. 'A special celebration cup of tea,' she said, putting it in front of us and handing us each a little packet of biscuits she got from her bag. Then she came over to me and hugged my neck, pushing my head into her breast. 'We should go out and celebrate with Nick,' she said. Georgina rolled her eyes but Helena carried on: 'I'll get him to bring Laurence – he's got a bit of a soft spot for you.' She nudged my arm with her elbow.

'Who, Nick?' I said.

'No, Laurence – he said he thought you were very pleasing on the eye.'

We all giggled. 'What the hell does that mean?' I asked her.

'I think that's Laurence's way of saying he fancies you,' Georgina said, biting into a biscuit.

'Yeah, Viv,' Helena said, 'you could end up a doctor's wife.'

'He's not my type,' I said, but I pictured myself in a twin set and pearls, opening a local fête and giving out the books at the school prize day. A pillar of society. Anything was possible now.

'He's got a girlfriend anyway – he's been going out with her since he was about six,' Helena said. Georgina held her biscuit up in the air like a medical specimen.

'Helena, why are the biscuits you bring in always stale?'

'They're from my dad's café,' she explained.

'So,' Georgina said.

'So, he wouldn't give them to me if they weren't stale. He'd sell them if they weren't stale.' I looked at my two friends and smiled as we dunked the soggy biscuits into our tea.

The lifts weren't working in my flats when I came back from school. I had stopped using them anyway. I stopped when Neanderthal Man moved into the flat below us. He was about six feet tall and six feet wide and had a tattoo on his throat of a dotted line with the words 'cut here' written along it. Every Saturday night without fail the police would be called to his flat, then after a lot of yelling and crashing he would be taken away in the arms of the law. But he always seemed to be back the next day, stalking about as if nothing had happened. One Sunday morning I saw him down Chapel Street market, standing under a Union Jack, selling papers for the National Front. As I walked past he pushed a paper in my face and said 'Do you want one?' and then started laughing. I was scared of being in the lift, the doors opening and Neanderthal Man stepping in. At least if I saw him on the stairs I could just put my head down and walk on.

I was looking forward to leaving the flats. I remembered

moving in, and how I thought it was like living at a holiday camp. But now the camp was filthy, with rubbish blowing along every balcony. All the corridors smelt of piss and on every surface words were scrawled or sprayed: fuck off, suck my cock, wogs out, Paki cunts go home. Every white polystyrene ceiling along the balconies was scorch-marked black with names. My name was there somewhere. I remembered doing it – sitting on Carol's shoulders holding up a lighter and giggling as we teetered about trying to get our names in a straight line whilst avoiding the falling drops of molten goo. For over a year the only names on the ground-floor balcony were Carol and Viv, and every time we saw them we knew we existed. Now every kid over five and underemployed had to display their name somewhere around the flats.

At night the well-lit streets of Finsbury Park seemed like a safe haven compared to the flats. Once you turned off the road on to the estate the night was blacker, the shadows bigger, the noises stranger. The lights from all the flat windows were as remote as television screens rising into the sky. Screams were common and ignored – a cat – just kids – *Starsky and Hutch*. I only felt safe when I was with Eddie.

I started walking up the stairs and met Olive as I rounded the second flight. She was standing at the top of the stairs waiting for Amy, who was holding tight to the railings of the banister, swinging her legs round and up on to the next step painfully slowly, while Olive rolled her eyes and said 'Come on,' as kindly as Olive could.

'Hi, Olive,' I said, grabbing Amy's hand and lifting, relieving her of some gravity. 'Guess what, I got into college.'

Olive sneered a smile and shrugged. But I wasn't going to be put off.

'I got into college, Amy,' I said, bending down. 'You can have my room to sleep in when I move out.'

Amy smiled and said, 'I got sweets.' She began looking for something in her pocket.

'Come on Amy,' Olive snapped. And I picked her up

and carried her the rest of the way.

'Aren't you pleased?' I asked Olive.

'Yeah – I mean it's good for you, although I wouldn't like to go back to school.'

'College isn't like school.'

'It is: you still have to do what people say – I couldn't stand that. I'm glad I don't have to do that any more.'

'It's not like that at college – they treat you like adults, because you want to be there.'

Olive sniggered.

My mum said, 'That's nice,' when I told her. She was taking off her coat but the doorbell rang before I had a chance to go into any detail. 'Who's that now?' she said.

'It's Eddie, I think.' My mum sucked her teeth quietly but I heard. 'Vivien, now you're going to college why don't you find yourself a decent boy?' she said.

'What, and bring him back to this dump,' I snapped back. She looked startled, like something had just burst in front of her face.

Mum never liked Eddie. She smiled at him and even asked him questions. 'So Eddie, how you like this hot weather?' And Eddie tried all his charm on my mum: 'It's a bit hot for me, Mrs Charles, but I bet it reminds you of Jamaica, eh? You must be used to it.' My mum usually ended any conversation with Eddie by rolling her eyes.

I had phoned Eddie at work to tell him my news. He wanted me to go round to his house for 'a knees-up to celebrate'. I said no so quickly that I felt bad and had to say that my mum and Olive wanted to celebrate with me at home. Eddie said 'I'll come to you then,' and put down the phone before I had time to shout 'no' again.

'Congratulations,' Eddie said, stepping forward through the door. 'I knew you'd get in.' He kissed me long on the lips and I had to pull away as I could feel Amy staring at us. She was standing totally naked in the hall.

'I go bath,' she said to Eddie. He knelt down to her height.

'Oh good, I thought someone had nicked all your clothes.' Amy smiled.

'Amy, get in here,' Olive shouted from the bathroom.

'Olive – my favourite Vivien's sister,' Eddie called.

Olive put her head out of the bathroom door.

'Hello, Eddie, what you doing here?'

'I'm celebrating with the college girl.'

'Oh yeah,' Olive groaned.

'Don't you think its good? Ain't she clever?' Eddie said.

'Yeah, it's all right,' Olive said. 'Come on, Amy.' Amy ran into the bathroom and Olive shut the door. Eddie looked at me. 'So you'll be leaving me then,' he said.

'It's not for ages yet,' I told him.

Eddie smiled. 'So where's the party?' He pulled out a bottle of Jamaica rum from the pocket of his jacket. 'I thought your mum might like this,' he said handing it to me. He pushed a book back down into his pocket and made sure I had seen. 'Oh, what you reading?' I asked.

'Just a book.'

'Let's have a look.' He took the book out and showed me. *Conan the Barbarian*, with an illustration of a muscly, long-haired man throwing a boulder at something. 'I read them for fun,' he shrugged. I nodded.

'Hello, Mrs Charles – so what do you think of the college girl, then?' Eddie chirped as we sat down on the settee. My mum was flicking through *Woman's Realm*. 'Nice,' she said without looking up.

'Where you going to live?' Eddie asked.

'What college is it again?' Mum interrupted.

'Canterbury Art College,' I told her.

'Art college – I tell her she should go to university, Eddie, if she's a clever girl.' Eddie nodded politely.

'I don't want to go to university, I want to do art,' I said.

'I know – I'm just saying,' Mum said, flicking at the pages of her magazine without really looking at them. I sat back and folded my arms.

'What's the long face for?' she asked me.

'Nothing,' I said.

'I hope you don't act like that when you're at college.'

'Like what?'

'Where did you say you were going to live?' Eddie butted in, smiling between us.

'I don't know exactly,' I said to him. 'I'll share a flat I expect.'

'Some nasty place I bet,' my mum said, glancing at me.

'No – why should it be nasty?'

'All right child, I'm not saying anything – it's just that art students don't have nice places.'

'What do you know about it?' I shouted.

'I know more than you think about these things,' she said.

'You don't know anything.'

'Will it be in Canterbury?' Eddie asked.

'What?' I snapped back.

'Will the flat be in Canterbury, near the cathedral or something?' Eddie said quietly.

'Well, you see you keep the place nice,' my mum said.

'What do you mean?'

'Don't get vex, Vivien – I'm just saying that you'll have to learn to keep your flat tidy – not like you keep your room here.'

I breathed out hard. Eddie went to speak, but I put my hand on his arm to shut him up.

'You don't sound very pleased that I've got into college. I thought you'd be pleased that one of your daughters is doing something with her life.'

'Of course I'm pleased, child, I'm your mother. I'm just saying that you'll have to learn to take care of yourself properly when you leave home. That's what a mother has to say.'

I sat back on the settee again and thought I was going to cry. So I pulled the book out of Eddie's pocket and began flicking through the pages. Nobody spoke. After a few minutes my mum said, 'I'll make a cup of tea.'

'No don't – I brought you this, Mrs Charles,' Eddie said,

nudging me. I handed my mum the bottle of Jamaica rum. She looked at it, unimpressed.

'I don't drink much, Eddie,' she said.

'Just a little one, Mrs Charles, to celebrate our college girl here.'

'You know, Eddie, I don't really like rum,' she smiled.

'I thought everyone from Jamaica liked rum,' Eddie laughed.

'Not me,' she replied, 'I prefer a nice cup of tea.' She went to the kitchen and Eddie whispered, 'Not much of a party, is it?'

Olive

It wasn't on an estate, it was on a street, in Wood Green, in a proper house. I ran round the place. I kept saying, Is it all mine, are you sure it's all mine? to the woman who showed me around. She laughed – yes. The bedrooms, the bathroom, the lovely kitchen with Formica tops which are easy to keep clean, and cupboards with little red handles. All the gold taps in the bathroom. Even the little garden where I could plant lovely flowers with bright colours and things that smelt nice when you walked past. They were all mine.

Amy's room had a big built-in cupboard. And my bedroom had huge windows that looked out on to the street. Everything was painted white. The bathroom needed a blind – a roller blind with flowers on. All the rooms were really big, and not just because there was no furniture in them. It was an old house with two flats – just modernized, the woman said. She said it hadn't been finished long. The front room had built-in cupboards that you could put a telly on, and a socket for the outside aerial for better reception. It was a housing association flat but not a high-rise, it was just on a street, like normal people's. I got transferred, the letter said. But it was all mine.

There was a big cupboard with slat shelves, an airing-cupboard for drying your clothes. And the kitchen had special taps for a washing-machine – red and blue. It had central heating with big radiators and a gas fire in the front room for extra heat in the winter. There were meters in a cupboard in the hall. And all the windows swung open so air got in at the top and bottom for better ventilation. All new – nothing old.

Even the floorboards were new and smelt of sawdust, but there wasn't any dirt anywhere.

The woman asked me if I liked it. I did – I did like it. Amy loved her room. She kept climbing in the cupboard, playing hide-and-seek. She ran into the garden with me chasing her and I picked her up and swung her round and we both fell down laughing.

Eddie and Vivien helped me move in. I didn't have much to move – just my mattress and Amy's cot and bags and bags of clothes and bits of food. Eddie kept picking Amy up and tickling her and calling her cheeky chops.

When we'd finished bringing everything in from Eddie's van, the place still looked empty. The mattress in my bedroom, the cot in Amy's and a few cushions in the front room – that was it.

'It's a really nice flat, Olive,' Vivien said, 'you're really lucky.'

'It's not luck,' I told her. 'I worked hard for this. No one has ever handed me anything on a plate.' I went to make us all a cup of tea, but the kettle had to go on a cooker and there was no cooker.

'We could suck the tea bags,' Eddie said, but we had orange squash instead, which we had to share out of the only mug. We sat on the floor and looked round and I told them what was going to go where as soon as I got everything.

My mum was the first person to ring the doorbell. She held her coat to her as she wandered through my flat. 'It's nice, Olive, but you're going to need a lot of things to fix up the place. I can probably sort out a few things for you that we don't need,' she said.

'No – I'm getting everything new,' I told her. I'd made a list. I needed a cooker, a fridge, a washing-machine, a table and chairs, a settee, a bed for Amy, a television, an ironing-board and iron, a wardrobe and chest of drawers for my room. Oh, and plates and cups and knives and forks and saucepans and dishes to put in the oven . . . carpets and curtains and a roller blind for the bathroom. And a swing for Amy, to put in the garden.

'Don't be silly, child,' she said to me, 'how you going to buy everything new – you don't have money.'

'Social security,' I said. And my mum sucked her teeth.

Eddie offered Mum a lift home. 'You can sit in the back of the van, Mrs Charles,' he joked, until he saw her face. I showed them all out. I held the front door and looked at the stained glass in the window-panes. I watched them walk through my front garden and close my gate behind them. Amy sat on the step shouting 'Bye, bye.' I shut the door and walked into my flat. Sunlight was coming in through the back door. The whole room had turned gold like something in a fairy tale. I put Amy to bed in her room: I sang 'Brown girl in the ring' to her and she sucked her two fingers and went to sleep. Then I went into the front room and sat on the floor near the window and looked out at the sky. It was very quiet.

Vivien

The day Olive left home she opened all the windows in the flat and parted the net curtains to let the sunlight through as she packed to go. She played Ray Charles at full volume. *Hit the road Jack.* She sang along and Amy smiled up at her mother's face, swung her hips, clapped her hands and lifted her legs in her first dancing steps.

I joined in – took my part, pointing at Olive like I always used to when we sang along when we were young. Me, the callous gold-digging woman and Olive the good-for-nothing hard-done-by man.

Olive smiled and put her hands on her hips as she sang that she would go and I finished by pointing dramatically at the door. Then Olive picked Amy up and swung her round as we all laughed.

Olive pushed clothes down into plastic bags. She got out an old suitcase that our dad used to use that had a piece of string as its clasp. She placed a clock, a mug, two tea towels and a spice rack in it.

'They're mine,' she said, when she saw me looking. She went to the record-player and put Ray Charles on again, and shrugged her shoulders and smiled at me. 'Seems funny to be finally going,' she said.

After Olive and Amy left, the flat fell into an eerie silence. It was like when my dad died: the whole place felt empty and still like a museum. Every room became a room without Olive in. She wasn't in the bedroom, she wasn't in the bathroom, she wasn't in the kitchen. For all my life Olive was somewhere around me, but now she was gone.

My mum and me spent our evenings watching the television in dull stillness. Without Olive we didn't know what to do. There was no reason to tut or roll our eyes – there was no reason to slam doors, no fights to get away from.

'You watching this, Vivien?'

'Not really; turn it over if you want.'

'No, it's all right, we'll watch this.'

And I missed Amy. I missed seeing her little back arched over as she picked up her toys from the floor. I missed hearing her muttering to herself and sucking her two fingers.

I had finished school. I always thought I would run out of Lady Stanhope throwing books in the air, declaring that I would never learn another thing again. Seven years of hell over – pop the champagne – bring on the band. But in the end the A-level exams picked us off one by one, with everyone drifting away as they finished them.

Georgina went to France with her family for the whole summer holiday. Helena went to Cyprus. And even Eddie was spending two weeks in a caravan in Clacton with his mum, dad and uncle Des.

'You can come if you want,' he had offered. But I decided to stay in London in Finsbury Park and mope round the flat watching *Sesame Street*.

My A-level results came through the letter-box in a brown envelope with the address written in my handwriting. A for Art and E for English – a spelling-book logic. I held the scrap of paper in my hands until it began to get limp and distorted with my sweat. I was trying to decide whether to tell my mum. But she'd want to know why I'd got an E for English. 'You should have done better at that Vivien – I thought you were clever.' Or worse, 'Tell me, what exam was this again?' *Well done Vivien, I'm so proud of you* was not in her vocabulary. And I was scared that I would get into a sulk and there'd be no Olive to break the tension with a 'Mind your own business' or an 'Amy, get here.' I didn't tell her. She didn't ask.

Georgina came back from her holiday with a tan and garlic

breath and tales of the six bottles of 'real' champagne she and her family had drunk to celebrate her two As and a B.

'Was your mum pleased with your A-level results?' she asked me.

'Oh yes, really pleased.'

She told me how her parents were taking her up to Edinburgh University to settle her into the halls of residence.

'They worry – it's a bit of a drag really. They're staying a week. I told them they didn't have to stay that long, but they're getting a hotel and looking round the city and everything. My mum keeps going on about leaving home being a rite of passage.' Georgina rolled her eyes at her parents' concern.

My mum looked at me like both my ears had just dropped off, when I asked her, 'Do you want to come down to my college with me?'

'What for?' she said, startled.

'Well, to see where I'm staying and that.'

'You got a place to stay?'

'Yes, a flat with another student.'

'Not boys I hope.'

'No, a girl.'

'What – you got a lot of stuff to take?'

'Well it's not that – it's just I thought you'd like to see where I was going to live and see the college and that. You could look round.'

'Can people just come in and look round?'

'If you're with a student – with me.'

'What, they just let anyone?'

'Parents always look round.'

'You've seen them, Vivien?'

'It'll be all right.'

She looked at me and swallowed. 'I'll have to think about that,' she said.

She went into the kitchen and started putting cups away. Then she called out: 'Yes, Vivien, I'll come with you. It'll be a nice trip out.'

'Oh great, Mum – we can go round the Cathedral. You'll like it, it's lovely – famous. It's where Thomas à Becket was killed.'

'Oh yes – that would be nice,' she said nodding and looking off into the air. 'Yes, I'll come down with you on the train. See where you're going.'

'I think you'll like the college – you could meet the tutors if you wanted.'

'They must be busy people, Vivien. I don't want to bother them.'

'Well, I can show you around.'

'If you think it's all right.'

'Yeah, I'm sure it will be all right. And then you can see my flat and meet the girl I'll be sharing it with.'

'Oh yes.'

'I haven't met her yet but . . .'

'Oh . . . yes.'

'Because, Mum, leaving home for the first time is a rite of passage.'

'Oh yes,' she said quietly, frowning a little, 'a passageway.'

Eddie didn't mind not going with me. 'Me big end's going anyway,' he said. 'I doubt if the old girl would make it down the motorway.' He lent me a suitcase. 'It's Uncle Des's – he won't mind.' It had a sticker saying *Torremolinos* right in the middle of one side which no amount of soap and water would get off.

I packed my clothes, folding everything carefully. I packed three of my dolls: Fluffy, Mandy and Toddy, and found myself wondering if they'd suffocate when I closed the suitcase lid on them. In anticipation of my full grant I bought a black dressing-gown with an embroidered Chinese dragon on the back and a bottle of Chanel Number Five perfume. 'Very sophisticated,' Georgina agreed.

As I packed I kept looking round my bedroom wanting to feel nostalgic, wanting to remember all the fun times. But none came. I was sure I must have smiled and laughed and sang in there, but I couldn't remember. All I could remember

237

were the angry shouting faces at the door; 'Where's my skirt, I never said you could borrow it,' or 'Tidy up child, the place looks like a pigsty.' I just wanted to get away.

Then the night before I was about to leave my mum said, 'Oh, Vivien, I've been meaning to tell you, I can't come with you tomorrow.'

My face stung with the slap of it.

'Why not?'

'I have to work – someone is sick.'

She always cared more about her work than me, even when I was little.

'But you said you would.'

'I know I did but it can't be helped.'

She never stayed home with me when I was sick. She'd get Olive to take the day off school or she'd just leave me with two Disprins, a bottle of Lucozade and strict instructions not to open the door to anyone.

'Couldn't someone else do the work?'

'No; only I know what to do – I'm a supervisor, you know, Vivien, I have to make sure everything is all right.'

She even left me at the hospital once when I got a metal splinter in my finger. She said she had to work, and just to go straight home as soon as the doctors and nurses had fixed me up.

'But you said.'

'I can't just drop everything to go gallivanting with you.'

'It's not gallivanting – it's my college. Everyone else's parents are going with them. Georgina's mum is going to Edinburgh for a week and Helena's dad is driving miles. Everyone is doing it.'

'It can't be helped.'

She never came to my prize days at school – not even when I was getting a prize and singing a solo. It can't be helped, she said.

'It's only on the train for one day. I thought you'd like it.'

'It doesn't matter, child.'

'You could have said before. I'll have to go all on my own now.'

She never stuck up for me – if kids teased me, if teachers were nasty – take no notice, she'd say, it doesn't matter.

'I'm sorry, but what can I do? And don't sulk, child.'

'I'm not sulking, I'm just fed up.'

She paid more attention to Olive than me, I was no trouble: I just had to get on with it.

'You're a big girl now. You don't need me. You're always saying I should treat you like an adult, like you're grown-up: well . . .'

'You just don't care, do you?'

'Of course I care.'

She didn't ask me about my A-levels.

'Funny way you've got of showing it.' I could feel tears in my eyes.

'Of course I care about you, but I have to work. I have you on my own, you know. I don't have anyone to help me. If your dad was here . . .'

'What's that got to do with it?'

'I don't know what you children want from me.'

She never loved me.

'I just want you to be like everybody else's mum.'

She turned away from me. 'Why do you have to make such fuss? You're big now, you can do these things without me.'

'Because you said you'd come.'

'I don't know these people, Vivien. I don't know what to say. You don't need me there – cha, child, don't make me mad. I have enough worry.'

'You said you'd come.' I let the tears slide down my face. She came towards me and put her arms out but didn't touch me. 'Vivien,' she said. 'I try me best, but you children, you live a different life. Come.' She put her hand on my shoulder but I shrugged her off.

'Cha child,' she said pulling away, 'stop this stupidness, you're a grown girl – you're acting like a baby. I can take you down the tube station. You want me do that? Don't stick your lip out at me like that. You want me take you down to the station or not?'

'Don't bother.'

She'd have been embarrassing anyway at my new college, in her old brown coat with the odd button on the front.

'Suit yourself – I can take you down the station, but I have to work and that's an end of it.' She walked out of the room and slammed the door.

Olive

Social security were useless. A man came round – eventually. I waited in for him for three days. Every day he'd say he was coming and then wouldn't turn up. So I'd have to phone him and they'd keep me waiting on the phone for hours. I had to use a phone box and I'd be stuck in there hanging on and feeding money into the machine. I went round to my mum's in the end: it was cheaper getting the bus and going round there, and I didn't get people giving me dirty looks and telling me to hurry up every minute.

So this little man arrived in a green anorak. He was only young, but had a bald head that he tried to hide by sweeping some hair over it. He didn't look me in the eyes once. He just walked round the flat, staring into every room, looking into every cupboard, without even asking. When he walked into my bedroom he looked at the double mattress on the floor and said, 'I understand from your file that you are a single mother – is that right?' I said I was, that my husband had left me, and he looked at the mattress again, raised one eyebrow and wrote something down in a book.

I told him the things I needed, and to practically everything he said: 'I'm afraid that is not considered an essential item,' or 'We won't be able to provide funds for that.' I got fed up. 'Well, what will you give me then?' I shouted, and he zipped up his jacket a bit more and said, 'Your attitude is not helping matters along, Mrs Flynn.' No washing-machine, no settee, no wardrobe, no blind for the bathroom, no swing for Amy. All I was getting was the cooker, a fridge and a bit of carpet, not even fitted: 'Fitted would be prohibitively

241

expensive at this stage, I'm afraid.'

But Eddie started bringing me stuff round. He seemed to come nearly every day with something, saying his mum didn't want it or someone called Des found it. Most of it was crap, but if I didn't like it I just shook my head and Eddie would usually smash it up there and then and put the pieces in the bin. Some things were OK; not what I'd have chosen, but . . . He brought me a glass-topped coffee table and a couple of foam armchairs that were covered in green corduroy. And I bought a poster by Salvador Dali called *Impressions of Africa* which I stuck on the wall. When the fire was on and something was cooking in the kitchen it began to feel really cosy.

Then a black woman moved into the flat upstairs. Charmaine. She had a little boy a few years older than Amy. I was pleased at first because the house was too quiet and empty at night. I thought we would be able to take it in turns babysitting and maybe even go out, the two of us, down the pub or to the pictures or just sit together talking about things. She was only a bit older than me. I went up to see her on her first day to say hello. The first thing she asked me, was 'Have you let the Lord into your life, Olive?' Then she went on for about an hour on how the love of Jesus Christ had saved her and how, if I let Him into my heart, His love would transform my sinful existence. I couldn't get out, she just went on and on, even when Amy fell asleep on my lap and I started yawning in her face. In the end I had to say I thought I could smell something burning downstairs.

She started having people round in the evening. Loads of well-dressed black people singing and banging tambourines and making a racket all night long. It started keeping Amy awake. I went up to complain, but when she opened the door she called me sister and invited me in, all smiles. I spent half an hour singing 'Down by the Riverside' before I could get away.

Every time I tried to tell her about the noise she'd say 'Come and join us,' or 'Read your Bible before you go to bed, and the Lord will take care of the sleep.' That boring. I believed in God and Vivien and me used to go to church when we were little, but you couldn't say anything to Charmaine without Jesus Christ creeping into it. I mean, bloody hell!

I started going to my mum's in the evenings – Amy liked it and my mum was all on her own since Vivien left. I wasn't lonely, I just wanted to get away from Charmaine and the Lord. And it stopped me having to put the heating on. I couldn't use the central heating. As soon as I put it on I'd watch the little dial on the gas meter whizzing round like some cartoon clock. I couldn't believe my first gas bill. I even rang them up. 'I think you've made a mistake,' I told them, 'a typing error.' And this snotty woman said, 'It's no mistake, Mrs Flynn.' I said I couldn't pay it – that I didn't get enough money to pay bills like that. So she said she'd arrange for me to pay it by instalments – in bits. But then they added the next bill to it. All my money just went straight to the gas board. Social security said I'd have to make savings. 'On what?' I asked them, but they didn't have any suggestions.

I made sure Amy was all right, that she always had something to eat – she loved her fish fingers and chips. But I sometimes ate up my mum's house instead. And I'd only have the gas fire on in the front room – I'd get Amy ready for bed and dry all the clothes in front of it.

My mum's house was always warm. We got on all right as long as I didn't stay too long. But getting home at night was horrible. We'd have to wait for a bus in the dark and the rain and the wind and the fog. There were always drunks on the street or someone singing and puking on the top of the bus. A man grabbed Amy's arm one night – pulled her like he wanted to take her off. I pulled her back and called him all the names I could think of. But after that she got scared when it was dark. She always wanted me to carry her, but I couldn't because she was too heavy. So I asked Eddie if he'd teach me to drive.

I thought I could get a little car and drive me and Amy

round. Or even get a job driving – delivering things – meals on wheels. Or I could learn to drive one of those big lorries and get a job doing that. I told Eddie and he thought it was a good idea, and we started the lessons.

He was scared at first. Nervous, I could tell. He kept grabbing the steering wheel and smashing his foot on to the floor even though I had the pedals on my side. The hardest bit for me was easing off the gas when you put in the clutch. 'Don't crunch the gears,' he'd groan. His van was an old cronk though, and sometimes he didn't come round because something had gone wrong or dropped off.

But I was a good driver. After a while Eddie started saying I was a natural: he just read the paper while I drove him round. I put in for my test.

I wrote to Peter and told him I wanted my car back, the one he bought for me, the one he stole when he left. I told him how I had my own flat and was learning to drive and would get a job, and how he did me a favour leaving me because now I was older, wiser and stronger.

Vivien

The door was marked with a black three. Had I known that as soon as I opened it twenty pairs of students eyes, female and male, would turn and look at me, I would have patted my hair down and checked my mascara. It was not the entrance I had wanted to make, puffing, sweating and cursing, but I was late.

I'd struggled down from Canterbury station with my bag that was acting like a petulant child – wanting to go one way whilst I wanted to go the other. 'Put your bag down over there,' Miss Schwarz said. She was sitting on a table at the front of the room in tight jeans and a huge white shirt with the collar up. 'It's Vivien, isn't it?' I nodded and placed my bag in a corner, then turned it round so the Torremolinos sticker wasn't visible. 'Have a seat – you haven't missed much.' I looked up and around: everyone in the room was smiling at me. I took a seat.

'We were just about to introduce ourselves. So what I want you to do is turn to a neighbour and tell them three interesting things about yourself.' The room tittered collectively. 'Now come on,' Miss Schwarz laughed, 'you must be able to think of just three things.'

It was then I remembered that I hadn't put on any deodorant that morning. I'd packed it the night before and had had such trouble getting my bag shut that I feared opening it again in case everything sprung out like a jack-in-the-box. So I just sprinkled a handful of Johnson's baby talc under each arm. But since then I had sweated. I had really sweated. I slid my hand inside my T-shirt as discreetly as I

245

could, rubbed it round my armpit and pulled it out. I was about to put my fingertips to my nose when someone said 'Hello, I'm Victoria, and that is Victoria, not Vicky.'

'Vivien,' I said.

'Vivien not Viv?'

'I don't mind.'

Victoria was a blonde woman with one of those faces that was so pretty it was boring. The sort of faces that if you were asked to draw them you'd just have to put everything in perfect symmetry and it would be a good likeness. Petite, turned-up nose, blue eyes and straight lifeless hair – they all looked the same to me.

'Number one,' she carried on, 'I'm from Northumberland.' I nodded while resting my fingers close to my nose.

'Number two – well, no, it's number three really, because number one should have been that my name's Victoria and not Vicky. I always insist on that.' I inhaled deeply.

'Number three, well, I suppose it's that I was debutante of the year a few years ago – no, don't say that, I don't want everyone staring at me, I haven't washed my hair today. Does it look an absolute fright? Go on – tell me the truth.' I stank of BO.

'No,' I said, moving away from her.

'Well, tell me about you. I know your name's Vivien but where are you from?'

'London.'

'Whereabouts?'

I was about to say Finsbury Park, but I looked at Victoria's immaculate red-painted fingernails, her tight, well-fitting jeans with a gold belt running through the loops, her soft pink shirt opening low down her breasts, the delicate gold chain round her neck and gold and pearl stud earrings and said 'Islington.'

'Oh Islington – I know it – do you know Frederick's? That restaurant in . . . oh, you know . . . you know . . .'

'Camden Passage,' I said. I knew Frederick's well. I used to look at the menu with Carol and we'd recite the dishes – smoked salmon with red peppers and limes, Parma ham with figs – and wonder what they tasted like as we ate a bag of chips walking down Upper Street.

'That's the place – my brother had a bit of a fracas there. Stupid really, he and some friends – someone's birthday – Giles, I think it was. Anyway it doesn't matter – but he hit the waiter and broke his hand. It was in plaster for weeks. Cost him a fortune tidying up the place. Do you still go?'

'No,' I said.

Miss Schwarz clapped her hands. 'Time's up.' Victoria leant towards me. 'Quick, tell me three things – quick, quick.'

I froze.

'Oh, doesn't matter,' she smiled.

Miss Schwarz pointed, and then in turn people were introducing Clare, Paul, Margaret, Jim, Ken, Cherry, Graham, Sarah, Chris, Chris, Chris . . . And saying interesting things about horses, gym tournaments, violins, cellos, drama clubs, karate, Japan, brass-rubbing . . . In parts of the country called Esher, Ashford, Virginia Water, Leamington Spa, Spalding, Perthshire, Tokyo and Peas Pottage.

Then: 'This is Vivien,' Victoria began, 'she's from Islington in London. She hasn't told me much about herself because I think she's a bit shy, but she has a wonderful cockney accent that I'm completely jealous of. And I think . . .' Victoria paused for dramatic effect, 'I think she's the person who's sharing my flat in Herne Bay who should have turned up last night but didn't – am I right?' She smiled a perfect span of teeth at me and everyone waited for my answer.

'Forty-one Hill Rise,' I said.

'That's it! I knew it!' she said. People laughed, and I thought, 'Oh fuck.'

The rest of the day moved in front of my eyes as fast as an old film. Our class went everywhere together like a chain-gang. We were in the canteen drinking tea and eating congealed shepherd's pie with beans.

'Tea's awful . . .'

'We'll have to get used to it . . .'

'I think it's quite good – I'll have it if you don't want it . . .'

247

'What's your name . . .'

'Where are you from . . .'

'Is that a private school or grammar . . .'

'I prefer technical drawing . . .'

'You can make a lot of money with graphics . . .'

'My parents are both artists in Cornwall . . .'

'I don't know what I'm doing here, I'm useless at art . . .'

I sat at the end of the table listening and watching as everyone sipped and crunched and vied for space in the conversation. I smiled a lot. I got up to go to the toilet to wash my armpits but as I pushed my chair back five eager girls said 'Oh, I'll come with you.' They all stood around the wash-basins looking in the mirror, fluffing and pouting. In the end I had to sit on the lavatory, spit on to some toilet paper and wipe it under my arms instead.

Then we were all in front of the window where the grant cheques were paid out. And people were arguing with the woman behind the desk, shouting their names, jumping in the air, crying, telling everyone they had to phone their mum and dad.

'It hasn't come, what am I supposed to do?'

'Is that all? I'm sure it was meant to be more than that.'

'Please look again, that's Prat with a silent "t".'

I got my cheque and said 'Bloody hell.' It was the largest amount of money I'd ever seen with my name attached to it. Four hundred pounds. I thought I'd won the pools. Victoria and a boy in a tweed jacket and tie whose name was James and who lived in Canterbury Cathedral grounds stood to one side of the window, chatting. They looked over at the commotion every now and again but it was obvious that they were in no need of a handout.

Then we all went off to the bank through the town in our little mass. And I walked with Sarah who was going to marry a farmer as soon as she finished college, and Margaret who had ginger hair, a face spattered with freckles and who went red as soon as you looked at her.

'National Westminster are giving pens and a student pad.'

'You get a book token with Lloyds.'

'Not Barclays – think of South Africa.'

'Yes, but you get a free folder and desk tidy.'

I'd never had a bank account before. My mum didn't have a bank account. Olive didn't have a bank account. I stood in the queue with all the others who liked the look of the pens and student pads best. I talked to Clare who said she was from Scotland but who didn't have any trace of an accent.

'Oh it's there sometimes – when I get carried away,' she said. She asked me if I liked Billy Connolly, then told me a joke about a shipyard, a welder and a hand-held tool, which I didn't understand. She laughed to herself, I smiled and pretended I got it.

'I'll play you some of his records – I'll bring them in for you,' she said as she walked to a window to be served. When my turn came a young man in a suit and a brown and mauve kipper tie showed me to a desk at the back of the bank. He asked me questions and made me sign forms. I thought he'd gasp when he saw the amount of money I had to deposit. But he looked at the cheque and said, 'We have to inform you at this stage that it is not this bank's policy to issue students with cheque cards.' I nodded, but didn't know what he meant.

When I joined my class outside, Chris (a boy with long dark hair and round green eyes that closed into little slits when he laughed) was waving his arms in the air saying, 'It's bloody useless without a cheque card. I asked them – I said what is the point of giving me a cheque-book if I can't have a cheque card?' Other people nodded in agreement and muttered about their banks. And I wondered what a cheque card was for, and wished I'd asked the young man with the kipper tie.

We walked back to college, meandering through the little streets and looking at the quaint old houses that seemed to be leaning on one another. With little doors that tilted one way and windows that tilted the other. Victoria grabbed my arm.

'Vivien, come in here with me a minute.' She pulled me in

the door of an antique shop. It smelt damp, like our old basement flat in Islington, and was choked full of things. Old things.

'Isn't it wonderful,' Victoria said.

It looked like a jumble sale after all the good things had gone. I followed Victoria around. She picked up pots, turned them over and read the bottom. She lifted old glasses up to the light. She opened wooden chests and cooed at cups and saucers. I wanted to go. Then she grabbed my arm, turned over a teapot and whispered in my ear, 'It's a bloody Suzie Cooper.'

'What?' I said.

She looked around her like she didn't want anyone to hear. 'Suzie Cooper for thirty pounds,' she said. 'Mummy will go mad for it.'

I understood. My mum would certainly go mad if I paid thirty pounds for an old teapot. She started trying on old fur coats from a rack of junk clothes. I began to sneeze from the dust as I stood there holding her teapot and assuring her that she didn't look fat in any of them. After about half an hour she said 'Right, this one,' and slung the coat over her shoulder and went to pay.

The woman who owned the shop told Victoria that there was a teaset that went with the pot, and Victoria squealed and hugged me as the woman went to get it. It took ages to wrap all the little things – the sugar bowl, jug, cups, saucers, cake plates. She ran out of old newspaper and started wrapping with that day's news. When the woman was finished she looked at Victoria and said 'That'll be a hundred and twenty-five pounds please.' I had to steady myself on the back of a chair, but Victoria flicked open a cheque-book and began writing. 'Do you need a card with that?' Victoria said as she handed over the cheque. The woman looked at the cheque and said, 'Not with that bank. Thank you.' And I wasn't sure, but I thought she gave a little curtsy to Victoria as we left.

We got back to college a bit late. We opened the door of

room number three and were confronted by an old man sitting stark naked in the middle of the room. 'Life drawing,' Miss Schwarz said when she saw my fright. 'Come on, hurry up – you're late.'

It seemed rude to stare at this poor man who looked like he'd collapsed exhausted on the floor. But we had to draw him for hours, with Miss Schwarz coming up behind me every so often and saying in a loud voice: 'Really get inside those wrinkles and rolls of flesh, Vivien,' or 'I want to be able to really understand how his penis is lying,' or 'You see how his nipple sags, unlike on a younger body.' I was embarrassed, but the old man just sat there motionless. At four o'clock he got up and put on a dressing-gown.

Everyone stretched and rubbed their eyes and held out their drawings at arm's length or walked across the room to get a distant view. I went to get my bag from the corner.

'Where are you going, Vivien?' Miss Schwarz called.

'Home,' I said, looking around me and then at my watch.

Miss Schwarz stared at me.

'It's four o'clock,' I explained.

She began to laugh. 'This isn't school, Vivien – we stay until six-thirty here.'

'Six-thirty,' I'd shouted before I had time to think. I must have looked horrified because Miss Schwarz said 'I'm sorry. Didn't you know?' I shook my head. 'I'm afraid,' Miss Schwarz began again, 'that it's eight-thirty on Wednesdays and Thursdays.'

I smiled. 'Oh great,' I said.

At six-thirty I struggled with my bag down to Victoria's car. She walked in front of me 'leading the way' and telling me how awful Herne Bay was and that if it wasn't for the fact that the flat was owned by a friend of her father's she wouldn't stay there a minute longer, because Herne Bay was so boring.

'Basically, Vivien, it's where people go to die.'

Victoria had a little green Mini. My suitcase wouldn't fit in the boot so I slid it along the back seat. We drove through Kent's country roads at about a hundred miles an hour.

Victoria kept both hands on the wheel and leaned her whole body over when we went round corners, like she was riding a motorbike. She only slowed down when I reminded her about Suzie Cooper in the boot. Then I saw the sea. 'Herne Bay is the arsehole of the world and Kent is the rest of the bum,' Victoria said as we pulled up outside a house on top of a hill. She walked on in front while I wrestled my bag out of the back of the car. 'Look at that,' she said, pointing to our neighbour's house. A sheep, all yellow-eyed and bald-headed, looked back at me.

'They're barking mad – they keep sheep in their garden.' I put my bag down and patted the sheep's head.

'Be prepared for an utter dump, Vivien,' Victoria said, opening the door.

It was a palace. Bigger than our flat in Finsbury Park – twice the size. It was the top half of an old house, with high ceilings and gigantic windows that looked out on to the sea.

'There's no central heating,' Victoria complained. 'It'll be freezing in the winter – I told daddy . . .'

The kitchen had glass-fronted cabinets full of glasses, plates, pots and pans, and a table and chairs with a lamp over the table that you could push up and pull down to the right height.

'Storage heaters, he said. I said the storage heaters don't work. I put them on but they don't heat up . . .' Victoria thumped the brown box on the wall. 'That's not hot, is it?'

There were antiques in the front room – a writing desk with lots of little drawers and gold handles and a brown wooden bookcase with impressive-looking old leatherbound books in it.

'It's a holiday home. I mean, who the hell would want to come on holiday here?' Victoria's room had a double bed and fitted wardrobes. My room was at the top of the flat, up a little staircase. It had a single bed, a sloping ceiling and was decorated in pink. The window had a window-seat with a pink cushion – you could sit and look out over the sea.

'Your bed's Queen Anne, apparently.'

'I don't mind,' I said. 'I really like the room.' Victoria looked at me, then round the little room, then back at me. 'Each to their own,' she said. I looked out of the window and wished Olive could see me standing in my beautiful pink room, in my lovely sea-front flat. I wished my mum was here to meet Victoria and say 'She's nice, Vivien; decent, a better class of person.'

'I need a drink,' Victoria said. 'I'll make some tea. Come down.' She closed the door behind her, then opened it again quickly. 'Oh yes, I forgot, there's a letter for you – it came this morning. It's on the chest over there.'

I opened the letter. It was from Eddie. As I looked at the childish scrawl I realized I had never seen his writing before; there'd been no need. I read the tiny joined up script: *I hope you got thier safeteley and the jurney was not bad.* I hadn't thought of Eddie since arriving at college, even though I'd cried before I left and said I didn't want to leave him. But now I thought of him with his tongue resting on his bottom lip as he composed his letter to me, and carefully misspelt his way down the page. I didn't want to notice the spelling mistakes. It was nice of him to write, I wanted to think. I love him, I wanted to think. I'm looking forward to seeing him, I wanted to think.

I am going to the pub now and I will think of you with every pint I drink. I am riting you a song, a love song and I will sing it to you at the weakend I hope.

Victoria called me in a high-pitched whine that seemed to rattle my doorknob. I folded up the letter and put it back in the envelope.

'Who's your letter from?' Victoria asked. She was sitting at the kitchen table carefully sticking together cigarette papers to make one long one.

'Oh, no one – just a friend.'

'Boyfriend,' she asked without looking at me.

'Sort of,' I said.

She struck a match and began burning the end of what looked like a small brown rubber. She crumpled it on to the papers. Then she noticed me watching her.

'Do you smoke dope, Vivien?'

'I've never tried,' I admitted.

'I don't believe you.' She stared at me, wide-eyed, then licked a cigarette and carefully took the tobacco out of it and laid it on top of the dope. She rolled it up, putting a tiny piece of card in one end and twisting the other until it formed a point. 'Well, now's your chance,' she said.

Olive

I passed my driving test first time. The examiner thought I'd done very well. He didn't actually say it, but I could tell he was impressed by me. I knew I'd pass, I knew I could do it because I had a very positive attitude. Vivien was jealous – my mum was shocked. 'It was easy,' I told them, 'you should try it.' I said I'd take my mum out for a drive to the country with Amy. 'In what?' she said. When I told her I was going to get my car back from Peter she just sucked her teeth. 'You and all your ideas, Olive.'

I telephoned Peter. 'It's not your car,' he said. And I said very reasonably that he'd bought it for me and that now I'd passed my test I needed it for Amy. And that he never gave me any money, so he could at least give me the car. 'I've sold it,' he told me. Liar.

Eddie said I could borrow his van. He always visited Vivien on the train because he said the van's motorway days were over. He said I could pick up the keys from his dad. I made loads of plans. I thought I'd move a few more bits from my mum's house to mine. Then I'd take Mum and Amy out somewhere nice where we could look at the countryside. And I'd go to the launderette and put the bags in the back of the van instead of lugging them home on the ends of my aching arms.

It was a Friday night. I found Eddie's parents' flat and rang the bell which played a tune. 'Hello, I've come to pick up Eddie's van,' I said to a man who stood there in a string vest and captain's hat. He stared at me and I watched his smile fade, the corner of his mouth slowly

255

closing up until he looked spiteful.

'Are you Eddie's dad?' I asked.

'I am.'

'Eddie said I should pick up the keys to his van from you.' He carried on staring at me.

'Well, how do I know who you are?' he said after a while. I just said, 'What?'

'Well, look at it from my point of view. Anyone could come along here and say that they wanted the keys to my son's van but I wouldn't be doing him any favours if I just let them have the keys, now would I?'

So I said, 'But didn't he say I'd be coming – Vivien's sister?'

'Ooohh,' he said for about five minutes. 'You're Vivien's sister.' He frowned. 'You don't look like her. He never told me you was a—' He stopped himself just in time, but I knew what he wanted to say. I put my hand out for the keys and left.

I'd never driven the van at night. I'd never driven anything at night before. It took me a while to get used to it, all the car headlights glaring at me. I went round a roundabout and as I came off I noticed a police car. I didn't think anything of it at first but then I realized it was following me. It started flashing its lights and drove alongside me with a man leaning out of the window waving his hand at me to stop. So I stopped.

The man got out of the car. He was young and white with hair that had a really straight parting down it, like he'd done it with a ruler. He wasn't in uniform but I could tell he was a policeman by his shoes. Lace-ups that no one else of his age would be seen dead in. He came up to my window and I wound it down. I was just about to say something when he pulled the door of the car open. 'Would you get out of the car, please,' he said, and sort of looked in the air while I got out.

'What've I done?' I asked.

'Phew! Where shall I start, miss. Number one, no lights.'

I explained to him that I couldn't see any better with the headlights on so I didn't bother. He laughed one of those sarcastic laughs that snorted out of his nose. He leant in the van window and clicked the headlights on then off again.

'You are joking, miss? I'll presume you're joking.'

'No,' I said. He looked at me and leaned in closer to my face.

'You have to have your lights on, miss. It's a very simple thing – it's called the law. Licence.' He held out his hand.

I felt stupid. 'Oh, I didn't know that,' I admitted. I didn't. Eddie hadn't told me that and it hadn't come up in the test. I was really surprised. 'You see, I've never driven at night before.' I wanted to explain. I laughed.

'Licence,' he said again.

'I'm waiting for it to come,' I told him.

'Oh dear.'

'I've only just passed my test.'

'You shouldn't be driving if you don't know what you're doing.'

'I do,' I said. 'I've just passed my test.'

'There's no need to answer me back.'

'I wasn't, I was just saying—'

'Where you going anyway?' His face looked hard and blank with eyes as lifeless as a corpse.

'I'm going home.'

A uniformed policeman called him from the car. 'Here, Bas, is she a bloke?'

Bas looked at me and said, 'I dunno, shall I check?' He laughed.

'That van's registered to an Edward Frank Desmond Cooke,' the other one shouted over.

Bas looked at me with his dead eyes and said, 'Oh dear,' again.

I'd had enough. 'Look, I borrowed this van from my sister's boyfriend.'

And he said, 'Oh yeah, what d'you give him then – a ride for a ride, was it?'

I thought I'd heard wrong. 'What?' I said.

He smiled, then said: 'You got any drugs in the car?'

I stared at him. 'No,' I said.

'That's odd, you niggers usually have bit of ganja on ya.' He said ganja so hard I felt his spittle on my face. So I told him to fuck off.

He stood back and up to his full height. 'Right,' he said. He looked in the car. 'Get that fucking bag out here and empty it, and keep you dirty black mouth shut.'

I went to get my bag and said 'Don't talk to me—'

'Just shut up, slag,' he said, and grabbed at the bag before I could get it. 'Right, open it up – let's see what's in it. He slapped it against my stomach. I went to open it but he snatched it from me. 'Come on, come on,' he tipped everything on to the bonnet of the van and started looking through my things – my purse, my make-up. He got my tampons and held one of them up in the air. 'What's this for?' He started thrusting it up in front of my face and grinning. He was pathetic. My comb dropped on the floor and he put his foot on it and then said 'Pick it up, then.' I bent down and when I stood up he was pushing the things back into my bag. I thought he'd finished.

'Can I go now?'

But he said, 'No, you can't. Not until you tell me what you're doing out. You looking for custom?'

I wanted to spit into his pasty fat face. 'I'm a married woman,' I shouted, 'I got a little girl. Now can I go now – I know my rights.'

'Oh you do, do ya?'

The other pig looked out of the window of the car and shouted 'Hurry up.' The other one said, 'Empty that bag.'

'I just did that.'

'Well I forgot what was in there. Empty it again, you lippy nigger bitch.'

I tipped the bag open and I noticed it straight away. I noticed it because it wasn't there before. A screwed-up piece of tin foil the size of a walnut. He grabbed it. He knew what he was looking for. 'Oh, what's this?' he said, peeling it open, all innocent.

I said, 'It's not mine – it wasn't there before.' But he was busy sniffing it. 'Smells like marijuana to me.' He pushed the little parcel in my face. 'Don't it smell like ganja to you?'

'I don't know. I don't know what it smells like,' I said. He raised an eyebrow and sniggered, 'Pull the other one.' He called his friend over who started walking towards us, talking into a radio. I could hear him saying they'd found suspected drugs on me, but he hadn't even seen it, not then.

'You put it there, you bastard,' I shouted. The other one was smelling it by now and shaking his head and smirking at me.

'Naughty, naughty,' he said. 'You'll have to spend a lot of time on your back getting out of this one, darling.'

People were driving past and looking at me. I looked around, I wanted someone to help me. I was being robbed. I started to cry. I told them that I'd never taken drugs, not ever in my life, that I was sorry about the lights and that I'd drive with them on in future and to please, please, please let me go because I had to pick up my little girl. And they said, 'Shut your black gob and get in the car.'

Vivien

Eddie used to come and visit me at weekends. Every weekend he'd turn up on the doorstep in his white afghan coat with his acoustic guitar over his shoulder and a grin on his face. I was pleased to see him after a week of college. A week of conversations about art; discussing the merits of the Impressionists, the Fauvists, the Cubists. Of listening to classical music during life drawing, and theories of why Sibelius symphonies always sound familiar. 'He repeats his initial refrain, de da, de da, de da, de da. Can you hear it Vivien?' Or talk of missing mothers or brothers or washing-machines or gardens to sit in.

There was no one in my group who was from a dilapidated council estate, who liked to eat Mother's Pride white sliced loaves and was more than used to washing all their clothes by hand. Who liked Radio One and knew what was top of the pops and said 'ain't' and 'blimey' when they forgot. There was no one who looked around themselves every morning and wondered how they got there. How they managed to be living in a flat that was nicer than one their parents could provide, with a woman who could rustle up something called a lasagne and got upset when she remembered that her father wouldn't let her have a pony when she was young.

Eddie would come down with tales from back home. Telling me about all the beer he had drunk: 'You could have lit my burps with a match,' or about the places we used to go: 'King's Arms is still the same. I'm jamming there next week. Doing someone a favour really, 'cause their guitarist got sent down for drunk and disorderly.' Or stories about Olive learning to drive in his van. 'We had to tie the exhaust on with a pair of your sister's tights – I hope you're not jealous.' Or: 'She's having trouble with the social, but you know Olive, she gives as good as she gets.'

'So what's been happening at college?' he'd ask, and I'd just shrug.

Eddie had never met Victoria because she went back to Northumberland every weekend for a party or a 'gathering of the clan' or just to get away from 'this bloody dump'. She'd pack her bag on Friday morning and sneak out of college at four. Then turn up on Monday looking flushed pink, well-fed and usually driving a different car.

Then one weekend she stayed. 'Everyone's away – I'm going to sample the delights of Herne Bay.' She invited three people from college round for Saturday lunch. So have you got it now, Vivien, lunch is in the afternoon and dinner is at night. We didn't spend a lot of time together, Victoria and me. She'd stay out until late at night during the week, at a pub or club which I was never invited to. I'd stay at home in front of one bar of an electric fire watching *Sale of the Century* on television.

'So you're the mysterious Eddie,' Victoria said.

'That's me,' Eddie replied, 'dark and mysterious.' He flashed a smile at Victoria who looked at me and said, 'I should stay here more often – see what you two get up to when I'm away.'

Eddie began to get more and more cockney as the evening wore on. Victoria looked enthralled and laughed at his jokes. By ten o'clock he was talking about having a pig's ear in his whistle and flute down the rub-a-dub-dub when he was boracic lint, but still managed to come out Brahms and Liszt.

'I know "up the apples and pears",' Victoria said.

'Yeah, but you don't say it right – you're too posh. But stick with me – I'll make a cockney of you yet,' Eddie promised.

'He's so earthy,' Victoria said to me when Eddie went out of the room to warm up some 'loop-de-loop'.

But then on Saturday morning Victoria wouldn't get out of bed. She was in one of her moods. She often got into moods. The first time it happened she was at college, scratching through wax on an etching plate, talking loudly about her brother's misdemeanour at Oxford involving a punt and a pole, when a phone call came for her. When she came back her face was stone grey. She picked up her bag and walked out of college. She wouldn't get out of bed for two days and she wouldn't speak to me at all. She just lay in bed smoking joint after joint until her room smelt like every Bonfire night I'd ever had. I thought I was going to have to phone her mum and dad, the Right Honourable Something or the Sir and Lady This and That, I couldn't remember. But then she emerged on the third day looking pert and pretty as if nothing had happened. 'I'm starving,' she said, and we never spoke about it again. I learnt to leave her alone.

'I'll get her up, I'll use my Eddie charm,' Eddie said. He walked into her bedroom before I could grab him back. 'What's up, Vic,' I heard him say. There was a bang and a shout of 'Victoria, you cretin,' and a red-faced Eddie rushed out again.

'What's up with her?' he said.

'Just leave her.'

'She's right down in the dumps. I know, I'll tell her a joke.' He went to walk in the room again. 'Leave her, Eddie.'

'It never fails. I will not admit defeat – I'll put a smile on her face if it's the last thing I do.' He began straightening his shirt.

'Leave her alone,' I shouted.

I walked into the kitchen. 'I'll have to make the lunch,' I said. It was the last thing I wanted to do. I hadn't invited any one round. I never did. I occasionally went round to other students' houses and ate spaghetti bolognese. And after we'd play a game of Botticelli, where someone would hold forth, thinking they were Napoleon, and everyone else would try to guess who they were with questions like 'Are you a nineteenth-century philosopher beginning with N?', to which the answer would be 'Ummm . . . no, I'm not Nietzsche.' I'd try to avoid most of the game by staying in the toilet, only coming out in time for my Earl Grey tea. 'Really, milk and sugar in Earl Grey, Vivien, are you sure?'

'Don't worry,' Eddie said putting his arm round me, 'I'll do one of me fry-ups.' Eddie's fry-ups consisted of egg, bacon, sausage, mushrooms and tomato, all fried to a charred mass until the different items were indistinguishable from one another. He served it on to plates before slapping bread into the cinders in the frying-pan and making it squelch up the remaining fat. Eddie would eat a mouthful then wipe the grease from his face with a tea towel.

'No you can't,' I snapped.

'Why not?'

'They won't like it.'

'Everyone loves a fry-up.'

I started to cry.

'Come on,' Eddie said. 'Well, what was her ladyship making?'

'I don't know – quiche or something.'

'What?' he asked.

'Exactly.'

By the time the doorbell rang we'd settled on rounds of egg and salad sandwiches: 'No, the brown bread, Eddie.'

Only Chrissy and Jim turned up. The Scottish Margaret couldn't come because her parents had come down to surprise her and had caught her in bed with Ken the Japanese boy. Chrissy knew Victoria before college. 'Is she in one of her moods?' she said, when she noticed her absence. I nodded. 'Bitch,' she added.

Chrissy was born in Barbados, although she was porcelain white with long brown hair that she kept plaited down her back. I liked her. She said she was a rebel, and on the first day we met she asked me if my parents came from Jamaica. I said yes, and she smiled and said 'I love the Caribbean.' We spent an evening drinking in the college bar, her elbow propped on the counter, guzzling pints of beer with whisky chasers, her telling me about her expulsions from boarding schools. 'So I told the mayor on prize day to stop looking at my tits – dirty old bastard.' She said art college was her last chance. Her father had threatened to 'cut her off' if she didn't stop hanging about with 'undesirable left-wing weirdos'. Her ambition, she declared, was to become an alcoholic.

Eddie grabbed the six-pack of beer she brought and they opened a can each. 'Are you at college, Eddie?' she asked.

'University of life,' he replied.

'Much more interesting and no exams.' They laughed.

Jim looked concerned. 'Is Victoria all right?' he asked me. Jim adored Victoria. It was sad to watch. He badly wanted to go out with her. But he was too ugly for her. 'Ginger eyelashes,' Victoria would say with a shudder. He followed her around college and she would ask him to fetch and carry things for her which he would perform like an eager golden retriever. He obviously thought this invitation to lunch was his chance to woo. He stank so much of Aqua de Silva aftershave that I could tell what it tasted like.

'Jim – beer?' Eddie said, holding up one of Chrissy's cans.

I drank my can fast and enjoyed the warm, shaking feeling that came up through my legs and made things seem not quite so strange.

We listened to Jim talk about Victoria. About what a wonderful artist she was. How good a driver. How down-to-earth, despite her background. 'She'll talk to anyone,' Jim told us with admiration. We all listened and Chrissy rolled her eyes as Eddie handed round the sandwiches and I looked at my watch. 'So what do you do, Eddie?' Chrissy asked. My heart began to beat so loudly I covered my chest with my arms to muffle it.

'I'm a musician,' Eddie signalled to his guitar in the corner.

'Oh, give us a song then,' she said.

Eddie tipped his head and swaggered to his guitar like he was Bob Dylan asked to play 'Blowin' in the Wind' for an encore. I tried to stop him with a look, but he didn't notice. We sat and listened to Eddie tuning up, but then realized after about fifteen minutes that that was it.

'Do you know any Crosby, Stills and Nash?' Jim asked.

'I don't like that stuff,' Eddie said. He also didn't like the other requests for Donovan, James Taylor, Steven Stills, the Beatles and, in desperation, 'Where have all the flowers gone?' Eddie strummed a loud chord: 'I'm a rock musician,' he said. I went to the kitchen to get some more beer, stopping outside the door to Victoria's room to give her the v-sign, the finger and the 'up yours' fist.

When I came back Eddie's guitar was on the floor. I breathed out.

'Here, Vivien,' Eddie said, 'your friends here don't know you're a cockney like me. They thought you was posh.'

I laughed: what else could I do? I'd let people believe I was from Islington – one of the big houses near Gibson Square. My father was an engineer, I'd say, my mother's in catering. I went to a grammar school. I let them make up the rest. 'No, she's a good ole salt of the earth like me – council estate. She likes a knees up, don't you, Viv?' He sounded like his dad. I laughed again as Jim and Chrissy stared at me with indulgent grins. There was total silence.

'Do you go back to London much, Vivien?' Chrissy asked.

'Not a lot,' I said.

'Well if you're back next week there's a march you might want to go on.'

'What sort of march?'

'Protest march for abortion – the woman's right to choose.'

Jim groaned.

'Shut up, you,' Chrissy said to him. 'It's an important issue for women.'

'I don't believe in it,' Jim said.

'What do you mean?' Chrissy said, raising her voice. Eddie picked up his guitar again.

'I believe that life is sacred.'

'Oh for God's sake, what about women, what about their lives? All those women whose lives are ruined because they've had a baby too young. What about them?'

'They should be more careful.'

'What about the men? It takes two to tango.'

'Well, it's the women that get pregnant. And that's just a fact. If there was a contraceptive pill for men I'd take it.' Chrissy looked at me and raised her right eyebrow. Eddie strummed louder and Chrissy had to shout. 'Oh, sure, I'd trust you. Don't you think women should have the right to choose if they want to have a baby or not?'

'I don't believe in abortion, that's all.'

'But,' I started tentatively, 'what sort of a life would an unwanted child have?'

Chrissy touched my arm in agreement. 'Exactly,' she said. 'Every child a wanted child, every mother a willing mother. That's why there's a march.' Jim made a face.

'What do you think, Eddie?' Chrissy asked. Eddie stopped strumming his guitar. 'About what?'

'Abortion on demand.' He looked in the air and thought; then said, 'I don't agree with it.' I covered my heart with my arms again. Jim patted Eddie. 'Good man,' he said.

'Oh God,' Chrissy moaned.

'No,' Eddie said, appealing for calm with his hands, 'hear me out.' My palms were making my jumper wet. 'I don't believe it should be on demand.'

'Well, do you agree with a woman's right to choose?'

'Yeah but listen,' Eddie carried on. 'I don't believe it should be on demand. I think you should have to say please.' There was another silence. Eddie expanded: 'I think a woman should go in and say nicely, "Could I have an abortion, please," not just run in and demand it.'

Chrissy began to laugh. 'You are joking, aren't you?'

But Eddie had a thoughtful face. 'No, I think it's very serious – I believe in good manners,' he said. Chrissy looked at me with her mouth open. So did Jim. And I would have died there and then on the lounge carpet if Victoria hadn't flung open the door and said 'Hi, everyone.'

Jim clapped at her entrance. She was in full make-up with

her hair freshly Carmen-heated-hair-roller-curled. She sat on the settee.

'So, what have you been saying about me?' she said.

I stood up. 'I'm making some tea, does anyone want some?'

'Ooh lovely,' Victoria said, 'Earl Grey?' I grabbed Eddie's arm. 'Come and help me,' I said.

'Women,' Eddie said, rolling his eyes. 'Can't do anything.' I dragged him out of the room before there was another incident.

I closed the kitchen door behind me.

'Eddie, don't you understand?' I whispered. 'It's not that the woman is running in and demanding it.'

Eddie looked at me with a frown. 'What are you talking about?'

'Abortion.'

'Oh that – well it's not ladylike to go round demanding things, it's bad manners.'

'It's not about manners,' I tried to explain. 'Don't you get it?'

He shrugged it off, then smiled and came across the room and put his arms round me. I struggled out of his hug.

'What's the matter with you?'

'Nothing,' I said, filling the kettle with water.

'Well, come on then, give us a kiss.' He grabbed me again and squeezed me. 'Your friends are a bit . . .'

'A bit what?' I said, pushing him away again.

'I don't know – just not much fun – serious.'

'They were trying to have a conversation.'

'Yeah, but . . .'

'But what?' I snapped.

'What's the matter with you?' Eddie looked at me with a serious face.

'They were just trying to talk and you're playing your guitar and making stupid comments about women having manners and telling them things and talking in that stupid cockney accent—'

'Excuse me,' Eddie interrupted, 'that's the way I talk.'

'Going on about the rub-a-dub bleedin' dub and trying to impress everyone—'

'And you used to be cockney once. What makes you so good now?'

'It's so embarrassing. You don't get even simple things.'

'You've got so high and bloody mighty, Vivien, since you've been here.'

'Don't you want to learn anything, don't you want to get on in life – do something?'

'Don't forget where you come from – you're just a working-class girl. What you getting so worked up about? You're not one of them.' Eddie jabbed his thumb over his shoulder.

'They're my friends now. I live in this nice flat and go to college and everything. I'm getting on with my life.'

'So,' he spat.

'So . . .' I was lost for words. 'So you're showing me up! I just wish you could be—'

'I'm me, Vivien. I can't be anyone else. I can't be all clever or arty. I'm me. So is that good enough for you or not?'

I looked in his brown eyes. The choice had become my old life or the new. I looked at him and said 'No, it's not good enough.'

Victoria opened the kitchen door with an 'Oops.' She looked from Eddie to me. 'Sorry, but there's a phone call for you, Vivien.'

'For me!'

The phone was in Victoria's bedroom. She had insisted on having one installed in the first few days we lived there, saying she'd die if she was incommunicado. I gave the number to my mum for emergencies.

'Yeah, and . . . could you make it quick – I need to make a call.' She smiled at me with only her mouth.

'Vivien, it's Olive.' Her voice sounded shaky, close to tears.

'What is it? Is it Mum – oh, not Amy?'

'I was arrested last night,' she said. For some reason I was relieved.

'Oh,' I said.

'What do you mean, "Oh"? Didn't you hear me, I was arrested. The bastards! I can't believe it . . . I hadn't done anything . . . but the bastard said I had . . . called me a black slag.'

She was crying and rambling and I kept saying 'Calm down, Olive, I can't understand what you're saying.' But she went on, oblivious.

'They planted it . . . I don't take drugs, you know that . . . I don't do that . . . I smoked some tea leaves once but that's not illegal . . . but they thought that just because I was black I should have drugs . . . and when I didn't they just put some there . . . and no one believes me – no one . . . and they treated me like a criminal but I never did nothing – nothing . . . and I had to phone Mum, and she don't believe I didn't have them . . . she says she does but she doesn't . . . she keeps looking at me . . . and she said there's no smoke without fire . . . they took my fingerprints and everything . . . and I told them, I told them I hadn't done anything . . . that they were planted on me, but no one believes me . . . it's my word against theirs, and who's going to believe a black girl on benefits . . . nobody, nobody!' She stopped for a while. I could hear her sucking hard on a cigarette.

'So, are you in prison?' I asked.

'No I'm not in prison,' she snapped. 'But I'm going to have to go to court.' She sniffed long and loud.

'But what happened?'

'I just told you,' she shouted, 'they stopped me in Eddie's van and made me empty my bag, which I did. Then they made me do it again and I thought it was odd and then there it was.'

'What?'

'The dope – a little round bit of dope all wrapped up.' She started to cry.

'Don't cry, Olive,' I said, patting my leg *there, there*, 'I'm sure it will be all right. I mean, if you're innocent then you'll be all right.'

Olive laughed a deliberate Ha! Ha!. 'God, Vivien, you're so stupid.'

'I'm not – if you're innocent then just tell them.'

'They don't believe me.'

'Well, tell them again – tell them exactly what happened.'

'Grow up!' she shouted.

'Well, what can I do about it?' I quickly retorted.

'It's just,' Olive hesitated, 'it's just that I feel . . . I feel . . . scared here.'

There was silence.

'What do you mean?' I asked.

She took a trembling breath. 'Well, I can't go to Mum's, not the way she goes on, I'd go mad, and I don't like being in the flat on my own. I know it sounds stupid. I mean, it's not that I'm not a strong black woman. I am. I am!'

'So what do you want me to do?'

'I wondered if I could come down there, just for a few days, with Amy. A week maybe, no longer, I just want to get away, out of London – somewhere quiet and . . . safe.'

I looked out of the window at the sun setting over the sea. It was leaving a beautiful, impossible sky-blue pink horizon. But as I thought of Olive in my flat, in my life here, a grey cloud drifted across the scene.

'No, you can't,' I said. 'There's no room.'

'I thought you said it was a big flat.'

'Well, it's not that big and besides, I share it with someone and they don't like people coming to stay.

'It wouldn't be for long.'

'No, I'm sorry, Olive.'

'Please.'

'No – I'll come back soon . . .'

She didn't let me finish before she started.

'That's so bloody typical of you. You little cow, you're so selfish, all you think about is yourself. What's the matter, do you think I'll be embarrassing? You make me sick, Vivien. You make me really sick. I knew you'd say that, I don't know why I asked. Now you've got all your college friends, now you've got your own flat, now you're all right. I knew you'd say that. Selfish, snotty cow.'

Suddenly I was shouting. 'Just leave me alone – just leave me alone Olive! I don't want you here – don't you understand – just leave me alone!' I began to sob from way down in my stomach and gasp for air like someone drowning. And I could hear Olive's small voice saying 'I don't feel sorry for you Vivien – cry all you want.' Then she put the phone down.

I wiped my eyes with my sleeve and the phone rang again. I thought it was Olive: I tried to take a deep breath, but it came in little staccatos and I quietly said 'Hello.'

'Hi,' a voice yelled, 'Vicky, it's Philip, you old tart.'

'I'll get her,' I said before the voice knew what was going on. I went into the hall and called Victoria. But there was no reply. I went into the front room which was empty – just cans of beer over the floor and an ashtray that was still smoking slightly. The kitchen was empty. There was a scrawled note on the table. *Gone to pub. You and Eddie come and join us.* I called out for Eddie. There was no sign of him – no 'Up here, Viv,' no 'Yes, that's me.' I ran up to my bedroom. 'Eddie, Eddie!' All his things had gone – his holdall, his white afghan coat. I ran into the front room panting like a dog and looked for his guitar through tears. It had gone too. He had gone. I sat on the floor in the still and quiet of the empty flat and looked out at the horizon.

I was alone.

Olive

Plead guilty! That's what the solicitor told me. Plead guilty to the charge of possessing cannabis, just to save them all a lot of time and bother. 'I believe you about the police planting the drugs, Olive,' she said. 'But getting a magistrate to believe you is another matter. Just plead guilty: you'll only get a fine – twenty, thirty pounds – and then you can get on with your life.'

She didn't understand, the little white woman in her white blouse, sitting in an office with a coffee machine bubbling and her university certificates on the wall. Her England is a nice place where people are polite to her, smile at her – ask her for directions in the street, sit next to her on buses and trains and comment about the weather. But my England shakes underneath me with every step I take. She didn't understand that I could be innocent. Oh no. I was born a criminal in this country and everyone can see my crime. I can't hide it no matter what I do. It turns heads and takes smiles from faces. I'm black.

She thought I wouldn't care about having a police record. That it wouldn't make any difference to my life. My husband would still have left me with a child to bring up on my own. My mum will still roll her eyes and suck her teeth when I open my mouth to speak. Plead guilty, Olive, even if you didn't do it, you're certainly guilty. Take your punishment and don't make a fuss.

But I've decided – I'm going to live in Jamaica. Live in the sun and watch Amy playing on beaches. I'm going to live somewhere where being black doesn't make you different.

272

Where being black means you belong. In Jamaica people will be proud of me. I've had enough of this country. What has it ever done for me except make me its villain? Well, I won't take it any more.

Vivien thinks she's escaped, with all her exams and college and middle-class friends. She thinks she'll be accepted in this country now. One of them. She's pleased with herself – turned her back on everything she knows. My little sister thinks she's better than me. She looks down her nose at me and thinks I've wasted my life. But I know more about life than her. Real life. Nothing can shock me now. But Vivien, one day she'll realize that in England, people like her are never far from nowhere. Never.

Vivien

The first time I went home from college, back to the flats where my mum lived, there was a mattress lying across the road. It had a hole burnt in the middle. Blue flowers trampled grey, fraying, with stuffing and springs poking through the charred-edged gash. The flats looked like some opposing army had finally seized them, plundering them of any value and then leaving. I wondered if they had always looked so raw and desolate, or whether I was looking at them with different eyes. With the eyes of a would-be artist who was getting used to looking for beauty in everything. My footsteps echoed against the walls and sounded like someone was following me. I kept looking around. I was nervous. Jumpy. Like a lost tourist.

Olive was in the flat on her own. I wanted us to sit down like the sisters in books, like sisters on the television, and talk excitedly to one another about our lives with giggly girlie hugs. But the truth was that I felt scared to be around my big sister.

I wanted to ask her what she was doing in my mum's house putting away washing-up like she'd never left home. I wanted to know why she wasn't putting away her own cups, getting on with her own life. I smiled at her. 'Hello, Olive,' I said, and she looked at me. A hard, squint-eyed, tight-lipped look – like she hated me. But she didn't speak. I wanted to know about the police, about the fine. Why did she pay it? Why, if she was innocent, did she agree to give them twenty pounds that she didn't have?

I wanted to ask her about Eddie. If she knew how he was.

Was he happy or sad, playing darts, drinking beer, getting pissed with his dad and uncle Des? Eddie wouldn't speak to me. I'd phoned him up on the day he left. He picked up the phone but when he heard it was me he put it down again. I phoned again, but then his sister kept saying he was out. I wrote to him – told him I was sorry for what I had said. But I didn't get a reply. When I finally spoke to him on the telephone his sentences were short and clipped – yes, he was all right, no, he wasn't coming down again. I asked him if he still loved me. There was silence enough for me to hear my tears dripping on to the metal cabinet in the phone box. 'I think the question is do you still love me,' he said. Then there was silence enough for him to say 'Goodbye Vivien.' I missed him though. *There's only one rock.* I missed him. *Stay with me I'll show you the stars.* I missed him. But not enough.

I hadn't seen Olive for months – there was so much to tell. But I looked at her mouth. Her two lips closed tight round a set of near-perfect teeth. I was scared to see those lips moving – frightened of what they might do to me. The room was hot and still like before a storm. 'Where's mum?' I asked. 'Out,' she snapped, then swung her body round and went out of the room. And then I knew that Olive was obviously not talking to me.

It had happened before. When we were young. She would spend her days giving me dirty looks, tutting when I spoke and pretending she could hear something but wasn't quite sure which direction it was coming from. I used to plead with her to talk to me again, to be my friend. I hated being shut out of her life. And I would promise never, never, never to do it again, that thing that I did, although sometimes I wasn't sure what it was. When she spoke to me again, even if it was a barked order from the kitchen, I'd smile to myself and breathe a sigh because it was over.

'Where's Amy?' I asked, as Olive marched back through the room.

'Out.'

'With Mum?' I said, trying to smile. Olive sighed, and I

smelt her breath as it brushed passed me. I looked round the front room. I had been away a long time – it looked unfamiliar to me. There was a new clock on the wall, white covers on the back of the settee where your head rests, and a smell of fried chicken mixed with a very faint odour of mothballs. Did we always smell like that?

The hands on the new clock didn't seem to move. Time stopped passing. Olive looked at me and for some reason tutted. I screamed, 'Oh for God's sake, Olive, what's the matter with you – grow up will you, just grow up.' The first flash of lightning before the thunder roars.

She looked at me a little startled. I wasn't playing the game. I wasn't sulking too – wandering round the flat avoiding her.

'Well, if you must know, Vivien, I feel sorry for you.'

My eyebrows went up involuntarily as I said, 'For me?' Why should Olive, my sister who had a child on her own, in a flat with nothing in it except the dream of where things would go once she could, in some mythical far-off time, afford them; Olive, who had no friends who phoned her or called to take her out and nowhere to go except to my mum's, to spend her time putting cups in a cupboard; Olive, who had to spend her days answering questions from people who needed to have questions answered before they would help her – why should she feel sorry for me? Me, I was getting on with my life. I was at college with certificates for exams passed and merits for jobs well done. I had prospects. I had decided. I was going to get a degree. I was going to get a good job. I was going to earn money and have a big house where the furniture was all of my choosing and every carpet fitted snugly against a wall.

'Yes, yes I do,' she said superciliously. She lit a cigarette and pulled a piece of stray tobacco off her tongue and said, 'I feel sorry for you because you don't know who you are any more.'

I must have frowned.

'You don't – you don't,' she carried on. 'With all your art

276

college and your new friends. You've changed, Vivien, you're just a little snob now. I remember you when you were little . . .' she started. She went through my life listing what she thought she saw. A right little swot at school . . . teacher's pet . . . little miss goody-goody who never did anything wrong . . . Mum and Dad's favourite, precious little brown-eyed girl. As she spoke she looked out of the window, round the room, anywhere but in my eyes, which were firmly fixed on her as she spouted her odd distortions about me. Her body twisted and turned as her hands moved to help her explain me away. 'You don't know what real life is like. You've had it so easy,' she said, then took a deep breath.

I sat back on the settee and had to tell my lungs to move in and out. I could feel the pricking sensation in my nose that warns of tears. Because she was my big sister and she was right. I had changed, I could feel it. I wanted so much from life now. I'd got big ideas. I didn't want to be ashamed of what I didn't have. Or proud of what I didn't know.

'You never had it hard like me,' she said with a vicious grin.

There was a silence. My big sister had always blamed me for her life. 'You're jealous of me,' I said.

Olive started shouting, 'I'm not jealous, I'm not jealous!' Flapping her arms about like a pigeon with a broken wing. The lit end of her cigarette fell on the carpet and she stamped on it hard to put it out.

'You are – you're jealous because you're miserable.'

'Shut up, Vivien, you make me sick. You've never had it hard, you don't know what it's like.'

'How do you know?'

'Because I know you and your spoilt-brat life – you never had to go through what I've gone through.'

'But it was your life, Olive – your choice.' She staggered a little like she had been struck. Eyes wide – mouth open. Lost for words.

I stood up. 'You act as if I was born in Buckingham Palace and you were born here. As if we grew up in different places.

Didn't have the same mum and dad. Didn't go to the same bloody school. But we did. We had the same chances, we started from the same place. And,' I pointed in her face, 'and you chose to lead your life and I chose to lead mine.'

'I didn't have a choice, I never had any choices, you had all the choices,' she screamed.

'It may seem like that to you, Olive. But it's not true – it's just not true.' She stared at me panting. I told her, 'Just because you had it hard, doesn't mean that everything has been easy for me.'

She pointed back at me. 'You think you've escaped now, don't you, because of your precious college. You think everything will be all right for you.'

'Yeah, yeah I do,' I said.

'Well it won't – you'll never be accepted. It won't be all right for you – one day you'll see – it won't.'

'You're just jealous, Olive.'

'What's all this noise?' my mum said opening the door wide. 'I can hear you shouting down the balcony.' Olive took no notice.

'Spoilt bitch!' she screamed at me.

'What's the matter with you two girls?'

'Stupid cow,' I shouted.

'Stop this now, you hear me,' our mum said, putting herself between the two of us.

'Little snob,' Olive shouted round our mum, as Amy stood in the doorway looking at us.

'Jealousy, jealousy,' I taunted.

'Shut up now you girls, you try my patience.' Mum held her hands in the air demanding silence as Olive yelled 'Stuck-up bitch.'

I put my fingers in my ears and started singing 'Sticks and stones may break my bones but names will never hurt me.' Mum mouthed at me to calm down and Olive's face distorted trying to find more words to spit. I started dancing on the spot, singing my song as loud as I could. 'Sticks and stones may break my bones but names will never hurt me.' Mum shook her head. Olive watched me for a while and sneered 'You're so childish' at me. So I poked my tongue out at her and she poked her tongue out at me.

Mum made us all a tea. There was no other word for it. Olive and I sat in a frosty silence, giving each other looks that pinned you to the spot. While Amy showed me her new two-headed doll: a smiling clown's face at one end but lift up the skirt to reveal a grumpy clown at the other. Mum pushed a new trolley through into the lounge. Her hair was a little bit greyer, her body a little bit smaller than I remembered. 'You'll like this, Vivien,' she told me. 'It's called a hostess trolley. You probably seen one of these with your friends in Canterbury.' She showed me all the compartments. 'Keeps food warm too.'

Then she wheeled it back into the kitchen and filled it with plates of sandwiches and cakes. Every plate had a white doily underneath the white triangular sandwiches and gaudy pink and yellow fondant fancies. 'Your friends use these?' she said, pointing at the doilies. I shook my head. She raised her eyebrows. 'Well, anyway, I thought you'd like things to be nice now.' She smiled as Olive's eyes rolled in their sockets.

'Now we can be civilized,' Mum said. She passed round tea in her best china cups and saucers that rattled together as they moved. The noise made me instinctively sit on the edge of my chair and think about vicars and sticking out my pinky. Mum looked at her family.

'Good. You finish all your arguing now? I don't know what you two find to argue about. How can two sisters be so different?' Olive and me sipped our tea and Amy sat on the floor fondling up the skirt of her moody doll.

'How's college?' Mum asked as she handed me a sandwich.

'It's good,' I said.

She smiled. 'You still share a house with that daughter of a Sir?' I nodded. 'I hope you make sure you do things right. I hope you don't give the impression that you come from a rough home.'

I looked at the doilies and the teacups in saucers and said 'No.' Olive sniggered and I took a bite of a sandwich. It was fish paste on Mother's Pride bread. I remember Mum and Dad discovering fish paste with 'oohhs' and jars of Sandwich Spread with 'aahhs'. Every sandwich they ate with those on made them feel somehow more English. But now it tasted too sweet to me: the bread seemed to mop up my saliva like a sponge. I had to wipe it round my mouth with my tongue and swallow hard. I was already used to brown bread.

'How long you staying, Vivien?' Mum asked. I felt like a distant relation come to visit. Out of place.

'Not long I hope,' Olive said.

'Olive, don't speak to your sister like that.'

'I'll speak to her any way I want.'

'Do you always have to make everything nasty, child – why can't you just be nice?'

'Well, you won't have to put up with me for much longer,' Olive said, and Mum said 'Cha' so hard that she had to put her hand up to her mouth to make sure her denture was still secure. 'Not that stupidness again,' she shouted at Olive. Olive turned her body to look out of the window and sighed a long huff. Mum leant forward to me with a sneer on her face. 'Your sister,' she began, 'your sister says she want to live in Jamaica. I ask you. She want to take little Amy and live in Jamaica.' Olive lit a cigarette and looked at the ceiling as Mum went on. 'She says it where she belongs because she black.' Mum leant back on her chair for a moment then sprang forward. 'I tell her she doesn't know what she talking about. She belong here. She born here. It's all she know. I tell her she doesn't know what it like in Jamaica.' She jabbed her index finger into her knee. 'It's not like here. But you know what she tell me? No. She knows that she will be accepted in Jamaica because she black. And I tell her, they don't want you there.' She became out of breath. Olive began to tut loud and frequent. 'All this stupidness,' Mum went on, 'I tell her you're just you – all this coloured stuff—'

'Black,' Olive interrupted.

'All this black colour stuff. I tell her "You're just you," and she belong here where she was born.' She took a breath. 'But no, she says she wants to go back with little Amy. Go back! I ask you, have you ever heard anything like that?' Amy stood up when she heard her name. 'I tell her, how you go back? You were born here, it's all you know. How you go back? I can go back but you children can't.' Her face became crimson. 'You don't know what it's like there. I know! I know! You children have had it easy . . .' Olive opened her mouth to protest but Mum carried on. 'But in Jamaica life is hard. You children don't know. And I thank God you don't.' She leant back on her chair looking from me to Olive. She'd finished. There was silence, then Olive muttered, 'Well I'm still going.'

Mum sighed. 'You must make a life here,' she pleaded with Olive, 'like Vivien. Get an education. Get a good job, then you wouldn't have all this trouble with who knows what. They would leave you alone. You could keep yourself to yourself. But you belong here. You tell her Vivien, you the sensible one. Listen to your sister, Olive, she knows where she belongs.' Mum kept looking at Olive but flicked her hand at me. 'Tell her Vivien . . . go on, tell your sister. Vivien, tell her, tell her where you belong.'

I looked at the old photograph of Olive and me on the wall. Two little girls with identical yellow bows in our hair and happy, smiling chubby cheeks. But now Olive's arms were folded on the world. She was angry with everything, with everyone. And I had grown too big for our council flat, but not sure where else I would fit. Where did we belong? I answered my mum the only way I could. I said, 'I don't know.'

Olive smiled at me for the first time. But my mum's face drained of expression as she said, 'Oh Vivien,' and the disappointment in her sigh drifted round and round the room.

Then Amy leant over the hostess trolley and stuck a whole fondant fancy in her mouth, squashing the last bits of pink icing and cream round her face. Olive leapt out of her chair and screamed 'Come here you,' and started chasing Amy, while my mum stood up and shouted 'Leave the child – she'll choke – leave her!'

On the train back to Herne Bay a white-haired old woman wanted to talk. I could see her trying to catch my eye, opening her mouth in anticipation. I looked out of the window, pretended to be asleep, rummaged round in my bag looking for something to read. Anything. But she still kept looking at me. 'Nice day,' she eventually started. I nodded. 'Are you going to Canterbury?' she asked. So I told her about my trip home to see my family and about my college course. 'Your family must be very proud of you,' she said. I smiled at her and shrugged. She stared at me then asked, 'Where do you come from, dear?' I looked at my reflection in the train window – I've come a long way, I thought. Then I wondered what country she would want me to come from as I looked in her eyes. 'My family are from Jamaica,' I told her. 'But I am English.'